For the Sake
of His Name

*the prophet Daniel's miraculous
life in Babylon*

by Cliff Keller

Copyright © 2015 by Cliff Keller.

Dedication

For the Jewish people, who began their long journey homeward in 605 BCE when the young prophet to be, Daniel, and his three good friends, Mishael, Hananiah and Azariah, were among the first of thousands eventually exiled to Babylon.

Contents

Acknowledgments

Much love and thanks to my wife, Marcia, for her encouragement, inspiration, faith, tireless proofreading and unrealistically high standards regarding my writing. Many thanks are also due Aleta M. Okolicsanyi and Diana Flegal for much reading and even more sound advice and criticism, some of which I accepted graciously. Anonymous regards go to other friends and family for their patience, faithful reading and encouragement.

For the Sake of His Name draws upon many resources in the public domain including, in addition to the Tenach, several non-biblical resources on ancient cultures and cuneiform writing. I am especially indebted to the Apollos Old Testament Commentary, Daniel, by Ernest C. Lucas, vice-principal and tutor in biblical studies at Bristol Baptist College in England (INTER-VARSITY PRESS, © Ernest Lucas 2002, US ISBN 0-8308-780-5), the content of which can be credited for having positively influenced much of what may be found to be accurate in this title with regard to chronologies, ancient cultures, languages and geopolitics and held blameless for any errors I may have made while in the process of fabricating this account.

Rather than using a single biblical resource for scriptural quotations or paraphrases in this novel, I have used several well-known resources, sometimes commingling their renderings for dramatic effect or readability.

Finally, the lion image used for the cover of For the Sake of His Name is from the photo, "Leo" by Mark Dumont, licensed under Creative Commons Attribution 2.0, https://www.flickr.com/photos/wcdumonts/14261850460/.

Introduction

HOW DOES ONE create an "objective" account of a string of miracles? For the Sake of His Name, a fictional rendering of the first six chapters of the Tenach's Book of Daniel, embeds the miraculous within a framework of facts. The exact dates may be debated but, in addition to the Old Testament accounts upon which For the Sake of His Name is based, Ancient Assyrian, Egyptian and Babylonian cuneiform accounts have established the historical veracity of the following beyond doubt;

❖ The northern kingdom of Israel fell to Assyria in 722 BCE and was wiped out.

❖ One hundred thirteen years later, the last competent king of the southern kingdom of Judah, Josiah, died of wounds suffered at the hands of Egypt's Pharaoh Necho II.

❖ Four years after Josiah's death, the Neo-Babylonian Empire led by then General Nebuchadnezzar II besieged and looted Judah's capital, Jerusalem, in the first of three campaigns spanning 19 years and ending with the destruction of the city and a third violent deportation of Jews to Babylon.

❖ Jerusalem's fall was the end of ancient Jewish sovereignty, the midpoint of Jewish history and the beginning of the redemption of modern Israel.

Once the "proven" and "highly likely" are set aside, the Daniel saga still confronts us with miracles. In an age when too many people prefer to believe that the observable universe sprang from nothing rather than give credence to a Creator, the inspired interpretation of dreams, survival in a fiery furnace, becalmed famished lions and supernatural handwriting on a palace wall may serve only to delight imaginations, yet they would accomplish immeasurably more when measured by the light of faith.

For the Sake
of His Name

I. Captives

1. Thy grief has just begun

MISHAEL WOKE TO the sound of drums. Outside his bedroom window the sky had begun to glow. The sun would rise soon but why should he care? Every day was the same.

After Babylon set siege to the city and Jerusalem began to starve, Mishael's parents had asked him to stay at home in bed and do nothing, even during the day. That had been easy. All Mishael's friends had been forced to do the same. There had been no school for months. Jerusalem's gates were shut against the enemy and her once crowded markets were abandoned, nothing to sell.

So it was easy to lie in bed as Mishael's parents had demanded but difficult to sleep. Everyone in town knew how a siege ramp worked; how, for a year, Babylon's clever stone gradient alongside the city's outer wall had grown higher every day. Everyone understood that, once the thing was completed, the enemy would storm up and onto Jerusalem's ramparts, flood into town and begin to...

Sometimes Mishael prayed for help to stop thinking.

He prayed that morning (to remain calm like his mother and be strong like his dad), as the drums beat still louder. Some nights during the last year he had lain in his bed listening, so frightened that he shook until his teeth clicked. Some nights he breathed in quick, frightened gulps under his covers hoping that no one would hear.

But the drums this morning sound different, somehow, he thought.

Mishael sat up in his bed and sniffed fire. Without another thought he dressed and ran outside, oddly unafraid. Out on the street he heard his mother call but had no time to stop. He had to be standing in the gate plaza when Babylon broke through the wall.

*

Mishael arrived at the siege point as Jerusalem's troops upon the ramparts dropped their weapons and ran. Rams pounded, stones broke and a pennant bearing the likeness of a bull began to course across the length of the outer wall with men bearing spears running close behind it.

1

"Get out of here, boy," a defender warned Mishael, running past.

"And go where?" Mishael asked, the question making such strong sense that it nearly calmed him. Smoke was everywhere, the noise had become maddening and several of the enemy had already jumped down from the ramparts and stood at ground level. Wave upon wave followed those; a hundred brutes, braying, then quickly a hundred more beating their chests, forming ranks and bracing behind shields against a counterattack that didn't seem likely to come.

Jerusalem had no fight left. It had been a difficult year.

Several of the enemy rushed past Mishael with swords raised but never struck him.

"What are you doing here?" a voice at Mishael's shoulder asked above the din.

"Daniel?" Yes, it was Mishael's friend, Daniel, calm as ever, which made no sense, but Mishael hugged him just the same.

*

They were stuck where they stood. Jerusalem's defenders had completely abandoned the plaza and retreated into town. A passing Babylonian officer poked at Daniel with his spear. When Daniel failed to flinch the soldier smiled (as if to approve) then spun and shouted to his men in a language much like Mishael's, "Take prisoners and gather them here, about these boys."

Soon Mishael and Daniel stood among a crowd of captives selected according to no apparent logic. Jerusalem's invaders simply ran about impaling some, ignoring others and arresting the remainder. Among those who were soon shoved into the growing herd came two more familiar faces squirming and flailing; Mishael's friends, Hananiah and Azariah.

"Be careful not to land a blow," Daniel cautioned as they struggled, "or one of them may run you through."

The boys took Daniel's advice. Their captors delivered parting quick kicks against their backsides and rushed away. The boys embraced awkwardly, then huddled to compare notes, finding they had each hurried to the plaza without knowing why, somehow unafraid, not having said anything to their families.

"What do you suppose that means?" Daniel wondered aloud. "It must be that we were meant to be together at this moment."

Mishael wasn't so sure.

"And so we are blessed," Daniel said, a peculiar notion under the circumstances yet pure Daniel, whose well-established habit of optimism seemed especially foolish that morning.

*

Though they appeared chaotic in all their outward behaviors, Babylonians could be amazingly orderly. Even their rage seemed to follow a plan. Mishael watched with grudging respect as the day wore on and the invaders surged repeatedly into the city bellowing and out of control only to reappear later having formed up in squads. These suddenly disciplined units would march back into the plaza rank and file leading prisoners as if on parade. After delivering their charges they would salute their peers, stretch a bit then break ranks and rush howling again toward town.

*

Still later, several empty ox-drawn carts passed through the ruined plaza gate and lumbered past the huddled captives. They passed again not long afterward, outbound, laden with holy articles from the Lord's temple. The boys, having stood in the hot sun for hours, began to choke back sobs. Daniel fought the black mood saying, "We must be here for a reason. I wonder, can we keep our faith?"

His answer came at once when the prophet, Jeremiah, appeared. The most disliked man in Judah stepped into the chaotic scene as if out for a stroll, ignoring a rising chorus of curses and jeers to step into their midst, raise his arms and look skyward (as prophets often do) but so fearlessly that even the guards quit their heckling to listen.

"O, Lord," Jeremiah bellowed, serious pain in his voice…

> *Jerusalem has sinned greatly and so has become unclean. Her filthiness clings to her skirts. Her fall was astounding; there was none to comfort her. Look, O Lord, on my affliction, for the enemy is triumphed… All her people groan."*

"Be still," a thundering voice answered him. Here came an enormous man striding Jeremiah's way wearing the dirtiest armor Mishael had ever seen. The soldier's big boots fell so heavily on the plaza stone that each impact echoed several times across the yard. His broad, black, squared-off beard made his jaw look like the business end of a shovel. He tore off his helmet, grabbed the hilt of his sword and roared again, this time in Jeremiah's face, "Here me now, old man, not one more word."

"Nebuchadnezzar!" the prophet shouted. (Everyone knew that name.) "You, general, are but the pawn of the God of Israel. Stop your mouth, I say."

Everyone gasped.

"Heed the Almighty's voice," Jeremiah roared, "rather than aspire to subdue it."

The general seemed as amazed as he was angry. "I am the almighty here," he shouted, drawing his sword to stir the air above the prophet's head, "and I charge you now, old man, make peace with your god for you are about to be enveloped in his light."

"No, prince of idolaters!" Jeremiah shot back at once, spit flying in the general's face. "Make your peace if you would live! The living God of Israel regards you and all fools who worship animals, trinkets, planets and base women as less than nothing. So, then, do I."

What a scene. Mishael peeked through his fingers while neither man blinked. Then, for no apparent reason, the mighty general from Babylon, most feared human in creation having recently orchestrated savage victories over Egypt and Assyria, lowered his blade slowly (allowing its razor edge to not quite graze Jeremiah's cheek) then, surprising everyone, he buck-snorted.

"Lieutenant," Nebuchadnezzar asked over his shoulder, grinning a little stupidly, "have you ever seen a more noxious race than these?" His lieutenant was too smart to answer but as the general continued to chuckle his men gradually relaxed and joined in. "Noxious but fascinating," Nebuchadnezzar mumbled when they had finished.

Jeremiah, unimpressed, turned his back on the general and began to stroll away. "O Judah," he wailed. "O Jerusalem, thy grief has just begun!"

"In that, old man," Nebuchadnezzar shouted behind him, "you are exceedingly correct." He wiped his filthy forehead with the back of his filthier hand, surveyed the city, by then almost entirely in flames, and nodded with pleasure. "This nation shall certainly pay."

Pay. The word stabbed Mishael's heart, remembering his mother's tears and father's grief the day Josiah died. Judah died with the king that day, all the prophets said, long before Babylon came and camped in the neighboring hills to set siege to Jerusalem.

"Pay," Daniel repeated, "because we've ignored God's commandments."

"Quiet, boy," a fellow prisoner barked beside him. "Don't cause trouble."

"Why silence the lad," another man hissed, "if he speaks the truth? False prophets promised Judah rain, wine and blessings and we fools gladly listened though we had been warned. Every last one of that brood of self-styled seers is a proven liar today. Judah bowed to idols, who can deny it? We killed babies to please cold planets, nodded at forbidden demons and honored common whores. Judgment has arrived just as Jeremiah, a true prophet, warned. The time for repentance has passed.

2. Traitorous Judah

NEBUCHADNEZZAR SPENT THE rest of the day cursing, shouting, and sending soldiers scrambling to do his will. He ignored the clutch of plaza prisoners until much later that afternoon when, as he passed near them, he stopped upon hearing a sound; a low, long quivering moan that had fought past Mishael's lips though he had tried so hard to be still.

The general pointed his sword at Mishael then ordered a man to, "Grab the crier."

When a guard yanked Mishael away Hananiah protested and Nebuchadnezzar, noticing, pointed and shouted, "Take him, too. And him right there," he added, marking Azariah, "that skinny cuss trying to murder me with his eyes."

With the three boys thrown at his feet, Nebuchadnezzar shouted in the plaza, "Traitorous Judah, may today be a worthwhile lesson to you. Egypt is not your friend and never will be. My father, Nabopolassar, king of Babylon, he is your great, great friend, truest ally and a too kind master." The general stopped to admire his voice as it doubled off the walls. "But even Nabopolassar, most gracious king of Akkad, has an end to patience. You refuse to pay tribute…? You plot with stinking Pharaoh behind my father's back…? Fine, now Babylon is here with its boot on your stiff necks after you've gone hungry for a year, taking much more from you now than if you had only given freely to Babylon." He kicked at the boys saying, "Make them stand and quit whimpering," and a guard goaded them upright.

"As a remembrance of this day," Nebuchadnezzar shouted, "and a simple, too kind warning, the king of Babylon now sees fit, in the manner of all great kings for millennia, to carry some of your own to Babylon as his slaves. There they will serve the nation all their days as the mighty king sees fit. We begin with these three handsome though highly uncooperative royal brats, I would guess, based on the stitching of their delicate, sissy clothes."

"This is why we rushed here?" Hananiah moaned.

"Quiet!" Nebuchadnezzar barked at him before turning back to the others. "See your errors, feeble Jews? Your women have been disgraced today while you have been forced to watch. Your brothers' bones are snapped like sticks, your homes wrecked and burning, your temple looted as I speak, all because of the treachery of your rotten king, Jehoiakim, who now sees his errors and has agreed this day that Babylon, not Egypt, shall henceforth be Judah's proper protector. You had better pray he keeps his word."

Nebuchadnezzar kicked at Azariah but Azariah jumped and made him miss.

"Shame on all Judah," the general yelled. "And be thankful that it is Babylon, not Assyria, here today to punish you, for those pigs would not have been as kind as I." He sheathed his sword and, while he seemed to stop to consider kicking Azariah again, Daniel stepped forward and cleared his throat.

"What's this?" Nebuchadnezzar asked.

Daniel took a step closer. The general leaned forward and yelled something coarse in his face, native Akkadian cursing, most likely, that Mishael could not decipher. But Daniel smiled instead of cowering and Nebuchadnezzar bellowed again, still louder.

Just as Mishael feared, Daniel's expression remained unchanged. Up on the ramparts several of the general's archers began to laugh. Nebuchadnezzar drew his sword a second time and threatened Daniel exactly as he had Jeremiah. "You mock me, boy, with that smile?" he said, shaking with anger.

Even the noise in town seemed to subside when, this time unlike the last, Nebuchadnezzar did not relent but rose to his toes and, in one swift continuous motion, brought his blade down with a whoosh and clang hard upon the courtyard stone at Daniel's left.

But Daniel did not move; he had not so much as blinked.

Nebuchadnezzar suddenly seemed delighted. "Did everyone see that?" he shouted, big grin again. "I could crush Egypt in a week with a handful of men with a fraction of this boy's stuff." He shot a hot glance up at his fun-loving archers on the ramparts and they quickly straightened up. "Or, I don't know," the general added, "it could be he's just stupid."

Everyone waited while Nebuchadnezzar mulled that over. "Enough," he said after a bit, "it will remain a mystery for now." He patted Daniel's head and added, "Take this strange one with us too. He seems to want to come along."

"Include women in this group," Nebuchadnezzar told his men, "pretty ones mostly but a few with good shoulders for work. Take strong boys, well-dressed men even if a little long of tooth and anyone who looks at all clever. And make sure they appear to have half a chance to survive the march." He started away but stopped and added, "Do what you like with the others. This day is nearly done."

*

Many of the candidates for captivity were rejected for not meeting Nebuchadnezzar's simple standards; not young, strong, pretty, well-dressed, no shoulders, too frail. Most of the rejected women among them were pulled toward town individually to suffer outrage; the men judged not up to snuff were led outside through the rubble-strewn gate.

"What will they do to them?" Mishael wondered aloud but his friends refused to guess.

In no time, hundreds stood beside the boys in a special cluster, bound for captivity in Babylon, they were told, provided they could do the distance.

The late afternoon air smelled of sweat, smoke and dust and even Nebuchadnezzar's amazing soldiers had grown tired. The guards allowed the future exiles to sit on the plaza stone but it was no comfort. Mishael tried not to think about anything that had happened and hoped especially not to cry.

"They won't destroy everything," Daniel said, "or harm everyone. The idea behind a captivity is to leave behind a nation too weak to revolt but which can still pay tribute."

"Jeremiah prophesied much worse," Azariah said.

They all looked at one another surprised.

"You're saying that this siege," Hananiah said, when Daniel nodded knowingly, "the starving, the dying, the humiliation…"

"Yes, it's only a warning from God," Daniel said, "to encourage Judah to turn back to him."

"And if we do not?" Mishael said.

"Then this is but the beginning of Judah's torment. The prophets say it, not me."

Mishael shut his eyes and prayed that Daniel and the prophets might be wrong.

*

That night the stars shone bright in the sky as if the world was good. The captives had been marched to a spot outside the city, a hill-side overlooking where the Kidron Valley intersected the Hinnom. Mishael knew a lot about that basin. Many Hebrew mothers and fathers had sacrificed their children to false gods there.

Several Babylonian bowmen stood guard around their camp, but why? Even if someone managed to escape, where would he run? It was July but a very cool evening. What seemed like thousands of enemy campfires flickered in the adjacent hills. Hugging himself for warmth, Mishael supposed he was the only coward in the camp. Hananiah had collapsed in the dirt, no complaining. Azariah sat frowning into space, angry and unafraid. Daniel, always doing the odd thing, had pulled a dirty stone from his pocket and stared at it by firelight.

In the shadows along Jerusalem's south wall stood the final proof of Babylon's superiority; neat lines of siege machines, mounds of armor and uncountable stacks of bows, arrows and spears. "We never had a chance," Daniel sighed, as if reading Mishael's mind.

"We were warned. Why didn't we listen?" Mishael asked, but even Daniel chose not to tackle that one. What was done was done.

*

What the boys had witnessed that day had been truly awful, but what they heard that night was much worse. An army doesn't camp for months on expedition only to grab treasure for their king, take a few prisoners then go home. The actual battle for Jerusalem had taken only hours; the remaining time became a sort of drunken furlough, encouraged by General Nebuchadnezzar and extending late into the evening as a sort of soldiers' reward. Unable to stop listening, Mishael's imagination refused to shut down. Horrid images flared in mind to match the screams he heard too clearly over the walls. O Lord, he prayed silently, please don't let me hear my mother's voice.

"Let's grab some rocks and charge these filthy pigs," Azariah hissed. "We'll crack their heads, take their weapons and rescue the people in town."

Even Azariah smiled when the futility of his notion struck him but Mishael's reaction quickly turned from amusement to pain, then tears, and though he despised his weakness he could not stop. He expected to be ridiculed by his friends but Hananiah and Azariah moved to his side and joined him in his grief, crying beside him unashamed. None of that for Daniel, though, who instead extended his hands into the cold evening air as if warming them at an invisible fire as he offered up advice... "We shouldn't fight this," he said. "It only makes things harder. Let's thank our God for sparing us. Then let's try to sleep."

Hananiah fell flat and shut his eyes. After a bit of grumbling Azariah did the same. Mishael followed closely after, wondering whether Daniel would eventually take his own advice.

*

At daybreak, most of the enemy units around them had broken camp and begun to march south, lifting a deep-throated pagan chant in chorus as they filed away. Upon waking, as his parents had taught him, Mishael offered up a morning prayer of thanks although he wondered why. These were confusing times. Rumors spread in their impromptu camp that Nebuchadnezzar's army was now on its way to Egypt. How efficient his troops were, loading up, lining up and treading into the low-lying fog in good spirits after a year-long siege, a night of shame and little if any sleep. Behind them, their abandoned campsites had cut ugly gashes across the hills; ruts of rubble, garbage and ash as far as Mishael could see.

A small force had remained behind with the captives to lead them to Babylon. These fellows were clearly angry to have stayed, no glory in prison detail, and they showed their frustration by mistreating everyone, including each other. Mishael listened carefully as they complained, hoping to learn more about what might happen but these fellows were much more difficult to understand when they spoke than the general and his officers.

One thing was clear; Babylon had lost patience with Judah and Jews. Every foot soldier despised them. All seemed convinced that

Judah's two-faced king had forced war upon Babylon by aligning with Egypt, her greatest enemy. Nebuchadnezzar's troops found King Jehoiakim's double dealing with Babylon so disgusting they were upset by how merciful their general had been.

"I would hate to see him angry," Hananiah said.

No one was able to smile. Where were their parents? Where were their friends? Who had survived the slaughter and who had not? The captives were not allowed to move freely among themselves so it remained possible that someone dear to them might be part of their herd but the odds for that seemed slim.

They spent that entire day and night stuck in place with nothing to eat or drink. The next morning the guards tossed stale chunks of flatbread and distributed brown water to drink in filthy fired-clay cups. The scraps looked and tasted awful but Mishael devoured all he could; the same for his friends. After eating they were ordered to stand, form ranks and count off. Finally, they broke camp and marched north.

They marched for days afterward, usually without food, up through Shechem and Samaria then beyond Megiddo. They eventually passed close to Tyre, then Sidon, and finally turned east toward Riblah where, Daniel told his friends, Nebuchadnezzar had recently established field headquarters.

Then came Aram, Rezeph and the great valley.

The journey lasted weeks. Vultures had circled above them from Megiddo, on. How many of their group died from exposure or starvation on the way? God only knew. When someone collapsed, he or she was left where they fell or their bodies were rolled aside. Once an older man tried to stop to help his fallen wife and was murdered on the spot.

O Lord, why? many wailed as they were goaded along.

"It is a sad but ignorant question," Daniel said one evening as they lay exhausted after a hard day's march. "We know why. God told Jeremiah then Jeremiah told us. But we continued to sin. And so..." He nodded at their pitiful surroundings.

Now, Mishael loved Daniel as a brother but he, Hananiah and Azariah had had enough. Correct or not, well intentioned or not,

Daniel's running moral commentary had become too heavy to bear. He had to stop and they told him so.

Daniel, being himself, agreed pleasantly, taking no offense. From then on each night after they obeyed their captors' orders by gathering wood, clearing brush and arranging a simple camp, instead of offering his friends perspective or suggesting further searches for meaning, Daniel sat and quietly polished the stone Mishael had seen him hold up to the light on the first night, rubbing it with the hem of his robe and fine white sand he had scooped up at Shechem.

"What exactly do you make of that thing?" Azariah asked Daniel one evening.

"It is a gem," Daniel said.

Tired as he was, Azariah laughed. "I remember," he said. "It's the brown pebble you found by the guard shack at the corner gate last winter."

"A stone, not a pebble," Daniel corrected, "and yellow, not brown. It is truly a treasure though you make fun. Some light already shines through it." He held it up, looking for a glimmer. "With proper polishing it will be brilliant someday, a thing of beauty."

"Yes," Azariah said, "a jewel. Grownups always leave them lying on the street."

"Just the same," Daniel said, holding up the piece again, "there is light in this thing, I can see it and you will someday too."

"You will show us," Azariah asked, "or Ya'el?"

Mishael caught his breath. The boys never mentioned loved ones since being taken captive, part of an unspoken agreement, but they all remembered dark-eyed Ya'el, daughter of the merchant, Ahiel, in Jerusalem, who always sparkled with a special freshness for Daniel. Long before Jerusalem fell Mishael had discovered Ya'el and Daniel holding hands. How he had envied Daniel's courage that day.

"She is my good friend," Daniel said. "I promised to give this to her someday after I had polished it bright."

"Do you think she lived?" Hananiah asked so softly they could barely hear him.

"For sure," Daniel said, biting his lip. "I know it." And he truly seemed to believe it. Mishael often envied the way Daniel stuck to his faith.

*

When their caravan passed south of Carchemish the boys knew that Babylon could not be far away. Each of them had heard countless stories about that wicked place; the idolatry, the carnality, the sorcery... They discussed their fears in whispers at night in camp. None of them could imagine surviving there so all their sessions ended with prayer. Daniel insisted.

At first Azariah thought it was foolish to pray. Their lives were wrecked, he said, and he felt justified in blaming God. But he gave in to Daniel's wishes and the four never failed to close an evening on the road by offering up thanks to the God of Israel for their lives, souls and futures just as they were. "We will follow the path of your will," Daniel would say to God and even Azariah added, "Amen."

Sometimes peeking side to side as they prayed, Mishael noticed by the dim light of the guards' campfires that their fellow captives, all of them much older, were watching them. Sometimes those former neighbors in Jerusalem, despite their sorrow, prayed with them too.

3. Like the color of pomegranates

THE MARCH ENDED after six weeks on the road. Survival had seemed so unlikely by then that the boys had stopped discussing it. But one evening, as they lay spent in the dirt after a shorter than usual march, a cool breeze blessing them, the boys heard music. Then they heard singing, then laughter. It made no sense; up till then everything they had done had been the same each day.

Along with its reputation for violence, cruelty and worshiping countless false gods, Babylon and Babylonians were also well known for their creepy commitment to order. Everything the army did was planned and repeatable. Now and then while they should have been sleeping the boys whispered about how, on the day that Jerusalem fell, the enemy first topped the wall like frantic animals but in the middle of their madness organized on the fly and began to follow orders.

That same mechanical quality was true of the captive guards. As they made camp each night one group, the same group, always manned the perimeter, another passed out bowls of a tasteless mash to serve as food and a third poured out clouded water for the prisoners to drink. The captives themselves were forced to do the heavy work when making camp. Every evening they were lined up, counted off and handed tools with which to clear brush, gather wood, start fires and dig sanitary trenches.

And that's how time passed. A day of plodding, camp-setting and troubled sleep became a week of the same. A week became a month. Captives collapsed and died from time to time. Terrain changed. Rock-covered hills turned into thick woods then fields of blowing grass. They walked narrow paths, crossed prairies and forded streams. The weather grew cooler and the look of the night sky changed. But their routine had stayed the same.

On that same evening they had heard music, everything changed. Having stopped well before sunset near a stream running through a glade of sweet-smelling clover, they were not called to perform their regular chores. Strangers rode in on wagons soon after and ladled out water in clean cups before silently serving what was, by comparison to their customary rations, tasty food.

Later the boys heard shouting; not battle cries but cheers. Mishael stood to look. At the edge of the clearing, scores of women rode into camp riding in mule drawn carts. Laughing and bouncing on their toes, they twirled veils in the air. Even before the carts stopped the girls had jumped down to the grass and run into clinches with the men.

"Their wives?" Mishael asked.

"Right," Azariah said, "or their sisters, come to chat."

Sometime during the march Azariah had begun to sprout a beard; only a few bent hairs on his pointed boy's chin but the faint growth was enough to make him look even more obnoxious than before. But even Daniel, on that strange evening, seemed to enjoy his odd remark.

The soldiers gathered and stacked wood without commandeering the prisoners then lit a huge fire. Soon the air was filled with crackles, black smoke and rising sparks. Several musicians had come with the women and they began to play. All the Babylonians danced. Like most of the captives sitting off to the side, Mishael, Hananiah and Azariah could not help but stare at the women's bare shoulders, flying hair and spinning skirts, but Daniel ignored the scene while he, again, polished his stone.

"Just after dark," he said later (as the guards' celebration wound down), "I saw in a waking dream two parallel walls, not composed of stone as in Jerusalem but made with square blocks, not cut but fabricated, bearing designs of many colors…"

"Colors?"

"…running for miles along an avenue."

Much later, when the blaze had all but died and everyone slept, the boys whispered about what Daniel's dream of walls might be. And why and how they might be colored?

"Tonight's party proves we're close to something," Hananiah said. "Walls or not that something must be Babylon."

After praying silently for courage Mishael spoke honestly. "Sometimes my vision blurs," he told his friends. "My feet bleed all the time and won't stop. I worry that I might pass out while we're marching like some of the men who have died already." He held out his arms, covered with scabs and stripes. "I'm scratched and bitten everywhere. Every joint in my body aches. So I'm thinking… I am wondering… I wonder if an end to this stinking march, even an end in Babylon, might be a blessing."

"They kill slaves in Babylon if they don't work out," Azariah said.

"God will provide," Daniel said.

The boys nodded together in the dark. God had to provide. Even Azariah had begun to encourage Daniel to speak seriously again, no restrictions, about whatever he liked. Azariah and Mishael and Hananiah had begun to listen more closely to Daniel every day. There was no denying the truth. Daniel had grown stronger while they had faded. He had remained peaceful while they so often cried like the children they were. No matter how nasty the weather, rough the terrain, bad the food or cruel the treatment, Daniel marched without complaining, finished his chores early every evening then cheerfully helped others.

Somehow he had even remained clean.

Their comfortable pretense had ended; the boys knew that odd behavior could not explain the amazing character of their pal. They began to accept, as Daniel had claimed all along, that the core of his strength was no more than his faith in God. Only a fool would not want that sort of comfort for himself.

*

The visiting women were gone in the morning. The bonfire around which they had danced had turned to ash. The clearing between the captives and the soldiers' tents stood littered with wineskins, shawls, a blanket or two, rope cords, odd sandals, two battle shields and, only paces from where the boys slept, an unsheathed knife. Some of the clutter marked trails from the campsite to the woods. When Mishael blinked awake in the morning only a few guards stood at the perimeter, some properly armed, some not.

"What a party," Azariah whispered beside him. "Did you sleep at all?"

Mishael didn't answer, embarrassed because he had shut his eyes early and remained unconscious all night. From the looks of Daniel and Hananiah, lying like dead men beside him, they had done the same. He stood and stretched, pleased that his legs felt surprisingly strong. How wonderful to have gotten more rest, plenty of fresh water and a bit of real food.

When the guards finally stirred the captives assembled on their own and formed ranks as always, ready to count off and hit the road again, but their yawning bosses ordered them to return to their spots and be quiet.

Something had certainly ended. Something else would surely begin.

*

That same morning Mishael heard that more captives had died during the night. Three older men had passed within hours of each other. Maybe they had been kin, Mishael did not know, but the boys remembered them as pleasant fellows who rarely complained.

"All three on the same night," Daniel said. "It was meant to be."

"It means nothing," Azariah spat. "Nothing means nothing. Nothing is meant to be."

Daniel patted his bitter friend's shoulder.

For the first time since they had been taken captive they were allowed to bury their dead. Daniel helped with the chore though careful to observe the Law. One of the three men who died had walked beside Daniel for several days and taken a liking to him. Two nights before his last he had handed Daniel a scroll. "Isaiah," the man had said. "Carried all the way from Jerusalem. Cling to the prophets, son, and may the God of Israel be with you all your days."

When Daniel showed his gift to his friends Mishael wondered why he seemed so happy to be burdened with it. No one understood. "I would have buried it with its owner to lighten my load," Azariah said.

"Shame on you for disrespect," Mishael said, because they had all been raised to honor the prophets, but Azariah refused to apologize. Mishael did not press it; he too would not have wanted to carry that bulky roll of parchment for even an hour. Why the old man had struggled to carry it for weeks, maybe at the cost of his life, was beyond him.

*

The captive guards preferred to shout orders to their prisoners in heavily accented Aramaic but always hurled their insults in Akkadian. On the morning after their party in the woods they spoke to one another in both languages, all excited, suggesting that something huge had happened overnight. Listening carefully, despite big gaps in their understanding, the boys learned that Nebuchadnezzar's entire army had marched past their camp late in the evening and entered Babylon. Nabopolassar, the general's father and king, had died suddenly in his sleep. So Nebuchadnezzar had turned from the brink of war against Egypt and double-timed his army home.

What a march that must have been.

But the captive band was in no such hurry to get to Babylon, it seemed. At midmorning Mishael bathed for the first time in weeks in the nearby stream. It was not the Euphrates, he knew, but for sure connected. How wonderful! Several guards threw hard chunks of yellow soap at him and other captives for sport. After they bathed they were given time to dry, then still more time to rest. When they finally broke camp in the afternoon they held to a mild pace upon a firm, wide road and soon passed spreading estates with pastures, barns, wells, fat animals and clever irrigation. Some of the nearby fields sprouted a nuggeted grain similar to that used to feed livestock in Judah. Then they saw Daniel's walls.

How had he known? They stood as tall and brightly colored as Daniel had said and lined both sides of the road, appearing to serve no purpose other than to decorate the avenue.

"Unlike our home," Daniel said, "there is little stone in Babylon. So they build with bricks, I heard them call them, like those our fathers' fathers made in Egypt as slaves. But these bricks are fired in furnaces, not dried in the sun. It makes them stronger."

"But why color them?" Hananiah asked. "The practice seems wasteful and dumb."

The odd-looking walls were littered with designs; birds, dragons and bulls depicted in red, yellow and blue, ugly, unnatural looking creatures, some with long curling tongues and human heads. But the hues of every one of them were magnificent. The yellows hid orange within them. The blues hinted at the green of sea foam on a cloudless day. The reds bled violet like at the edges of rainbows. One color especially caught Mishael's eye; it was red but not quite red, purple but not really, a lot like the color of pomegranates. How could ordinary people produce something so beautiful? The novelty made Mishael smile but several adults in their party began to wail, "Behold Babylon, wicked city of which the prophets warned, O help us, God of Abraham!"

"They've snapped," Azariah said.

Or, they know something we do not, Mishael thought.

The road turned from hard packed earth to a broader lane paved with dark red bricks. The boys walked along with their jaws fallen open as the scenery rapidly changed. Each time they spotted the new pomegranate color they pointed and laughed as if free and at home. Even Daniel seemed to enjoy the experience. But later, when the wind changed, they could smell the city. Their mood changed at once. Mishael hung back hoping no one would see him shaking. Daniel slowed to walk beside him. "Everything," he kept saying, "will be okay."

4. A coronation

MISHAEL'S FIRST GLIMPSE of Babylon came as they crested a rise in the road, the tip of a glittering tower with pennants and a bonfire up top. The soldiers cheered when they saw it. The great ziggurat! they sang out with disturbing reverence. Mishael soon heard voices wrapped in the wind and rips of strange music. He had expected to be terrified when Babylon finally hit him full face but he felt drained instead, every inch of him in pain and so hardened somehow against fear. But at their first glimpse of the tower, Daniel, of all people, fell shuddering to his knees and began to wail and pray. The boys stopped beside him, unsure what to do as a guard rushed toward them lowering his spear.

"Quick now, Daniel," Azariah whispered, "we are upsetting the men with the weapons."

Daniel revived, stood and dusted off. "Sorry," he said, "I was frightened."

"Afraid," Azariah challenged Daniel as they began to move again, "of a place?"

"A place where men worship planets, prostitutes and farm animals," Hananiah said. "You claim that doesn't concern you?"

Azariah refused to answer. Sometimes he seemed so lost, so wounded by what he had witnessed in Jerusalem, he had by then lost all light from his once shining eyes except when he was angry, which was often.

"It's hard to keep faith," Daniel said, putting a hand on his friend's shoulder, "but we must. Judah's sin demanded punishment, the prophets say, but all will work for good."

"What is my sin, Daniel?" Azariah asked, pushing Daniel's hand away. "What did I do to bring ruin to Jerusalem? What did we do to deserve to never see our families again?" He wiped away a quick tear. "Nothing works for good that I see, only heartache. So yes, Daniel, I'm having a tough time feeling rosy about the future no matter what you or the prophets say."

A bitter moment but Daniel replaced his hand and Azariah let it be. They walked side by side not speaking for a while, none of them knowing what to expect or how to act. Fear, bitterness and even a desire to die seemed like reasonable options to Mishael.

*

Upon a broad, clever bridge, the captives crossed what was certainly the famed Euphrates, landing on the far side to intersect a perimeter road paralleling Babylon's outer wall upon which, up top, countless turrets, pennants and patrolling bowman were arrayed. The lane from the bridge led to, then through, an enormous decorative gate still under construction. The captive guards began to shake their fists and shout once across the river, praising all sorts of oddly-named gods. Mishael grinned just a little despite the increased chaos and his fear seeing that their long, bitter march had somehow turned into a parade.

All around the entry gate men in turbans and women wearing coils of rings broke from their haggling at several kiosks to stop and watch the captive caravan pass. A cheer went up when, from nowhere, the big-wheeled carts the boys had first seen in Jerusalem lumbered past them into the city brimming with stolen treasure.

"Judah has learned her lesson!" someone cheered.

A boy jumped up into the lead wagon and held high gold and silver goblets, plates and platters from the temple for everyone to see. His irreverence was too much. Mishael fell to his knees—let the guards kill him if need be—and it might have happened had not Azariah yanked him to his feet before one arrived. The wagons rolled on, into the city and Judah's shame was complete. The captives' march had finally ended in the shadow of the great gate beside its two looming towers.

"This thing must be fifty feet tall," Hananiah said, "and a hundred across."

"It is named for Ishtar," Daniel said, squinting to read something, "after a goddess who these people believe helps women have babies and armies win wars."

Up top, artisans on scaffolds arranged colored bricks into images more varied, larger and even more colorful than those the boys had seen outside of town; flowered vines, winged lions, rams with crooked horns and twisted tails. Long wood beams lay stacked beside the gate mouth tethered together with rope, waiting to be hoisted up and swung between the towers. Daniel read aloud from an inscription...

> *I hung doors of cedar adorned with bronze at all the gate openings. I placed wild bulls and ferocious dragons in the gateways...so that people might gaze upon them in wonder...*

But there was no time to wonder. A man rode up on horseback and ordered the captives to count off again. Obviously an official, the bald, powerfully built fellow wore a white linen tunic tied at the waist with a black cord, a white mantle, jeweled cylinder seal about his neck and several gold and silver finger rings. Though not dressed like a military man he carried himself like an officer. With a quick wave of his hand he ordered the prisoners to turn and face him. After the captives straightened ranks the horseman dismounted and strutted past them twirling a crop. Suddenly he stopped, pointed at a healthy-looking adult and shouted, "Nippur."

A guard hurried up and pulled the man aside.

Next, the man in white shouted, "Birs Nimrud," pointing to another. This second fellow too was set apart. The process continued. Some were picked for Nippur, some for Birs Nimrud or Sippar. Some were passed by with no mention. But when he came to Mishael, Hananiah and Daniel, the man in white eyed them carefully, dismounted and forced open Mishael's mouth to inspect his teeth then snapped his fingers.

"Yes, O master," an underling said, rushing up, "Yes, O Ashpenaz."

"Send these to the school," Ashpenaz said, and guards led the three boys at spear point to a separate spot closer to the gate.

When Ashpenaz stepped past Azariah without selecting him, Daniel gasped quite softly but, as if Ashpenaz had heard him, the man in white turned back to regard Azariah a second time. Azariah refused to open his mouth for him, so Ashpenaz enlisted a burly soldier to pry it open with a sizable stick. "School!" Ashpenaz shouted after a peek inside and guards pushed Azariah into the huddle with his friends.

"Without blemish," Ashpenaz muttered before moving on.

"Two days ago," Mishael whispered, shuddering, "my face was covered with blotches."

"You had nothing to fear," Daniel said. "We are ordained to be together. How else do you explain that when Jerusalem fell we left our homes and rushed to the same spot?"

"I don't know," Mishael sighed. "Why don't you just tell me?"

"It was meant to be," Daniel said, nothing original. All the same Mishael was thrilled that his complexion had cleared.

For quite a while afterward Ashpenaz continued to dispatch captives here and there according to his whim. The boys watched him at work and, after a while, Daniel proved to be quite good at guessing where the man in white might send them.

*

From the beginning of the march to Babylon the women had walked and suffered separately. The boys knew some of them; neighbor ladies, some married, some not. They had been prodded to keep pace each day but rarely were able. Most evenings they staggered into camp well after the men but the male captives were not allowed to mingle with them or even to help them set up camp. Though they always bedded a good distance away Mishael heard their sobs the first several nights as the guards passed among them routinely. But after a week or so of marching the captive women had become as dirty and foul-smelling as the men so their tormentors lost interest.

That morning in camp, after the women had bathed at the river they were given oil for their skin and ribbons for their hair. The guards confiscated and burned their marching garments while they bathed and, after taunting the ladies in their nakedness, offered them no choice but to beg for new, revealing clothes of garish Babylonian cut, color and weight. So dressed, they were presented at an auction.

Ashpenaz ordered them to stand on platforms and submit to examinations. Once bidding for the women began Ashpenaz left them and led the boys through the Ishtar Gate and along an avenue the natives called Processional Way.

No time for goodbyes, the boys headed into the city while their brothers and sisters from Jerusalem awaited assignments for forced labor, slavery or worse. At a more elaborate market inside the city, merchants hawked spices, wares, cloth, grain, trinkets and roasting birds. Drums beat and pipes played. Everyone seemed to be shouting.

"This is no ordinary day," Hananiah said. "It couldn't be."

"I overheard the guards," Daniel told his friends. "Today, general Nebuchadnezzar becomes Babylon's king."

The reached a sunlit, park-like quadrangle that the guards called Esagila. At its center rose the ziggurat they had seen from miles away. Ashpenaz ordered the boys to stand well back. "No noise," they were warned, "and don't move."

"He doesn't want to miss the ceremony," Daniel explained.

The people called the tower at Esagila, Etemenankia, The House of the Platform between Heaven and Earth. It ran maybe three hundred feet on each side. Mishael counted seven levels to its top, stacked like flat stones, each a little smaller than the one below it.

Thousands stood all around the tower waiting for something to happen.

Suddenly the music stopped, the crowd quieted and a ceremony began. A roar went up as the crowd spotted Nebuchadnezzar, the once filth-covered general who had wrecked Jerusalem, now sunlight clean and dressed in flowing robes, bounding up the ziggurat stairs like a great cat, two at a time, to become Babylon's new king.

Trumpets sounded and the crowd cheered when Nebuchadnezzar reached the top, raised both arms and shook his fists. "*O eternal ruler,*" he began to pray in a booming voice…

> It is you who has created me and you have entrusted to me sovereignty over mankind. According to your mercy, O Lord, which you bestow upon all, cause me to love your supreme rule. Implant the fear of your divinity in my heart.

Grant me whatever may seem good before you, since it is you that controls my life.

"Fascinating," Daniel whispered. "In Judah, this man had no peace or good will within him, yet now…" His voice faded when a man dressed even more splendidly than the king, a sort of holy man, stepped from the structure up top the ziggurat and launched into a rhythmic chant with his hands raised toward the sky.

After the old priest set a crown on Nebuchadnezzar's head the king spoke again. When he finished, Nebuchadnezzar raced down the steps, jumped onto an ivory paneled litter and was borne off on the shoulders of half-naked slaves. His path from the square passed close to the boys. Seeming to recognize them, the king turned and glared at each in turn with wild eyes. Not even when he had marched bruised and starving toward Babylon, had Mishael felt so helpless, intimidated and alone.

5. Don't test your god too often

AFTER THE CEREMONY the boys marched through the city and out through a portal leading to a neighborhood beyond Babylon's wall. Soon after, they passed under an arched gateway and into a courtyard of a compound. A barracks, it looked like. More prisoners from somewhere stood assembled as if waiting for them. The boys joined their ranks and counted off. Ashpenaz addressed them.

"Nebuchadnezzar, King of Babylon, servant of Marduk, master upon whose whim your lives depend, sends greetings," he said. He turned to face the boys. "You are lucky," he told them. "Old Nabopolassar, the king's father, may his spirit reside in peace forever, did not favor your people or your god. But his son has a special interest in you Jews; he values your alleged cleverness and discounts your sour natures." Ashpenaz paused. "Are you listening? I am your master now, your benefactor, your protector, your sun, moon and stars. There is nothing as stubborn as a Jew, I have learned. Not a creature on earth. Look at the evidence. You have only one god and even he abandoned you. So says your own prophet."

"Jeremiah," Hananiah whispered.

"That's his name!" Ashpenaz snapped. "He warned you repeatedly, right?"

The boys lowered their heads.

"Now, this is an elite school," Ashpenaz went on, "but do not be impressed with your good fortune. Few of you if any will sniff the king's service, understand? Only the elite among the elite. Most, if you work very hard and cause no trouble, can look forward to administrative jobs in the provinces. Others less talented may learn trade skills and eventually do construction. If you fail here and dare embarrass us for having selected you... Let me advise you, simply, do not do that."

He removed his gloves, beat them against his thigh and examined the rising dust. "Melzar," he yelled, and a wiry little man ran forward and bowed at the waist.

"O Master?" Melzar said.

"See that these bathe then assign quarters. Tell them the rules. Organize them into classes and devise schedules." He smiled crookedly then pointed at the boys. "Pair these children from Jerusalem with the Phoenicians and Sepharites."

"In their studies?" Melzar asked.

"Lodging too," Ashpenaz said. "They will either make up ground, or not."

Melzar led everyone to the baths then to an empty barracks where he ordered all but the boys inside. "I'll be back," he told them. "Choose beds. Cooperate. Make no noise." He led Mishael and friends to a building occupied by intense looking fellows who glared at them as they stepped inside.

When Melzar began to mutter, Mishael asked, "Is there a problem?"

"These are men, not boys like you," Melzar said, "and well advanced in their training. This school is competitive. Understand? You must compete with them. It will not be fair."

"God is with us," Daniel said.

"Good for you," Melzar said, "you have a god. Except for Jews I've never met a soul without at least three. But an even break may serve you better."

Their new lodgings had forty beds, Mishael counted, twenty to each side of a center aisle. Along that aisle the inmates had hung several reed curtains painted with images of snakes, bears and stars. While the boys chose cots at the rear Melzar recited a list of rules and punishments. Afterward they reassembled in the courtyard where Ashpenaz delivered more warnings.

"You will not see much more of me after today if things go right," he said. "If they do not go right, if you cause trouble we shall cut off a finger, a toe or you'll die. If you get sick we'll cut off a finger, a toe or you'll die. Fall far behind in class? You'll do labor in the Hatti. Argue with an instructor and you will do labor in the Hatti. If you complain…"

"Labor in the Hatti?" Azariah guessed out loud.

Ashpenaz stopped, smiled coldly then spat in the clay at Azariah's feet. "We train Phoenicians, Avrites and Sepharites here, boy," he said, "slaves from Moab and Dor as well. Any of these are as clever as Jews." He stopped as if daring Azariah to disagree. "If it had been my choice I would not have brought one of you back to Babylon. The men of Assur were dogs in their day, the earth is well rid of them, but they knew how to treat your kind."

Azariah understood Ashpenaz's reference to the northern kingdom which had been wiped out by Assyria over a hundred years before. "Now gone completely," Ashpenaz smiled at Azariah, "am I right?"

Wisely, Azariah held his tongue. Ashpenaz started away, barking over his shoulder that there would be a last assembly later that evening. The new students would begin their routine the next day.

Once back at the barracks, Daniel suggested that they try to sleep. Mishael dropped into his cot—hard as stone yet a luxury—and shut his eyes, too sapped of strength to worry. It would soon be time for their next meeting. Who knew what might happen then?

*

Melzar came for the boys earlier than expected and led them to the front gate where Ashpenaz stood waiting, clearly upset. "You are trouble already," he said. "The king has ordered that his Hebrews should eat from his table, a privilege granted only to a few and usually earned." He turned to Melzar. "I warned you. They are your problem now." He turned back to the boys. "By the king's word you will eat better than the others and I hope you choke. Nebuchadnezzar embraces an odd superstition but don't be encouraged, no instructor here will favor you. None will tolerate tricks, maneuvers, or demands for special treatment."

That was clear enough, no need to test the wind, but when Ashpenaz turned to leave Daniel followed him, forgetting the guidelines regarding fingers and toes. "Please, sir," he said, and the bald man stopped. "I would like to discuss our food."

"Have you heard anything I've said?" Ashpenaz asked.

"In our faith," Daniel said, "we're forbidden to eat what has been consecrated to false gods."

"Forbidden because of your faith?"

"Correct."

"Do you hear this, Melzar?" Ashpenaz asked.

"I have observed this one since he arrived." Melzar said. "He's not quite right."

"It would defile us," Daniel said, "and we must not eat it."

"You are either brave, boy, or stupid," Ashpenaz said in a surprisingly mild voice. "If it's courage I can admire it. If it's dullness we will see soon enough. But I tell you, I fear the king. He would end me if you or one of your friends turned up sickly or pale."

"I do not believe what I have witnessed," Melzar whispered when Ashpenaz left. "My master does not chat with slaves, much less explain or apologize. He kills them, most often, if they are foolish enough to step out of line, sometimes after torture." He sighed, looking for sympathy. "Or he orders me to do the rotten job."

"God intervened," Daniel said, "the real one."

"If I were you," Melzar said, "I would not test my god too often in this place."

"I ask that you, Melzar, test us," Daniel said. "For ten days give us nothing but pulse to eat and water to drink..." Azariah stuck a finger into his open mouth and pretended to gag. "...then compare us to the men who eat the royal food and treat us in accordance with what you see."

"You somehow avoided a slit throat just now," Melzar said, "but don't begin to imagine you can maneuver here for favor. You have no rights. I will certainly not risk my life for a slave, helpless or not, boy or not."

Mishael felt relieved, in all honesty, because he had always enjoyed a good meat dinner, but that evening in the dining hall Melzar's servers brought the boys only beans and fruit.

"What's this?" Hananiah asked.

"Undefiled food," Daniel said, winking.

Melzar came up to their table later and whispered, "Lentils for energy, blueberries for eyesight and memory, raspberry for brain function. But if one of you even sneezes you'll be eating the king's food and drinking his wine."

Azariah sneezed to be funny. Melzar hurried away.

"What just happened?" Hananiah asked. "Both Ashpenaz and Melzar said no yet we sit here eating yes. Why did Melzar risk his life?"

"We are not alone on this journey," Daniel said, his mouth full of beans, "it is the kindly work of the God of Israel."

Faith was how Daniel explained everything. And though it seemed unlikely, he had been right every time since their trouble began.

*

On the boys' first morning in class an instructor named Suusaandar changed their names. When would the evil end? After King Josiah had died from his wounds at Megiddo Mishael had lived in constant fear of war. Later, when Babylon came to town, he nearly starved to death. Before reaching the age of fifteen he had lost his home, his family and nearly every friend yet somehow he had managed to survive; so Mishael was stunned by how much it hurt him when Babylon took the very last thing he owned.

"Excuse me?" Mishael asked Suusaandar in Aramaic, not quite believing what he had heard.

"Meshach, your name will be," the instructor repeated while entering the disgusting moniker into the elite-school roll. "After Mi-sha-aku, which means, a mighty god." (The Sepharites laughed when Mishael's lower lip may have quivered, only briefly.)

Suusaandar cleared his throat and said to Hananiah, "You will be called Shadrach, Aku's command," but Hananiah turned away, seeming not to hear.

In Suusaandar's next breath Azariah became Abednego. "Nobody knows exactly what that means," he told him, "but it's a popular name in the land and you shall bear it."

Daniel was given the name, Belteshazzar, meaning Bêl guard his life. Mishael expected a scene then, perhaps a flat refusal, but Daniel surprised his friends by making no fuss at all, explaining later, "It makes no difference what Babylon might call me. I know who I am."

"Shadrach, Meshach and Abednego," Azariah crooned with an unconcerned smile, cheering Mishael somewhat. "You have to admit, when recited together, they have a certain rhythm."

"Never concede anything to Satan," Daniel scolded, and Mishael's sadness revived.

*

Suusaandar's course covered cuneiform writing. The boys' ignorance of Akkadian proved worse than they had feared. They were lost. The Babylonian system, they discovered, included over 500 symbols and scores of complex rules for their use. The boys found themselves two months behind and Suusaandar offered not hope, but antagonism.

"I prefer Phoenicians to Jews," he told the class though no one had asked him. "They're smart as whips and never trouble. You boys feel superior?" he asked Daniel. "Catch up, then, on your own."

"Are you guys beginning to feel unloved?" Azariah whispered to his friends, but Mishael was too depressed to even smile inwardly.

After class, all of them renamed and feeling low, Daniel proposed a short-term solution to their potential problem (which he characterized as appearing to be highly ignorant). "Let's hold our peace, keep questions to ourselves and pretend that we understand," he suggested. "The less we say in class the more confident we'll seem, the less likely Suusaandar will be to call on us. I sense that he, resenting the king's interest in us, will not want to showcase our skills."

Azariah was skeptical of course, he doubted everything, but Daniel's plan worked. The boys nodded in their ignorance day by day and their silence seemed to intimidate Suusaandar. The practice of pretending to be intelligent became addle-brained fun, especially for Daniel, who had somehow learned a few things in that confounding class.

"But eventually they will test us," Azariah said, "and then what?"

Nobody knew the answer. But, as Daniel put it, "We must deal with each day for what it may yield and leave the long-view to the Lord."

Azariah inhaled to argue but Hananiah wrapped him in a choke hold and refused to let him speak. It was entertaining; all three of Azariah's friends were sick of him and his negativity.

*

After ten special-diet days passed Melzar was stunned by the boys' health, glow and fitness after eating nothing but beans and fruit.

"You look fatter," he said, all surprised. "Tell me truly, you have never tasted the king's wine or nibbled a bit of blessed meat?"

Daniel assured him, never, but Melzar had his doubts. Melzar did not seem to like the boys but he didn't seem to hate them either. Often he whispered advice, confusing the boys further. "The God of Israel has made him our ally," Daniel told his friends one night in the barracks. "If we continue in faith, Melzar will also protect us later."

"Protect us from what?" Hananiah asked.

"The Phoenicians are fine with us now," Daniel said, "because we remain silent and in the background. They cannot imagine that we'll someday become their serious competition."

"Neither can I," Azariah said.

"Right now, the less Suusaandar finds it necessary to contend with us, the better," Daniel said. "But when we catch up and begin to excel..."

"Do you really think we will?" Mishael asked, because he could not picture it.

"...the Phoenicians will become our enemies. They will oppose us for a long time."

"So we'll live!" Mishael gushed.

Azariah rolled his eyes. "How would Daniel know?" he said. "He's not a prophet."

That comment led to an awkward pause.

Mishael said, "Not yet."

What a humbling moment. They all began to shiver then slid to the barracks floor between their beds to pray in hushed tones on their knees. From then on, though they rarely mentioned what they had just seemed to learn about their friend, they agreed to listen more respectfully to whatever Daniel said.

Maybe he would someday be a prophet?

*

A month passed. On a given day Mishael might feel a rush of joy for having remained alive. On another, grief would nearly cripple him for the same reason. But whether his spirits rose or fell it became clear that he and his friends had begun to learn wondrous things. What a place, that school in Babylon. Stepping past any open classroom door on that breezy campus one overheard snippets of mathematics, law, medicine, languages, military science and civil administration. The collected wisdom of ages of Babylonian inquiry, some of it evil but much of it fascinating, were Mishael's to weigh if he might only survive.

Many of the elite school's instructors shamelessly taught magic, divining, mysticism and alchemy. And though these sinful pursuits were among the most popular among the students captured from the nations, the boys sought protection from their influence in prayer. But what was prayer? Mishael had begun to wonder. As a child he had prayed every morning and evening to please his parents, offering up recitations to Someone, he suspected, who lived in the sky. But back then, safe and secure at home in Jerusalem he had moved from thing to thing unworried about the sky, the world or the future. But after losing everything he regretted that his prayers as a child had not been more frequent, thoughtful and sincere.

"Maybe God allows bad things to happen to add intensity to our prayers?" Daniel said.

Azariah threw his hands up to object but that made sense to Mishael. If he had learned anything as a child in Jerusalem, Babylon's siege and sack of the temple had proved that the God of Israel demands respect. Those who have no hope but him pray often, urgently and well but those who accept life's blessings as their due, who benefit from all his goodness yet fail to seek him in prayer with all their hearts, minds and souls, risk waking some sunny morning to find Nebuchadnezzar at their gate.

*

One late night in the barracks, Daniel woke his friends in their cots and whispered, "I've been thinking, praying and listening to the guards' conversations. We're getting by here now by pretending to understand but to thrive when our testing begins we must get past the alphabet, arithmetic and folk tales. We'll need to do real math. We must learn to read well enough to interpret Babylonian laws, literature and philosophy at their highest levels."

"I can't count to sixty yet," Azariah said.

"If they don't eliminate us beforehand our language training will last a year," Daniel said. "To be chosen for the king's service we'll also need to know and interpret their scripture."

"They have the Word?"

"Tens of thousands of words about planets, animals and spells."

"I refuse to read any of it," Azariah said.

"Well, right now you can't," Hananiah sighed. "That's our problem."

So they pledged to study in secret every night in the shadows between their beds. And they did. Though they worked hard nothing changed at first. Classes continued and they fell into a numbing routine. It did not help that everybody knew that the king favored them as sons of Judah; that Nebuchadnezzar constantly pestered Suusaandar, their principle instructor, by asking, "How are my Hebrews doing?"

My Hebrews. Maybe because of the king's overworked phrase, Suusaandar both warned and threatened them one day. "Everyone in this elite school has been chosen to compete not only for high station but for survival too," he said. "The king needs talent, not mouths to feed, so do well here, students, or likely die." He broke into a tight-lipped grin. "This training, slaves, can be looked at as an opportunity to advance but it is more correctly perceived as a struggle to survive. I promise, you students will hold privileged slots in this academy only so long as you appear to be worthy. Accomplishment is your best and only way to survive."

"They would never kill us," Azariah said later.

"Not now," Daniel said, "while the king is so interested in our welfare but yes, later, if we fail."

Mishael thanked Daniel sarcastically for his upbeat opinion. Daniel missed the intended irony and answered, "You're welcome," having no idea how depressing he could be.

6. Night studies

AS TIME PASSED, instead of making peace with his new life in Babylon Mishael's sense of loss haunted him more each day. After long hours in class and still more effort spent studying in the barracks every night, he would sometimes lie in bed afterward, completely spent, and hope to die. But Daniel insisted that they were blessed. That was how he always thought no matter how bad things seemed to be. "Our situation could be much worse," he offered one afternoon after his three friends had taken turns complaining.

"We still have each other," Mishael supposed, trying to be agreeable.

"And we still have our God."

Mishael winced upon hearing poor, angry Azariah's sure cue to rise up and object. "Where is God then?" Azariah shot back. "Where has he gone after turning us into orphans?"

They had stopped to talk near the entry arch. The sun had not quite set and its low, reddish light had lit the blowing dust and filled Babylon's air with what looked like sparks. "To find him," Daniel said, "you must look in his direction."

"Everywhere I look," Azariah shot back, "I see thugs who want to break our necks. Everywhere I sniff, I smell Babylon. I hear threats of mutilation almost every day and I know for a fact that this entire school would be thrilled if that happened."

"Yes," Daniel said, "all this evil about and look, thanks to God we still thrive!"

Azariah wrote Daniel off as he always did, as hopeless, and that was how their days passed; a meal, classes, a short break, more classes, an argument between Daniel and Azariah, a final meal of plain lentils then hours of hushed study huddling in the barracks. As Daniel had predicted their skills eventually improved. Every evening at twilight, while their Phoenician bunkmates and a gang of Sepharites sat in the fresh air by the main gate watching wagons pass or telling stories, the boys began their studies by praying on their knees...

Blessed art thou, O Lord our God, King of the universe, who provides for all our needs.

They drilled for hours every night, whispering even after their rivals returned and slept, crediting the God of Israel for their surprising energy. Gradually, they began to understand the cuneiform. It seemed miraculous. Daniel said it was nothing less than so. After two more months of pounding the language they could follow the Akkadian tongue quite well, even to grasping idioms. Armed with their new skill they began to eavesdrop unaware on their guards and faculty, hearing many things not intended for their ears.

Even then they memorized, repeated, analyzed and reviewed new phrases every night.

Daniel proved best at the language because he seemed immensely gifted at recognizing and manipulating patterns. Akkadian fell subject, object, verb. Hebrew most often went verb, subject, object. By forcing himself to purposely think out of order and noting certain similarities to Aramaic, which they all understood, Daniel was first of the four to become fluent but, slowly, they all began to hear, read, speak and understand the strange Akkadian tongue beyond even Daniel's expectations. So they agreed one night that the time had come to make a move in class. It was time to demonstrate their new abilities to Suusaandar so not to be expelled, or worse.

But exactly how should they go about it? And when?

"Once we establish ourselves as legitimate contenders for appointments to the king's court," Azariah said, "the Phoenicians will want to kill us."

Mishael hoped that Daniel would laugh at that notion but Daniel agreed.

"If we move too soon," Daniel said, "we will alert and threaten our competition."

"If too late..." Azariah said. He made a slashing gesture across his neck.

They agreed to leave the timing to God, Daniel's suggestion, because things always worked out God's way anyway, and so they held their peace in class and waited for a sign. But no sign came at first.

As more time passed the boys had grown so skilled that even Mishael, easily the slowest learner of the four, became impatient with the pace of learning. He had been tempted many times to speak up and show Suusaandar and the others how much he understood but something always held him back. "If nothing happens soon," he said, "they'll cull us out and dismiss us as dumb."

"When we least expect it the moment will arrive," Daniel said.

And so it did. One cool afternoon as a light breeze blew through the classroom windows Suusaandar asked during a drill, "Who will render what I've just said, Akkadian to Aramaic?"

The star of the class to that point, a muscular, full-grown Phoenician from ArSuun named Philosir, sat up front hesitating, stroking his chin.

"Come now, my geniuses," Suusaandar said, "soon everything we shall say will flow in the heavenly tongue, or else. Those of you who cannot keep up will be digging wells in the districts or building huts in the Hatti." He smiled and wriggled his brows. "Or worse."

Suddenly Daniel said, "You said, although the men of Akkad were disrespected in Egypt, Nineveh and the Hatti for nearly two centuries, the courage and leadership of mighty Nabopolassar, may he rest in peace forever, restored Chaldea's place as first among the nations, beginning at Carchemish summer last."

The room fell still. Suusaandar looked down at his sandals, sniffed then mumbled, "Correct." Though the king's special interest in his captured Jews was well known, the boys' failure to produce up till then had given their rivals hope. "Now this," Suusaandar muttered. "Clearly, somebody has been studying and holding back."

When a surprised Sepharite, undistinguished in the school and politically unaware, turned in his seat to congratulate Daniel for his clever go at the translation, big Philosir rose in his chair and glared.

The proceedings had simply stopped. Suusaandar's disappointment hung in the air as thick as fog. Mishael, Hananiah and Azariah traded shrugs. Was that it? Had their long awaited silence-breaking come and gone with a thud? But Suusaandar slowly revived. "I have wondered exactly when you fuzzy-faced boys would show your hand," he finally said. "No one could be as thick as you four have seemed, nodding at everything, whether it was right or wrong."

The class laughed, but only a little. "Good for you, then," Suusaandar said, "but I wonder how far you have really come." He closed his eyes and recited something at a blazing clip then said, "Tell me, Belteshazzar, what did I just say?"

The particular passage Suusaandar had recited, maybe part of an Akkadian poem, spoken quickly and laced with tricky words and phrases, was far too difficult for Mishael to tackle but Daniel nodded and began…

"All the desert blooms in adoration," he recited. "Azure skies span the eastern plain. Akkad glimmers sacrosanct in the light of the false god Marduk's glory."

False god?

"False god?" Suusaandar repeated Mishael's thought, blinking rapidly. The guards lounging along the back wall snapped erect as the instructor whipped his reed pointer into splinters across a table top. "False god?" he shouted a second time, bolting toward the rear of the room to where, as should have been no surprise, Daniel remained as composed and calm as he had been in Jerusalem when Nebuchadnezzar threatened to split him in two.

"Recite again, correctly," Suusaandar hissed.

Mishael needed air. He wanted to suck in every ounce of air in the classroom, in all Babylon, then blast it out again to shout, Praise the God of Israel! so proud was he that Daniel had bravely spoken the truth. Who was stupid Marduk after all if not a fable, a planet, a weak, numb light in the cold sky that the Master of the universe had made?

"Again, Jew, I say," Suusaandar demanded, "and this time, if you wish to keep your teeth behind your smug little smile, recite the passage exactly as I have dictated."

Daniel sat perfectly still, hands folded in front of him, not blinking. It became suddenly clear to Mishael, to everyone, Daniel did not intend to speak! The guards began to fidget. All of them knew that the king personally followed the progress of his Hebrews. How would it go, then, if Suusaandar harmed one of them against the king's will?

The pause became embarrassing. It looked like Suusaandar's rage would get the better of him but when the livid instructor's hand dropped to the hilt of his dagger and he began to draw it out an odd thing happened. The Phoenician, Philosir, began to recite the same passage aloud, stumbling some but ending as dictated, "…in the light of Marduk's glory."

Again, nobody moved.

"Correct," Suusaandar said softly, dropping his weapon back into its sheath.

"Suusaandar has saved face," Azariah whispered. "Philosir made it possible."

Suusaandar returned up front, confused perhaps, for sure frustrated, clearly not certain whether he had won, lost or broken even. "So, Belteshazzar," he said, his voice lacking its usual confident edge, "the king will be pleased to hear of your progress." He scooped up the fractured pieces of his pointer and tossed them aside in disgust. "But hear this, Jews," he said, "if you are half as wise as you may feel just now, understand that the king of Babylon will never favor insubordination over the workings of this prized institution. We have rules here. We employ keen remedies against those who break them, lawful and customary, yet many entail torture before death. So…" He stopped and smiled. "Consider my message a word to the wise."

Mishael caught himself grinning in the same carefree manner as his friend. He had not understood until that moment how much he thoroughly hated Babylon. But good faithful Daniel, sweet Daniel… Daniel had faced his would-be masters and not flinched. He had challenged them by being faithful to the God of Israel and they had backed away.

Mishael wished to shout, Hallelujah! And though he did not shout, he dared any of his Phoenician or Sepharite classmates to notice his new, bold look.

How wonderful to be alive again, he thought, because now, thanks to Daniel's courage, he no longer feared dying. How grand to stand in truth with his brother because it was the righteous thing to do. He would not be corrupted. He would not bow down. He and his friends would continue to pray, to work, to learn and grow, all the while refusing to embrace Babylon's filthy myths, deny the faith of their fathers or eat food consecrated to harlots, asteroids and wild animals.

He would never forsake the God of Israel.

*

Once the drama concerning their progress ended, the boys' attention turned to survival. Daniel had made no friends by establishing his advanced literacy. After word spread regarding his confrontation with Suusaandar the other instructors also labeled Daniel a troublemaker; Mishael, Hananiah and Azariah as well, by association. Still, with their learning now finally exposed, the boys quickly moved past the Phoenicians in status in the class. All of their rivals, especially Philosir, understood that their ambitions to one day graduate and join the king's council had been put on notice by the scholarliness of their Hebrew rivals.

"We now seriously threaten their futures," Daniel said. "But if we hold back… If we can manage to appear to be only a little ahead in class… If they do not totally lose hope of retaking the lead…"

"Then they may not try to kill us," Azariah finished for him.

"Yes," Daniel said in a cheery tone, as though he were discussing the weather instead of the odds of their being murdered. "And we'll also be able to overhear more from the guards and staff if they think we know less than we do."

Daniel's tactic worked. The Phoenicians began to spend less time socializing at the gate in the evenings and began to study harder. With increased competition the pace in class quickened. Suusaandar, proving to be a teacher after all, seemed to enjoy the new energy that had evolved, so he began to spice up the language lessons using uncommon phrases and idioms. "Let's see who can keep up," Suusaandar would say. The boys were always game.

Though Philosir and his friends studied every night afterwards in the barracks it was too late for them. By then the boys could do Akkadian in their sleep. They could speak, interpret, cipher, reason, measure, weigh… But in keeping with Daniel's plan they also became skilled at balking when Suusaandar moved too fast though they were miles ahead of the Phoenicians and daily widening the gap.

Rather than rely upon what they had already mastered, Daniel increased the pace of their studies—sometimes they worked all night—but no matter how long they drilled in the shadows they always felt fresh the next day.

"God has given us tremendous energy," Daniel explained.

God's hand in their growth and strength seemed so obvious that even Azariah agreed. But then he would ask, why? "Why does God bother to help us now," he challenged, as always a little bitter, "after making us orphans?" His friends sighed. Patience and continued prayer, they hoped, would someday allow Azariah to accept God's chastening with a peaceful heart.

Their memories had improved too. Daniel and Hananiah could recall and recite whole notices posted in Akkadian on the compound walls. Mishael and Azariah could repeat word for word, absolutely certain and error free, snippets and phrases of casual speech they had overheard during the day. Late evenings, in whispers while their rivals slept, the boys analyzed and interpreted everything. But they continued to demonstrate only enough learning in class to stay ahead of the Phoenician leader, Philosir.

Suusaandar had no idea how far the boys had really come. The proof of his deception came clear whenever he spoke to his peers or to monitors from the king's court rapidly, in high Akkadian, clearly comfortable that his words were secure.

But the boys understood everything.

"Philosir, the Phoenician, deeply resents the Jews," Mishael overheard Suusaandar tell a king's man one day. "But I suppose Nebuchadnezzar will be thrilled," he sighed. "His Hebrews are proving him right."

"Are his favorites in danger, then?" the king's man asked.

"There's only so much we can do," Suusaandar smiled, and they laughed together.

Clearly only the king's interest had kept the boys alive. "But what more can we do?" Mishael asked his friends. "We are delivered into captivity by the arm of the Lord. He will preserve us, or not, according to his will."

"Exactly," Daniel said. "So expect miraculous protection."

For lack of a better plan they agreed to do exactly that. Soon after they agreed, their strategy was mightily tested.

*

One early morning, pitch dark, Daniel shook Mishael awake while he lay in bed, nudged the others and motioned for them to follow him outside. Daniel never broke rules. Leaving the barracks during sleep time was a finger-toe-death trespass. Mishael's heart raced as they tiptoed toward the rear but Azariah snickered like a wicked child, eager to swim upstream.

Usually a guard sat at the exit but that dark morning they found only an empty chair. Daniel tried the door. "It's open," he whispered, "because it had to be." He cracked it a notch farther. Azariah cackled again. Risking his neck thrilled the misguided boy.

Out they went, no one in sight. The sky lay blue-black over the compound, full moon and brilliant stars capping the earth's pale rim to the east proving daylight was near, glorious to behold, but the air chilled Mishael to the bone.

They huddled for warmth along the barracks wall. "Why did you wake us?" Mishael asked. "We could lose our noses."

"Pray for a moment of privacy," Daniel said.

"We've conspired inside with privacy for months," Hananiah said, "why take this risk now?"

"Pray," Daniel repeated and the bickering stopped.

"I had a dream," Daniel said when they finished, "a vision which confirms what we've overheard. We must stay together always, every minute, from now on. If not we will be killed." Azariah grinned and rubbed his hands together, like someone was about to hand him a cake.

"Stop that," Mishael hissed, "we do not all share your death wish."

"Suusaandar hates us," Hananiah said, "but he knows that the king is watching. He also seems to respect that we've caught up. I can't imagine, Daniel, that he would harm us now."

"He's not our problem," Daniel said. "In my vision, Suusaandar stood between us and a shadowy figure easily five cubits tall, with black eyes and huge, hairy fists holding high a flaming sword."

"Philosir," Mishael and Hananiah murmured together.

"I'm sure that the Phoenician has figured out our game," Daniel said. "He understands that he can't beat us in the classroom and so has hatched a murder plot. Tomorrow will be critical. Let's skip the exercise period and stay close to the staff. They will protect us; if we were harmed in their presence the king would have their heads."

"Why doesn't Philosir simply murder us in the dorm?" Azariah asked.

"Witnesses?" Mishael said. "Certain punishment?"

"Philosir would never risk his neck to do the deed where so many could see," Hananiah said. "The others would not protect him if they were tortured."

"Let's kill him first, then," Azariah said. "He sleeps defenseless now!"

"Wonderful," Hananiah said, "and regarding his thirty friends?"

"We are already safe," Daniel said.

The boys stopped to stare at him.

"If we are so safe, Daniel," Azariah said, "why are we out here freezing, risking our pinkies to discuss it?"

Daniel ignored him. "Let's thank God for the warning," he said, "and he shall provide."

They all knew better than to argue. They prayed again, no burden at all. Thanks to Daniel they had thanked the Lord so often since being captured that Mishael had begun to enjoy it, sometimes able to see much more with his eyes closed than open.

The boys rose from their knees and pledged from then on to eat, exercise and study together always. By day they would stay near their instructors. They would cross the campus only on the main paths (never between buildings or where foliage might hide them from view). By night in the barracks they would remain within site of the rear door guard.

Philosir and his mates would never find an opportunity to harm them.

7. Excellence

T WO YEARS PASSED. The boys remained safe. With no reason to hold back after Daniel's protective vision the boys felt free to demonstrate all that they had learned and soon left their competition in the dust. Despite their huge lead in class they continued to study day and night. Though Philosir and his friends grew increasingly hostile, the boys provided no openings to do them harm. Owing only to their excellence (for they were not at all well-liked), Daniel, Mishael, Hananiah and Azariah became celebrities in the school. When they spoke, other students listened, and their instructors listened as well.

Suusaandar proved to be an educator at heart. In the face of their excellence he no longer required his star pupils to attend regular classes. Instead, he arranged a series of special lectures featuring magicians, sorcerers, military men, officials in the king's court and astrologers. The boys absorbed everything that was informative, valuable or good and rejected that which was not of God. And they grew continually in wisdom.

Mishael was not happy in Babylon, he could never be, but like his friends he had begun to become a man. Each of them had grown a head taller since being taken captive, each had developed a passing beard and wiry muscles. More importantly, each of them had matured emotionally, so there were many less tears.

Mishael prayed continually, ate only pulse like his friends and competed regularly at athletics in the yard. He had learned to shoe, outfit and ride a horse. He could lift large stones, climb ropes and scale structures. He had become a whiz at math, could speak and write well in three languages and knew several odd dialects spoken in the East and across the Hatti. In a measured way his growth and new abilities thrilled him—men handled things differently than boys— but an unnamed anxiety continued to haunt him.

"Why so?" Azariah asked.

"Philosir and his buddies still hate us," Mishael said. "They want us to die, are determined to make it happen and are only biding their time."

"Let's pray, then, that they are quickly dismissed from this school and sent west to do construction," Hananiah said.

"It won't happen," Daniel told them, sounding more like a prophet each week. "They are brilliant men, really, though evil, and they'll remain our enemies for decades."

Mishael smiled despite the bad news. At least Daniel believed they would live for a while.

*

The boys always listened politely during their specially arranged lectures but refused to engage in discussion with Babylonian astrologers, priests, seers or magicians, and for good reason; their instruction was of the adversary.

Babylon had also taught Mishael that Satan lived, for her holy men and magicians performed many supernatural deeds. For centuries, with the adversary's help, Akkadian mystics tracked the sun, moon and stars and divined to advise kings, all the while recording their creepy observations in well-maintained diaries. It was all wicked nonsense, often unreliable, but sometimes not. Daniel had cautioned his friends neither to disregard nor value the local mystics' immoral powers. "Worthwhile revelation comes only from God," he said, "yet sometimes these men are disturbingly accurate. But because their gifts are not from God it is important to ignore them."

The seers of Babylon manifested the real but lesser powers of Astarte, queen of heaven, Baal, ruler of the universe, son of Dagan, rider of the clouds, Marduk, Nabu and on and on... But these wicked gods were only extensions of the evil one himself, hating mankind but also willing to confer favors on his devotees in order to corrupt their souls.

So the boys steered clear of black arts, continued to study and grow and never abandoning their hopes of returning to Jerusalem. Daniel, of course, surpassed everyone in everything yet remained humble, prayerful and kind.

Sometimes Mishael could not stand him.

II. Babylon

8. The king's dream

EARLY ONE MORNING, King Nebuchadnezzar of Babylon sat up in his bed and roared. He had not yet turned thirty; he had lived in perpetual abundance both as a general and a king and he had never known defeat. Yet he could not sleep. When no one came running to serve him he bellowed again, a wild noise that thundered in the halls. (The harsh echoes pleased him briefly, like a sneeze might thrill a child.) Amytis, his queen, once herself a haughty princess among the Medes, feared nothing ordinarily, but on that morning she ran from the room.

That pleased Nebuchadnezzar too. A wise king never made excuses for his passion. He shouted a third time. When his attendants finally approached he said, "I cannot sleep. I've had a troubling dream and fear an evil spell has been stuck to me. Summon my magicians, enchanters, sorcerers and astrologers."

"Which of them, O king?" one asked.

Nebuchadnezzar grabbed an enormous clay pot beside his bed and threw it across the room. "Bring them all," he yelled as it shattered against the wall, "and bring them now."

*

It fell upon Arioch, captain of the kings' men, to dispatch troops across Babylon to round up every wise man in the land. Arioch took every royal command seriously, including the dumb ones, and so he treated this charge from the king with a keen sense of urgency. But after hours of effort his men had managed to bring only a handful of seers to the palace.

The king refused to wait longer. Arioch had no choice but to present those he had collected and hope for the best. Among those rounded up was Nebuchadnezzar's chief astrologer and High Priest of Marduk, Enshunu, who himself had crowned the king. Arioch knew quite a bit about the famous old wizard. Enshunu had also served under Nabopolassar, the king's father, and he had dazzled all Babylon with demonstrations of supernatural power. He was said to have ended two droughts, to have cast several crippling spells on the Medes (back when they were enemies) and reliable sources testified that the priest could see in the dark.

Maybe Enshunu would satisfy the king?

After a big cleansing breath Arioch marched into the royal bedchamber and said, "O king, some you have summoned await, including the High Priest of Marduk himself."

"Some?"

Arioch swallowed hard. "It's been a hectic morning, Sire."

Nebuchadnezzar shut his eyes. "You, old soldier," he said, "once served my father well. Yet you and I never campaigned together."

"My loss, Majesty, surely."

"Nor have we experienced the intimacy and trust that naturally accrue to brothers at arms, eh?" The king paused briefly for drama then added, "What do these facts suggest to you?"

"They suggests to me that you and I have not shared the camaraderie that one might…"

The king raised his hand and Arioch stopped. "What are these, Captain?" he asked, his eyes resting upon a bowl of fruit beside the bed.

"Dates, Majesty," Arioch said, "and figs, pomegranates and nuts still in their shells."

"I know that, you fool. Where did they come from?"

Arioch shrugged.

"A simple question for you then, Captain. Answer carefully. Is this stuff poisoned?"

In a just world Arioch would have laughed in the king's face and asked, Are you serious? Instead he stammered, "The royal taster knows his duty, Sire. I'm sure…"

"You are sure!" the king howled. "How wonderful! You have no idea, soldier, how safe it makes me feel to know that the captain of my guard is sure." He spat. "I'll show you how sure I am. Go now and arrest the taster fellow, take him to Esagila and behead him at a public ceremony on suspicion of poisoning the king."

"He has a wife, Sire," Arioch said, "and two small girls."

"Then warn him," Nebuchadnezzar screamed at the top of his lungs, "that someone will soon die miserably if these dreams of mine don't stop mangling the royal sleep."

"Of course, O king," Arioch muttered, averting his eyes. "And the high priest?"

"Bring in everyone now," Nebuchadnezzar sighed, "before I go completely mad."

Arioch left the room at once, suspecting the king had already lost his mind.

*

The king's bedchamber was a high-ceilinged suite with lion profiles sculpted on its walls. Rows of huge clay pots dotted its polished floor (though one less than earlier as a result of the king's fit). Bright tapestries framed an opening onto a patio at the far end of the room. From there one could see the great ziggurat and half the city. The king stood out on that patio while waiting for his seers, inspecting the progress of a magnificent terraced project he had begun for his queen; an elaborate garden.

"It's magnificent, O king," Arioch said when he returned.

"Where's the priest?"

The captain bowed then led in a handful of magicians, Enshunu first. Nebuchadnezzar had never liked the pompous old man but Enshunu had been a favorite of his dad's. Before the king could speak Enshunu said, "Sire, I've had a vision of your upcoming campaign."

"Have you?" Nebuchadnezzar asked. He crossed the room and sat in a large chair in the corner (Amytis called it his little bedroom throne) and tried to speak evenly, without raising his voice. "And what did your vision reveal?"

"A great and lasting victory over Egypt," Enshunu said, "provided Nabu, son of Marduk and Sarpanitum, grandson of Ea, god of wisdom and writing, are appeased."

"Sarpanitum!" Nebuchadnezzar said. "Hi, ho! I'm encouraged by that."

"Most certainly, O king," Enshunu said, missing Nebuchadnezzar's sarcasm. "All Babylon knows that had your father, may he rest in peace forever, not fallen ill and died untimely, the army under your superb generalship would have crushed Pharaoh Necho's ragged band and stuck Egypt in our pocket."

Nebuchadnezzar smiled a little. The wily priest certainly knew his flattery. "Ordinarily, Enshunu, I would run with your praise," he sighed, "but today I have an awful headache."

"Headache, Sire?"

"Splitting and, more importantly, I am unable to sleep unmolested by a dream."

"I understand, O king," Enshunu said, "but your coming victory in Egypt, Sire, headache or no, is sealed in the courses of planets, in cast bones, in sacred chicken guts, all provided..."

"Enough," Nebuchadnezzar said. "You speak nonsense. Rotten Necho has had ample time to retrench and rearm his sissy army since I whipped him. I'm haunted I tell you, by a sense of opportunity lost..." He stopped to clear his thoughts. "But that's not why you're here."

"...provided, of course, that you, the king, continue to please Marduk," Enshunu finished.

The king pressed his temples as he spoke. "What the royal treasury eventually doles out to you and your pal, Marduk, for colored smoke, frilly eunuchs, so-called temple virgins, jewels and embroidered pennants is a matter for another day." He raised his fist then lowered it slowly. "I've had a dream, priest, I say, and I want to know what it means."

Enshunu smiled confidently. "Such stress over a mere vision, Sire? You have gathered here many of the finest Chaldeans in the land..."

"And more are coming, O king," Arioch hastened to say.

"...but, with all humility, I, your own high priest have proved myself to be skilled at divining every manner of late night manifestation. So please, O king, send these honorable souls back to their lesser gods. Marduk spawns all dreams. I can read them all."

Nebuchadnezzar sat and said nothing. Arioch had never seen the king in poorer humor.

"Tell me the details of the thing, O king," Enshunu said, "and I shall comfort you."

"No, priest," the king said, "it is gone from me."

"Come again, Sire?"

"I've forgotten it." Nebuchadnezzar said.

It seemed to please Nebuchadnezzar, then, to see Enshunu squirm. "Use the power of which you boast to tell me what I've seen." He eyed the other practitioners in the room. "If you clever fellows cannot give me what I ask then all of you and your ilk shall surely die."

*

Hananiah, in his view, was by far the most normal of the four friends who had miraculously become the king's Hebrews in Babylon. It was not vain of him to think so, only accurate. Who would brag about being ordinary? Daniel was unbelievably wise. Mishael, sadly, was embarrassingly weak. Poor Azariah was cursed with a terrible temper and worse judgment. But Hananiah was steady. Hananiah always did his job without complaining. When there was work to do he worked; when prayers were in order he prayed. That was it.

"But you are never your happy self anymore," Mishael had often complained.

True enough. Before the morning Jerusalem fell Hananiah had never before set eyes on a cadaver. Before wild men breached the city's walls he had never imagined rape. Credit Babylon, then, for changing him from cheerful boy to cold observer in less than a day.

Hananiah sat in a small classroom one morning doing exactly that, coldly observing, while he and his friends waited for a guest lecturer, the high priest Enshunu, to appear. Suusaandar stepped in instead and said, "Today's session has been canceled. There's been a thing at the palace that has required the presence of Enshunu himself."

"A thing?" Daniel asked, but Suusaandar, instead of answering, handed them tablets.

"Study these council notes, especially those regarding Sidon and Tyre," he said. "Be prepared to discuss the findings therein as if to advise the king." On his way out he added, "I'm off to the citadel to learn what's up."

The boys divided the tablets and read for a while. Hananiah was pleased by the cancellation; he had had no desire to listen to an evil old mystic squawk about burning entrails. After a while he looked up from his reading and said, "Tyre is bad business, well-fortified and resourceful. The king should steer clear." Mishael whined about several unrelated things. Daniel listened to every word carefully, nodded a bit then stroked his chin.

"Our king is always planning some attack," Hananiah continued, "Egypt always heavy on his mind, but he allows so many flatterers to advise him that he rarely does anything except pick on weakling states in the Hatti."

"And your point is...?" Azariah asked.

Hananiah pushed his tablets aside and propped his feet. "My point is twofold. I am bored beyond belief and this day, though only morning, is already shot. My advice to our king after scanning this learned garbage is to fire two thirds of his help and grab a long lunch."

As Hananiah and his friends laughed, several heavily armed riders galloped into the compound and pulled up not far from their open window. "Arioch's troops," Mishael whispered, "king's men."

King's men, Babylon's grittiest soldiers, were not to be taken lightly. The boys listened at the window as the lead horseman spoke. "All Babylon's wise men, including instructors and students at this school," he said, "are to be arrested and taken to Esagila for immediate execution."

Suusaandar, who had not yet left campus, rushed out from a classroom to meet them. "I'm an instructor, not a seer," he told the captain in a pleading voice, "this is certainly a mistake. No one at this institution has ever practiced black arts."

"Orders are orders," the rider said.

Several of Suusaandar's teaching peers joined him in the courtyard and began to contend with the fellow too. A squad of barracks guards double-timed to the spot to investigate and, after some heated chatter, sided with their counterparts from the citadel, orders being orders after all. The boys stepped outside as other students did the same and a small mob formed in the yard surrounding the king's guard.

"My duty is clear," the captain said, drawing his sword and sweeping it over their heads. "Along with every priest, magician, seer and enchanter in the realm, every teacher and pupil here shall be done in too."

Because the soldier spoke Akkadian not every student understood. But Philosir and his band, knowing the score at once, quickly slinked away. Daniel led his friends off too, behind a classroom building.

"Start praying," he said, and they did so. Then Daniel stepped in view and motioned to a school guard, asking, "What has happened?" The guard claimed ignorance at first but then, as souls so often did around Daniel, he reversed his field and opened up. "The king can't sleep as I understand it," he said. "He had a dream which he cannot remember and which no one can describe. So, in his anger, he blames your kind."

"Our kind?" Hananiah asked.

"Mystics," the guard said. "And mystic trainees, I guess. Arioch's men say that the king's regular revelators, even Enshunu himself, have failed to tell his dream."

"Interpret his dream," Daniel said.

"No, tell it," the guard said, laughing. "Nebuchadnezzar gave old Enshunu not a clue." He whispered, "Everyone in Babylon knows that the top man can't sleep. On a better day he might have only kicked something." He turned up his palms. "Such it is with kings."

"So, Nebuchadnezzar is going to…"

"Kill you all," the guard finished, "because none can tell his dream."

"But no one can do that," Azariah said.

"And so you all shall die. It will be a ton of work for us." With that the soldier squeezed Hananiah's shoulder and began to lead him away. "Out in the courtyard with you all now," he said, "it's my duty to help out. No fuss and follow me. Tomorrow, at Esagila, you are all to be beheaded." He sighed. "Understand, these poor king's men are sorely pressed for time, having only begun to scour the provinces knowing Nebuchadnezzar is a stickler for detail and won't settle for less than all of you. There's only a handful of you bone-readers in chains now. A drop in the bucket. I had no idea this nation was so full of your kind."

"We're slaves for goodness sake, not wise men," Azariah said.

"King's orders," the guard shrugged. "Now be good and follow me."

*

Philosir and his mates were arrested too. Suusaandar and the other instructors resisted at first but, when encircled by men with spears, they gave in and allowed themselves to be bound like everyone else and herded toward the dining hall. As Hananiah and friends marched in step with them, Daniel stopped in his tracks. For some reason their guard stopped too. "Please tell the captain there is no need to kill anyone," he said. "I shall tell Nebuchadnezzar his dream and the meaning thereof."

"You couldn't possibly…" Hananiah began, then stopped, embarrassed. Mishael had lit up with hope when Daniel spoke. Even Azariah seemed encouraged by his words. Why had he, Hananiah, lacked faith? Did they all not believe in the same, powerful God?

"Consider this," Daniel told the soldier, "if you pass on my claim to the king and I prove able to truly do as I say, won't you, then, be a hero to the nation and his majesty?"

The soldier seemed to consider Daniel's proposal but said nothing. Once assembled inside the dining hall the prisoners were ordered to line up and count off—Babylonians loved to count off—after which a king's man circulated among them and began to record their names. When a Phoenician bolted from the ranks and tried to escape through an open window, a guard drew his sword, gashed him and blood spewed everywhere. The near riot that followed forced the guards to run everyone back outside. As they filed out, Daniel passed the same soldier and repeated his offer to interpret the king's dream; but the man didn't seem to hear.

"He will do it," Daniel told his friends. "The God of Israel is with us."

Hananiah prayed that it was true.

*

The king's men reassembled their prisoners along an outer barracks wall. The wounded fellow was dragged there too, still bleeding, his wound serving as a vivid example to the students and teachers of who not to cross. Soon the wounded man stopped moving. Then he stopped groaning. Shadows lengthened. The afternoon air turned cold. The guards found and stacked wood and built fires at a distance at which they stooped and warmed their hands.

"Why no news?" Mishael whispered much later. "Why just stand here?"

"Try to stop thinking," Azariah told him, "there is no benefit to it."

Mishael had never felt more helpless. "We marched for weeks eating stale bread, drinking muddy water and shivering in the night only to be murdered at a pagan shrine?" he asked his friends.

Daniel answered simply, "No." He pulled out the odd stone he had promised to the girl, Ya'el, in Jerusalem and he began to polish it. He had done so every day, usually while they studied together at night in the barracks, rubbing it with cloth and fine sand. It still didn't look like much to Hananiah, perhaps a bit less dingy, perhaps a bit less rough.

"Pray with me," Daniel said, and they began at once. No one is more eager to pray than the condemned.

The Phoenician prisoners mocked them but found no real joy in making fun. They too would likely die in the morning. As the boy's wrapped up, the king's captain approached out of nowhere and looked straight at Hananiah, still on his knees.

"Belteshazzar?"

"No, him," Hananiah said, swallowing hard and pointing at Daniel. Arioch was a scary man.

Arioch turned to Daniel and said, "Jew, repeat your claim for my ears."

"Since you are the king's official," Daniel said, "let me ask first, sir, why has King Nebuchadnezzar issued such a harsh decree?"

Arioch seemed ready to explode but then, as if a switch had been throne to disarm him, the captain calmly confirmed what the boys had heard. "Take me to the castle, then," Daniel said, "to seek permission to interpret the thing."

Arioch cut Daniel's bonds, snapped his fingers and they were gone.

"What just happened?" Azariah asked.

"It seems plain to me," Mishael grinned. "Our friend is off to see the king."

*

Night fell. The boys slept fitfully with their chins stuck in the dirt and their hands bound behind them. Not long afterward the school gate screeched opened and a chariot clattered in. The driver pushed Daniel out into the compound then turned his rig and headed away. When Daniel stumbled to a stop a king's man grabbed him, tied his hands again and led him back to the pack. "Did you see the king?" Azariah asked.

"Half a minute," Daniel said. "I got a bath beforehand, though, and that was nice, but Nebuchadnezzar never looked my way."

"What did you say to him?"

"If he would give me the evening to pray, I promised to tell the king his dream by morning." They stared at Daniel's steady eyes by firelight. "And he agreed," Daniel said.

The boys prayed together the remainder of that night. Hananiah sneaked peeks at Daniel now and then hoping for some sign of success and, seeing nothing, he prayed still harder. Arioch returned early the next morning, stepped past his men at breakfast to where Daniel remained on his knees and he said, "The king has granted the time you requested, Belteshazzar. Now your game is up. He remains as angry as I've ever seen him. I promise, when you fail, boy, Nebuchadnezzar will make you wish you had died a thousand times before he has his revenge. What say you?"

Daniel stood, stretched as best he could then smiled pleasantly. "Praise the name of God forever and ever," he said, "for he alone has all wisdom and power. He determines the course of world events. He removes kings and sets others on the throne. You have told me what we asked of you, O Lord, and revealed to us what the king demanded."

"Are you saying...?" Mishael began, his eyes full of hope.

"I'm saying, my friend," Daniel nearly shouted, "all glory to God, I've got it!"

The boys began to celebrate. The other students and instructors had no idea what to do.

"Stop, you foolish Jews," Arioch shouted. "Say you, Belteshazzar, that you can truly tell the king's dream?"

"Not I," Daniel said, "but the Lord, my God, through me."

Arioch stepped chin to chin with Daniel. Neither fellow blinked. It was not yet light that morning, the sun just creeping up, so the condemned strained to watch the staring match between the Israelite who claimed to have received a gift by which they might be saved and the soldier tasked to kill them. Then, by the faintest light, they saw the captain crack a smile.

Even the Phoenicians cheered.

Arioch raised his arms for quiet. "If you fail, boy," he told Daniel, "I swear you will die much more slowly and painfully than all these others."

The Phoenicians cheered again.

The campus lay draped in shadow, doomed to be closed forever if Daniel failed at his task but bitter endings were routine in Babylon. Parallel grooves leading away in the dirt proved that, establishing that the dead body of the wounded Phoenician had been dragged away during the night.

Daniel dropped to his knees and prayed again. The boys kneeled beside him, asking God to deliver a miracle through Daniel as he met with the king. And they remained on their knees until Arioch cut Daniel's bonds and ordered him into his chariot for a second ride to the palace.

9. Recalling Daniel's courage

ON HIS WAY to see the king a second time, Daniel wanted to laugh out loud, the morning air felt so fine on his face. But his excitement vanished when he and Arioch passed several wise men standing along the roadside bound and waiting to be taken to Esagila.

"Every one of them will be beheaded," Arioch said, "and their homes demolished in a day." He shrugged. "There are hundreds now in custody and many more to come. I simply don't have the manpower. So, boy, though I don't believe any man can do what you have promised, I truly hope you succeed. But I expect the same end for you and your friends as for these seers; except of course you slaves have no homes to knock down, which is nice."

Arioch slowed the pace as they approached the citadel gate. "I've heard rumors that you and your Hebrew pals are among the most brilliant in the land," he said, "and yet you look simple to me, boy; like you do not truly understand what is happening around you. Have you not listened? Has it not struck you? Do you lack the wisdom to understand that very soon you will surely suffer and die?"

"It is wise to rely upon the Lord," Daniel said.

"Marduk," Arioch nodded, afraid to disagree.

"Marduk," Daniel said, "is but a cold, mindless planet that roams the evening sky..."

"What's a planet?" Arioch asked.

"...but the spirit of the God of Israel is within us when we call on him in prayer."

"Within us?" Arioch came back. "I can see and handle my gods any time I wish. Our sacred stories tell of the greatest of them, Marduk, growing large and fiery in the sky in the shape of an enormous bull, stirring the seas and causing the whole world to shake. I keep replicas, facsimiles and likenesses and honor them in turn for protection and look, I am whole. You tell me, where was your Hebrew god when Marduk's mighty men sacked Jerusalem and took treasures from his temple? Where is he now, boy, while you wait to die? His unseen power cannot save you."

They arrived at the gate. Attendants rushed up and saluted. Arioch led Daniel inside.

"God does as he pleases," Daniel said when they were alone again. "Marduk does as God pleases, for he is nothing but an object under the one God's control. Yesterday Babylon conquered Judah, I know not why but remain trusting. Today, if it serves the Lord that I survive, then the vision He has provided me regarding the king's dream will prove true and it will amaze your king. It will have pleased God to save me, my friends and even the wise men of Babylon. And it will also prove that God has chosen to sustain your king for now, for even mighty Nebuchadnezzar does his bidding."

"Nonsense," Arioch said. He led Daniel into an antechamber. Servants approached to prepare them both to see the king; perhaps a second bath.

"Your king has served the God of Israel before," Daniel said, "and he shall again."

"Junk like that," the captain snapped, "will get your head stuck on a pike and planted on the roadside, boy, Assyrian style. When you fail here today I will tend to you myself. No man or boy should mock Marduk. None can tell another's dreams."

*

Daniel's second meeting with the king was much more formal than the first. Nebuchadnezzar received him and Arioch on the ground floor of the citadel in a spectacular chamber filled with polished engravings, exotic pots, ornate tapestries and upholstered chairs. Daniel had passed a second time through the palace baths where he again combed his hair and slaves rubbed his limbs with oil. But for this occasion attendants had also given him a bright linen robe to wear. The king sat waiting for them on a tall, jeweled throne. The queen sat on a smaller armchair to his left.

Daniel gasped when he saw Amytis, struck by her beauty.

Arioch drew his sword. "Slave!" he said. "Avert your eyes."

"I meant no offense," Daniel said. "The queen reminds me of a dear friend in Judah."

"With your forgiveness, Sire," Arioch said, bowing to the king, "I present the captive, Belteshazzar, who claims to know the king's dream. I have warned him that…"

"I know you," Nebuchadnezzar interrupted, eyeing Daniel. "I suspected as much last night. Yes, I do know you." He turned to Arioch. "Captain," he said, "this is the very boy I have mentioned to you who never blinked on the day I sacked Jerusalem." The king raised his arms as if holding a sword. "I started to slice him head to toe, seriously, remember me saying? I'm not sure why I stopped." He lowered his arms. "I guess I took a liking to his spine. He never so much as twitched, I say, when my blade passed this close to his head." The king made a narrow gap with finger and thumb to demonstrate. "And so I let him live. Him and the wild prophet I also spared that day."

"Jeremiah," Daniel said

"Yes! That's him, an insane fellow too," the king said. "And you… You're taller now and wiry like a man but for sure the same kid. You grinned like you hadn't a worry when I bellowed in your face. How long has it been, a year…?"

"Nearly three," Daniel said.

"Well over two years!" the king laughed. "But my point is I've neither seen soldier nor officer, Captain, not in my army or the armies of Assur, curse them all, or in all of disgusting Egypt, ever, anywhere, in all my days with the absolute stone cold nature of this plucky Hebrew here."

"I think it's that he's numb, Sire," Arioch said. "They're all a bit addled down there."

"Truly," Nebuchadnezzar sighed, "and I may yet kill him."

Daniel smiled.

"There he goes again," the king said, "can you believe it?"

"And your dream, O king…?" Queen Amytis reminded.

Nebuchadnezzar's gleam faded. "You have had all night, boy. Do you know it?"

"Not of my own power," Daniel said, "but through the strength of the one true God."

With that, Amytis cursed and left the room. The king shrugged.

"I wanted her to see this," Nebuchadnezzar whispered, "but my lady's high-flying roots extend back to the Magi, you see. She adores the old-style gods of the Medes." He frowned. "And she really, thoroughly hates Jews though I swear I am unaware of a single past contention between her people and yours." He shook his head and sighed. "Certainly the Medes never had my problems with the Jews. But enough! This is simple, boy. You've made the boast now tell the dream. Tell me exactly what it means. I swear if you cannot you will die first and most awfully among the countless priestly parasites in this land who test my patience and the treasury with holy blackmail, claiming to be favored by the gods."

"O king," Daniel said, "there are no wise men, enchanters, magicians, or fortune-tellers who can tell the king such things."

"That has been confirmed," Nebuchadnezzar said.

"But there is a God in heaven who reveals secrets and he has shown King Nebuchadnezzar what will happen in the future. Now I will tell you your dream and the visions you saw as you lay in your bed."

The king began tapping his fingers on the arm of his chair.

"While your majesty was sleeping you dreamed about coming events. The Revealer of mysteries has shown you what will happen. And it is not because I am wiser than any living person that I know the secret of your dream but because God wanted you to understand what you were thinking."

Nebuchadnezzar waved his hand. "I know how you people are," he said, "and I truly wish not to be rude, but I get all that. You had better not be stalling, boy. It will not save you, I promise. Tell me, son, do I look to you even a little like a patient man?"

"No," Daniel admitted.

"Well, there you are!" the king said. "Now, quickly, all glory to whomever, go on."

"Your majesty, in your vision you saw in front of you a huge and powerful statue of a man, shining brilliantly, frightening and awesome."

Nebuchadnezzar's nostrils flared. Hand over mouth he mumbled, "That's right."

"The head of the statue was made of fine gold, its chest and arms were of silver, its belly and thighs were of bronze, its legs were of iron, and its feet were a combination of iron and clay."

The king stood up out of his chair. "Captain, leave us," he said, his voice barely a whisper. "Go find the queen now. Even if she objects, Captain, even if she is at bath, bring her here now, as you find her."

"The queen, Sire...?"

"Drag her by her hair, Captain, need be."

Arioch left the chamber quickly, muttering. Not long afterward Daniel heard Amytis shout something loud and rude in the hall. The captain led her inside stuttering mad but Nebuchadnezzar ignored her complaints, motioned toward her throne and warned, "Sit, woman, and not another word!"

Amytis jerked free from Arioch, cursed him under her breath then sat beside the king as ordered. Arioch hurried out, booming the chamber's big doors behind him.

"Continue, Belteshazzar," Nebuchadnezzar said.

"Daniel," Daniel corrected.

A wave of anger crossed the king's face. "Daniel, then," he said, "but let's you and I keep that little nuance to ourselves." He turned to Amytis. "Relax, my lady," he told her, "it's important to them, and prepare to be amazed. We must listen to every word this young man has to say."

10. Women

DANIEL FINISHED RECITING the king's dream while Nebuchadnezzar and the queen listened in wonder. "But I am bound to say," Daniel added when done, "all that has been revealed to you today is because it is God's will, the God of Israel, his alone, not Marduk or any other false god."

"I am to be a king over many kings, you say?"

"By God's hand, O king, you have received sovereignty, power, strength and honor."

Nebuchadnezzar beamed.

Amytis stood and said, "His beliefs mock us and our gods. Can't you see that?"

"And yet," Nebuchadnezzar said, stroking his beard, "while fat Enshunu and the other so-called holy men in town, who are, by the way, standing in chains this moments with their fates in this boy's hands… While they wailed that I had asked the impossible, this Belteshazzar, this Daniel…" He sighed. "Tell me, sweet bride; if not for his god how could he know my dream better than I remembered it myself?"

The queen folded her arms and looked away.

"Stubborn woman," the king said. "I know what I've seen. I am not so hateful or impractical that I cannot recognize a big, bouncing miracle when it smacks my face." Then he jumped off his throne, threw open the chamber doors and shouted in the hall, "This young man has done the impossible." Amytis began to weep. Nebuchadnezzar laughed, stepped to Daniel and hugged him.

"I absolutely hate this!" the queen screamed.

"And I love it," the king came back. "Leave us, woman, go somewhere and organize your thoughts. Consider what you've just been honored to witness, for grief's sake."

"Women," Nebuchadnezzar shrugged, as Amytis ran from the room. He shut the chamber doors behind his bride and insisted that Daniel sit beside him on her throne. "Tell me about Jerusalem," he asked, after Daniel cautiously lowered himself into the queen's plush chair. "Tell me about your journey here, your friends who came here with you and your experiences in my school."

*

The sun was well up. The boys had not moved from their spots in hours. Hananiah heard a king's man apologize to Suusaandar in the yard for harsh treatment but, he explained, Arioch wanted the prisoners to be ready to move chick-chock. "When a king wants blood he wants it now," the guard said, "better yours than ours."

None of the condemned was peaceful, of course, but Suusaandar looked truly pitiful, ready to cry. Even as he sat waiting for his own execution Hananiah enjoyed the instructor's pain. "He spends one cold evening with an empty belly and the threat of a quick death..." Hananiah whispered.

"...and our pompous instructor is quaking like a girl," Azariah finished for him.

"He is human like us," Mishael said. "Have we lost our hearts?"

"What kindness have these beasts shown us?" Azariah asked. "They mock our faith. They've changed our names and laugh at our condition. Yet each of them was raised by a mother and grew up fat with family and friends. Did any of them, even once, demonstrate a shred of compassion for us as slaves?"

"No."

"And where, Mishael, were Babylonian hearts during and after the siege of Jerusalem? When our loved ones who had not yet starved to death died from abuse in the aftermath and on their way here? Now these jellyfish whimper because they caught a chill and missed a meal? They wet themselves for fear of losing their gizzards when we've lost everything? It's comical, I say. I feel more pity for Philosir and his goons than for these arrogant Akkadians. May every one of them choke and die."

"But we'll die with them," Mishael said.

"So what?" Azariah said, and he had a point. How strange, Hananiah thought, that in such a short time he too, like Azariah, had grown so cold. "I've no pity for them either," Hananiah said. "We'll face our end like men."

"Daniel would never agree with any of that," Mishael said.

Hananiah's shoulders sagged at the mention of Daniel' name. He had been gone too long. "Accept it," he sighed, "Daniel has failed, and soon..."

He was interrupted by the faint sound of...music?

Flutes, pipes, whistles, drums?

"A dirge?" Mishael asked.

"No, you fool, listen," Azariah said, "that's peppy music."

The main gate opened. Daniel strode in on foot, dressed in a bright white robe with a spiffy looking horse and chariot parked behind him just beyond the archway. Three armed men entered alongside with several musicians close behind playing a silly tune. The king's men at the gate blocked their way but, after a quick discussion with their peers, stepped aside. As Daniel crossed the yard to his friends the other students and teachers stood with difficulty, their hands still bound behind them, and listened drop-jawed as Daniel said, loud enough for all to hear, "Gentlemen, we are acquitted, every one of us is free!"

Instructors, Amorites, Sepharites and Phoenicians shouted for joy and began to hop about, hugging one another while Daniel's pipers played. A filthy Sepharite kissed Hananiah's cheek! Even the king's men seemed pleased by the new development after having been saved from a great deal of work. But Daniel's rival, Philosir, led his cadre of allies into a murmuring huddle immediately after the first flush of relief had passed.

When the celebration lost its steam Daniel addressed the others. "Shadrach, Meshach, Abednego and I..." (He winked at his friends as he used their heathen names.) "...are bound to the citadel for interviews with the king. By his decree, our time has passed in this school."

Even Suusaandar clapped his hands. Though he had first hated the boys, then tolerated them and then, grudgingly, shown respect, Suusaandar seemed truly grateful that Daniel had saved his life. Affirming that, as soon as a guardsman had his bonds, Suusaandar coaxed the boys aside and offered advice, nodding toward Philosir and his men.

"It appears that you boys have won the king's prime posts," he said, speaking high Akkadian for security, "but, trust me, you cannot yet imagine the power that accompanies those positions. You will make important appointments. You shall have influence, wealth and ready access to the king's ear but you shall also contend with a thousand false friends and subtle enemies, none of them more threatening than that Phoenician who hates you especially, Daniel. Be wary. Consider everyone a threat. Trust only each other."

When they each shook Suusaandar's hand (a little sadly, after all) and started away, Hananiah wondered, briefly, if he would ever come to miss the slave school.

*

The ride to the palace was a wonder, Hananiah's first unsupervised moment in three years. Daniel's escorts, actual armed-to-the-teeth and tough-as-nails king's men, were not there to threaten but to protect them! Two soldiers led their party and one followed behind, ready to confront anyone who might get in their way. "This rig, driver, horses and all, are assigned to me," Daniel said, "and they come with a reserved spot in the royal stable."

The boys looked at one another in disbelief. How could this have happened in only hours?

"Obviously King Nebuchadnezzar is a powerful man," Mishael said.

"God is powerful," Daniel said, "Nebuchadnezzar is his servant."

Of course Daniel was correct but Hananiah could only thrill at every nuance of their breezy ride from the edge of death at the slave school to the nation's glory seat, the citadel at Babylon, thanks to Daniel's faith, the eccentricity of a sleepless king and, most of all, the God of Israel.

*

On their way to the palace Daniel described the king's dream to his friends in detail. "Then I said to him, you are a king over many kings. The God of heaven has given you sovereignty, power, strength, and honor. He has made you the ruler over the inhabited world and has put even the animals and birds under your control. You are the head of gold." Daniel paused to smile. "Nebuchadnezzar loves gold, so that thrilled him. Then I revealed the fates of the four kingdoms represented by the statue in his dream. I told him that they will precede an everlasting kingdom, the kingdom of God."

"The Hebrew god?" Nebuchadnezzar had asked.

"God Himself," Daniel answered, "the only God. The dream is true, its meaning certain."

The king bowed at Daniel's feet. "Everyone," he shouted, and several servants rushed in. "You will offer sacrifices to this young man and burn sweet incense whenever he appears."

"Do not be mistaken," Daniel objected, "all the glory is God's."

Nebuchadnezzar sighed and scratched his head. "How refreshing," he said after a bit of reflection. "Enshunu and his cronies demand small fortunes for sniffing bones and mumbling over poultry guts. Truly your God is the God of gods, the Lord over kings, a revealer of mysteries, for you have been able to reveal this secret."

"I wanted no credit for myself," Daniel told his friends, "but the king said that if I successfully passed a formal interview, it's the law, he would put me in administrative charge of the provinces. I saw no evil in that. Then he ordered these soldiers to protect me and sent us to get you." Though Daniel was pleased he seemed almost apologetic. "I'll also have an office in the citadel," he explained, "and the king tried to give me jewels."

"You refused rubies and such?" Hananiah asked.

Daniel held up his little stone from home. It had become much less ugly after three years of constant polishing. "Truly," Daniel said, "I have the only gem I want."

"So we are safe at last?" Mishael asked.

"No safer now than before," Daniel sighed. "Security comes only from God."

"But we'll for sure eat better," Azariah said.

They arrived at the palace. Before heading upstairs Daniel said, "I told the king that you three are as learned as I. I asked him to consider giving you high stations. He agreed. You'll manage districts under me if all goes well. I hope you don't mind. I'll also be in charge of his wise men. The four of us will serve on the king's council."

Hananiah was so happy he began to cry. "Look at me," he said, dabbing his eyes, "I've turned into Mishael." They laughed, then cried, then hugged, then of course fell to their knees on the polished palace floor to once more praise God for his mercy.

*

The citadel at Babylon surrounded five courtyards. The inner, residential complex included a reception hall, the king and queen's personal suites and an adjoining dormitory for concubines. Two vaults behind the throne room contained circular wells. These supplied fresh water for the ritual washing of all who wished to see the king; so, before going upstairs, Hananiah, Mishael and Azariah washed with a resinous soap as Daniel had twice earlier that day. They prayed again together as they waited in the foyer before the king's door. While they were at it, the big bald man who had chosen them for the captive school years earlier, Ashpenaz, appeared and bowed to them!

"Look at this," he said softly, shaking his head. "I would have bet my best mount that you four would be murdered in your beds inside a month." He laughed. "But your success has accrued to my glory! The king has summoned me this day to reward me for selecting you to the school. Suusaandar has benefited too, promised that if you perform as expected he will get a promotion, an engraved citation and a royal badge for accomplishing your training."

"We are so happy for you both," Azariah said.

Ashpenaz laughed at his sarcasm. "More truth?" he said. "I picked you boys for your good teeth, clear skin and fine clothes, nothing else. It's policy." He nodded at Daniel. "I once was certain that subtle grin of yours, Belteshazzar, was proof that you were feeble. And yet, thank Marduk, here we are."

"No thanks to Marduk," Daniel said, "but to God."

Ashpenaz sighed at mention of the God of Israel, but did not argue.

*

Their interviews with the king lasted quite a while. "Never," Nebuchadnezzar said afterward, "have captives done so well." But there happened one scary moment when the king had asked Amytis, whom he had ordered to attend, to read from a Median scroll of poetry in her native dialect. Hananiah did not understand it all but it was clear that the selected passage contained references to the false gods Farnah, Arta and Vourunâ. Hananiah held his breath as Daniel translated to Akkadian, remembering that his friend had once felt compelled to insult Suusaandar rather than render Marduk's name properly.

"But there was no need this time," Daniel told Hananiah later. "No one in Babylon, not even Amytis, believes any longer in the frivolous gods of the Medes. The same will happen to Marduk and the others."

Good, then. The king was ecstatic and even Amytis admitted that Daniel knew his stuff.

"No students have ever impressed me as much as Belteshazzar, Shadrach, Meshach and Abednego," Nebuchadnezzar announced afterward. "I hereby appoint them all regular members of my council. In all matters requiring wisdom and balanced judgment I find the advice of these young men to be ten times better than that of all the magicians and enchanters in my entire kingdom."

Naturally the boys were thrilled. Daniel had saved their lives, the lives of the other students and the lives of every instructor and wise man in Babylon. He had maneuvered himself and his friends out of the captive school and into powerful jobs.

Then they learned that their new assignments would keep them apart.

"Belteshazzar will administer the entire kingdom," the king said. "He will remain in Babylon. Meshach will run the southern district and live near Uruk. Abednego is hereby dispatched to Nippur. It's the rule, boys. An administrator must live in his district."

Hananiah was sent north to Sippar. How quickly the seeming permanence of their companionship had ended. How awful, Hananiah thought, after years of never being out of each other's sight to learn in a flash that their time together had ended. They all shed tears, even Daniel, and pledged to keep in constant touch.

*

No longer a prisoner but a man of rank and privilege, Hananiah's every earthly need vanished. Once he began to get paid (in ledger entries of barley and silver equivalents) he arranged for food to be stocked, prepared and served in his new quarters in Sippar exactly as he had remembered it being done at his father's table in Jerusalem.

Mishael and Azariah did the same but Daniel continued to drink only juices and water and eat only pulse.

"Why?" Hananiah asked.

"My struggle has only begun," he said.

That was so him.

The boys discussed it. "Should we eat only plain food too?"

"Nothing would please me more than to bless the wine and bread on Erev Shabbat," Daniel said, "in the same manner as our fathers. But that is not my path. It is best that you continue as you first thought best. You shall surely honor God in all that you do even as you enjoy your meals." He smiled, not his normal look but a delighted expression revealing a little mischief. "And a spectacular opportunity to glorify him, I know, will soon come your way."

None of them understood that last, glorify, part, but they agreed to eat meat. They were still orphans, still lost, but blessed to work in comfort and sleep safely in their homes for a season after lifetimes of disappointment and loss.

The boys soon plunged into Nebuchadnezzar's service with all their energy and found plenty to do. Babylon had no peers among the nations and seemingly no limit to what she might accomplish, having amassed power and wealth rivaling even Egypt of old. There were countless highways, houses, schools, fortifications and monuments to be built, armies to be equipped and trained, land to cultivate, diplomacy to test, treaties to sign and wars to wage. The king's council managed every bit of it.

Daniel oversaw it all.

11. Seventy years

THE KING'S COUNCIL met twice each month, most often at the palace. Daniel ran the meetings. He began each with prayer, silent prayer when Marduk followers were around, but on those rare occasions when they met only with Nebuchadnezzar they prayed as they pleased. The king seemed fascinated by their beliefs.

"Only one god?" he would say.

"He is all that exists," Daniel would answer, "all that any man needs."

Nebuchadnezzar would chuckle about what he called their "differing points of view" then get down to business, always, because he had enormous gifts, accomplishing a raft of things. But not all council work was rewarding. As events became clearer, Babylon faced a serious problem. Once again, the cause of that problem was Judah.

"They're flirting with Egypt again," the king cursed one afternoon. "If they keep it up I will make them pay."

Pay. That word again.

It seemed that every soul in their homeland had lost his mind. False prophets in Jerusalem had painted a wonderful future for a shaken people; rain, big harvests, lasting peace and a return to the glories of Solomon. Given all that good news, even after Babylon had taught Judah what should have been a thorough and bitter lesson, Jews in Jerusalem ignored the prophet Jeremiah's inspired advice in favor of others' shallow promises. Judah grew to expect a quick return to the blessings of old and the people were moved to violence against Jeremiah, who had passed on God's instruction for the exiles to settle in.

"This captivity is long," the prophet had spoken bravely, "build ye houses, and dwell in them; and plant gardens, and eat the fruit of them."

"According to Jeremiah," Daniel sighed, "our exile will last seventy years."

"We'll all be dead by then," Hananiah said.

Daniel grinned and shook his head no but then failed to elaborate.

"After all the trouble he's caused in Jerusalem," Azariah said, "it amazes me that old Jeremiah isn't dead by now. What's kept the people from stoning that sour old guy?"

"He did not cause the trouble," Daniel said, "he only foretold it as God had burdened him. So the Lord has protected him against his every enemy."

They sighed and sat back remembering. It did seem clearly miraculous that Jerusalem's unpopular prophet, Jeremiah, had survived.

*

King Josiah had succeeded to the throne of Judah at age eight when King Amon, his father, was assassinated for practicing idolatry after the fashion of the Assyrian kings. Josiah held things together in the land until, at age twenty-two, Jeremiah began to prophecy in the name of the Lord and Josiah's priests rediscovered Moses' lost Book of the Law in the temple.

Hear O Israel, it said.

...the Lord is God the Lord is one!

What wonderful words. True repentance flowed in Judah for quite a while afterward. Once he had read every word of his priests' amazing find, Josiah gained God's favor by destroying many of the pagan groves and idols in the land. He scoured the temple and banished false gods. But even then, with the immense job not complete, Jeremiah warned the nation that grief would follow if the people lacked remorse and idolatry failed to cease.

Repent, repent, repent! Jeremiah had railed tirelessly. No one enjoys bad news, especially when delivered with the tactlessness of a raging prophet; so when, fifteen years after his reforms began, Josiah died a wasted death in a questionable battle, all Judah blamed Jeremiah for his death.

"But if we had repented back then," Daniel had argued during their days in the captive school, "Jerusalem would still shine and we would not be slaves. But when things are going well people rarely take hard advice."

Jeremiah had started out on the wrong foot by announcing, as the Lord had charged...

*set thee [meaning Jeremiah!] over the nations and over the
kingdoms, to root out, and to pull down, and to destroy, and
to throw down, to build, and to plant.*

Who did he think he was? everyone asked. How could this ordinary man from nearby Anatoth claim to be ordained to serve not only Judah but the entire world? Jerusalem's other so-called prophets mocked him, claiming that bright days, not trouble, were the nation's due. But Jeremiah prophesied that the Lord would bring evil and a great destruction from the north. Of course the people exploded in anger. His negativity was too much. But, just before Josiah died, there came a season during which all Judah was forced to wonder, could Jeremiah be right?

*

Hananiah was a small child when Josiah's fatal crisis struck. Rumors had spread that the armies of Judah's three greatest enemies, Assyria, Babylon and Egypt, were about to clash in the north; Egypt and Assyria, often rivals, apparently intending to team up against the rising threat of Babylon.

King Josiah announced plans to take his army to Megiddo and intercept Pharaoh's force on its way through Israel to do battle in the north. Even as a child Hananiah had understood that this was not Judah's fight. On the morning that the end began, Hananiah heard cheering in the streets.

Despite misgivings of war, people always seemed to enjoy a good show of force.

*

Here's why everyone in Judah had been so worried. For over a century Hebrew prophets had warned Judah about Babylon by name, even before Babylon had begun to emerge again as a power. Despite King Josiah's continuing reforms the people had ignored those prophets, had continued to embrace child sacrifice, idol worship, cheating at weights and measures and ignoring the needs of the poor.

Still vividly alive in Judah's collective memory was how Assyria had decapitated and raped its way through the northern kingdom over a century earlier. Those Jews who were not slaughtered then had been scattered into foreign lands where they intermarried, embraced idols and disobeyed God even more.

They were lost.

No one wanted that fate for Judah. Even before Isaiah began to prophesy a hundred years earlier the prophet Amos had, with perfect accuracy, warned…

> *I will sift the house of Israel among all nations, like as corn is sifted in a sieve, yet shall not the least grain fall upon the earth. All the sinners of my people shall die by the sword.*

Though God had also promised not to utterly destroy the house of Jacob, this was no comfort to Judah when Josiah led his army toward a confusing battle.

Even Pharaoh Necho had warned him, claiming to have heard from God…

> *…What have I to do with thee, thou king of Judah? I come not against thee this day but against the house wherewith I have war: for God commanded me to make haste: forbear thee from meddling with God, who is with me, that he destroy thee not.*

But Josiah took an army to Megiddo and left a bewildered nation behind. Spirits fell in Jerusalem when no word came back regarding his fate. Then one day the news spread through the city that the clash between Josiah and Pharaoh had begun. Josiah had been mortally wounded, some said soon after, and the army had headed home in defeat.

*

One day, rumors flying everywhere, Daniel persuaded Hananiah and friends to go with him to the main gate to learn the truth, weaving their way through a bickering throng. Crops had failed, water had grown scarce and commerce lagged exactly as Jeremiah had prophesied. Could the rest of Jeremiah's grim message be true?

Shofars sounded from the ramparts shortly after the boys arrived. Up went the gates. Clouds had spread low overhead for days, tailing from down the nearby mountains onto the plain toward the western sea. All Judah had hoped these meant rain but, when Josiah's bewildered troops first appeared staggering homeward in the hills, everyone understood why the world had lost its light. Judah's army was in ruin.

Shouts and more shofars hailing their return echoed through the city but the ragged troops were a long time coming. Mothers, sisters and wives rushed out to meet them, sobbing as they went, grim-faced and choked with fear, their skirts held high to help hurry over the rocks, bushes and brush that littered the slopes, eager to learn the fates of their husbands, brothers and sons.

Hananiah heard the returning soldiers' tales. Josiah's army had arrived at Megiddo in time to bar Pharaoh's way. Necho sent an envoy on horseback under the Pharaoh's personal flag and he repeated Necho's claim; Egypt's battle is not with Judah this day. If Josiah would but allow Egypt's army to pass, no Hebrew blood would be shed.

Pharaoh had aligned his men on the ridge common to the valley with Mount Carmel to their left, banging on their armor, blowing horns and shouting as they dared Josiah to decide.

"Tell Pharaoh, return to Egypt or advance and die," Josiah had answered.

Advance Necho did.

A lament went up among those listening, "What of our king?"

Hananiah remembered the ground shuddering and thunder rolling as a ragged band of men crested a hilltop with the answer, accompanying Josiah's body as it lay in a bloody sling. It seemed like everyone came streaming out from the city then. The already eerie darkness grew still deeper, no light on the slopes as poor Josiah appeared all but dead. Everyone turned and slowly looked behind them, toward the tower.

There stood Jeremiah alone atop the ramparts. How had everyone sensed he was there?

The prophet's hair blew in the air like a madman's in a sudden, unrelenting wind. The boys strained to hear Jeremiah's voice though fearing what he might say. But the prophet spoke not one word that afternoon, nor would he utter another until the wounded king had died.

All that week, from Megiddo to Beersheba, the air cracked and flashed under the same black sky but never a drop of rain.

Four years after Josiah died, Nebuchadnezzar, still a general, defeated the combined forces of Necho and Assyria at Carchemish, but Necho managed to escape and return to Egypt with his army still intact. So the king's obsession with Necho was easy to understand. Though Nebuchadnezzar was the most feared man in creation, he had never conquered Egypt.

*

In council, because of Pharaoh Necho's continued meddling in Judah, all the king's advisors except Daniel and his friends urged Nebuchadnezzar to attack Egypt immediately. The king ignored the boys' advice and soon assembled a splendidly-equipped army, tens of thousands of men, to march south against his hated foe. Bands played, the nation celebrated and the army tramped off to war. But Nebuchadnezzar and his troops were soundly beaten.

Everyone hoped that the king would skip the council meeting at which, as required by Babylonian law, they would review the official record of his misadventure, but Nebuchadnezzar chose to attend (after recovering nicely from his wounds).

"Short and sweet," he grunted as he fell into his seat to hear the recitation.

Enshunu cleared his throat to read… "In the month of Kislîmu," the high priest began, "the king of Akkad took the lead of his army and marched to Egypt."

"Did you write this, Enshunu?" Nebuchadnezzar interrupted.

"Is something wrong?"

"Will you answer a simple question?"

"Yes, O king," the high priest said, "it's my job."

Nebuchadnezzar waved his hand and the priest continued.

"The king of Egypt heard it and mustered his army. In open battle they smote the breast of each other and inflicted great havoc on each other. The king of Akkad turned back with his troops and returned to Babylon."

Nebuchadnezzar pounded the table. Everyone held his breath. "You said we would win, priest," the king hissed. "Every one of you so-called military experts and pumped up seers said it would be so. Goat innards and the like all pointed to certain victory, you claimed."

"But Daniel did not predict victory, O king," Azariah said. "He advised against the attack."

Nebuchadnezzar slammed the table again, rose halfway out of his seat then shouted, "Fair enough!" He fell back and said softly, pointing a big, stubby finger at Daniel, "I will never ignore this man's advice again."

No one believed him though that seemed to end it; business was conducted as usual but there was a new bitterness to Babylon's king after he had lost so decisively to Necho. He had been routed, regardless of how mildly Enshunu had told the tale.

"Nebuchadnezzar is consumed with Pharaoh," Daniel told his friends one day, "and he's missing bigger things. While the king focuses his attention southward disturbing reports circulate regarding a people who call themselves Persia."

"Persia?" Mishael repeated. "Who are they?"

"It lies well east of Elam," Hananiah said, "and is rumored to be gaining strength and vitality beyond the frontier and across the plain. They are courting our allies, the Medes."

"From out of the dust one day," Daniel said, "and Koresh will be his name."

His friends blinked at him.

"Recall the Isaiah scroll," Daniel said. "I have held on to that gift since our march here. The prophet wrote of a Koresh, a gentile further identified as God's anointed, who will say to Jerusalem, thou shalt be built; and to the temple, thy foundation shall be laid."

"But Jerusalem is already built," Azariah said.

"And Solomon's temple stands," Mishael added. "So, for Koresh to build Jerusalem and lay the temple's foundation..."

Daniel looked sadly at his friends. "The whole city, then, would need to be leveled and the temple demolished sometime in the future for this word to prove true."

"Isaiah has never been wrong," Mishael said.

"Nor shall he ever be," Daniel added.

That sudden revelation stabbed Hananiah's heart.

It did not take long for what seemed like confirmation of Isaiah's words to follow.

*

A bitter report concerning Judah came to the council soon after. "The Jews have balked again at paying their agreed tribute," the king said. "Once more they pursue Egypt's friendship behind my back." He looked around the room. When his eyes met Hananiah's the king's features softened and he apologized. "I have no choice," he said. Then he excused his Hebrews from the meeting so that the remaining councilmen could vote to approve another siege of Jerusalem.

Azariah argued that he and his friends should protest by resigning their posts on the spot but Daniel reminded him of the word from Jeremiah…

You must submit to Babylon's king and serve him.

So they did, painfully, while Babylon attacked their homeland a second time. And in time Jerusalem fell as before. Enshunu read another report.

"In the seventh year, the month of Kislîmu," he began, "the king of Akkad mustered his troops, marched to the Hatti-land and besieged the city of Judah. On the second day of the month of Addaru he seized the city and captured the king."

The king's advisors applauded. Nebuchadnezzar stood and bowed.

"The king led away as prisoners the Jerusalem officials, the military leaders, and the skilled workers, ten thousand in all," Enshunu read.

"Ten thousand," Azariah gasped, "forced to make the same bloody march that we…?" he stopped, out of words.

Nebuchadnezzar nodded. "A bitter lesson," he sighed, "that had to be learned."

"Only the poorest people were left behind in Judah," Enshunu read on. "The king took their king, Jehoiachin, to Babylon, along with his mother, his wives, his officials, and the nation's most important leaders. He also led away 7,000 soldiers, 1,000 skilled workers, and anyone who would be useful in battle."

"Judah's new king," Nebuchadnezzar told the board, "is called Zedekiah."

"Your man?" Enshunu asked.

"He had better be my man," the king growled, "or he'll be Judah's last."

12. How war works

WHEN THE MEETING ended Nebuchadnezzar asked his Hebrews to stay behind. When alone with them he spoke frankly about the second siege. "It did not go well for your people," he said, "much worse this time than last."

Hananiah looked away as the king spoke. Outside, the sun's fading light lay upon Babylon's shining rooftops like a glowing shroud. How unjust to hear such sobering news on a warm, glorious day.

"Serving as your advisors," Azariah said, "we have lived comfortably while our brothers in Jerusalem starved another slow death. Maybe it would be best if we did not hear this."

"We should listen to everything the king will say," Daniel said. "It is a courtesy."

Nebuchadnezzar continued, sparing no detail as he recounted the pain and suffering that preceded Jerusalem's second fall.

"Why did you allow it then?" Azariah said, failing to address the king respectfully. "Why did you again permit murder and rape and carnage and looting?"

"That's how war works, son," Nebuchadnezzar spat. "As for who allowed it, how stand Jerusalem's idiot king and his flat-faced son in your eyes? They ignored my many warnings and bet on Egypt. Again." He rolled his eyes. "Egypt! Knowing well that that vile, inbred nation—my goodness you were all slaves there once, your story goes… Egypt in its history has never benefited a Jew. It's my guess that onto eternity it never will."

Nebuchadnezzar could be terribly cold at times but Hananiah sensed that the king was truly sorry for what he, in his mind, had been forced to do. His account, the bitter detail of it, comprised both confession and apology.

"Is our prophet, Jeremiah, among the captives," Mishael asked, "or has he died too?"

"I spared him," the king said, "again. I let him choose; struggle in Jerusalem among the remaining poor and feckless or thrive in mighty Babylon in a place of honor serving me." The king chuckled. "He cursed me again and chose to stay."

"A good and holy man," Daniel sighed.

"A man who spoke the truth to your people and was hated for it."

"And who will speak even more and be hated more," Daniel added.

It was Mishael, shortly after their meeting with the king, who shocked his friends with an angle they had not yet considered. "If I heard correctly," he said, "Nebuchadnezzar still did not destroy the temple. He did not completely level the town." He stopped as they blinked at one another. "So, if the temple stands even now, if the city remains intact and a king still sits on Jerusalem's throne…" He stopped with teary eyes to look at Daniel.

"Then," Daniel said, "according to the Word, there will be even greater suffering in the future." He closed his eyes. "Babylon's second assault on our homeland was not its last. Jerusalem and the temple will be utterly destroyed. Thousands more of our captured brothers and sisters march toward Babylon now, suffering as we once did. We will help them as best we can when they arrive but remember, no matter what the future may bring we will serve this nation, Babylon, as the Lord has directed."

They all agreed. What else could they do?

*

Egypt continued to raise Nebuchadnezzar's ire by exploiting the bad judgment of Judah's King Zedekiah, encouraging him to double deal against Babylon. After two sieges in eight years and the mass deportations of many of its most gifted citizens, Jerusalem's economy had tanked. The people blamed Babylon, not themselves, for everything that had happened, including diminished rainfall and a crippling blight which had wiped out vineyards and crops. Jeremiah, who had been thrown into a cistern for speaking God's word, voiced another caustic judgment against them as soon as he was released…

> *I will deliver Zedekiah, king of Judah, and his servants, and the people, and such as are left in this city from the pestilence, from the sword, and from the famine, into the hand of Nebuchadnezzar king of Babylon, and into the hand of their enemies, and into the hand of those who seek their life: and he shall smite them with the edge of the sword; he shall not spare them, neither have pity, nor mercy.*

"Jeremiah said that?" Nebuchadnezzar asked at a council meeting. "Because I have to tell you fellows, sometimes that is exactly how I feel about Zedekiah's growing treachery. What is it with your people," he asked the boys, "their willfulness, fascination with Egypt and their run of stupid kings? Why don't they listen when their god speaks to them so clearly?"

Hananiah hung his head. There was no good answer. The burden of his understanding of Jerusalem's eventual destruction was almost impossible to bear.

"Should we try to persuade Nebuchadnezzar not to attack a third time," Mishael asked his friends later, privately, "or would we then be opposing God's will?" They turned to look at Daniel, who rarely frowned but did so then, speaking while rubbing his temples.

"We knew with certainty, from Isaiah," he said, "that the holy city and the temple would someday be destroyed. Now we know from Jeremiah that it will happen at Babylon's hand while Nebuchadnezzar is king. And so..." His voice trailed off for a moment. "And so it appears that we three will likely live to see it."

"So that's it?" Azariah asked. "It is spoken! There's nothing we can do to help our people?"

"God's word is absolute," Daniel answered. "His will is beyond our understanding."

"But what if Judah repents?" Mishael asked. "What if we go to the king and do our utter best to persuade him to hold off and then..." He stopped and looked desperately at Daniel. "Go to the king, Daniel, please. Ask him for time. We can pray day and night for Zedekiah to open his eyes and accept Babylon's dominion as God has commanded. We can ask God, through Zedekiah, to lead all Judah to repent."

"And maybe then Jerusalem will be spared," Azariah said.

"I will meet with the king," Daniel said, "but only with your understanding that I will never pray for anything contrary to God's will. And neither should you."

The four prayed together, long and hard, for a miracle of mercy to somehow spring from Daniel's meeting with the king.

*

Nebuchadnezzar and Daniel met soon after to talk about Jeremiah's prophesy consigning Jerusalem to oblivion. "I like that crazy character," the king said. "He has entertained me since that day, what...? How many years ago? When he dared to spit in my eye..."

"I was there," Daniel said.

"Yes, I remember!" Nebuchadnezzar said. "The first siege. I almost killed you too."

"Jeremiah is a true prophet..."

"And he himself," Nebuchadnezzar nearly shouted, "has sealed Zedekiah's doom."

"The truth flows from the mind of God," Daniel said, "not the will of his prophets."

"Are you saying it will not be?" Nebuchadnezzar challenged.

"There is an irony, O king, would you agree," Daniel said, "that you, the King of Babylon, so admire a Jewish prophet who in turn reviles you and who, at the same time, is hated by his own people?"

"Most people hate anyone with a potent point of view," Nebuchadnezzar said. "They make them feel bad about their pansy selves. I suppose it's the same with your better Hebrew prophets. I've heard the reports. Those fools in Judah tried to kill your man, Jeremiah, for speaking truly but show me a prophet or king who says only what the people want to hear and I'll show you a coward. No, Jeremiah was right. Zedekiah has turned on me. Jerusalem will pay again sooner or later and, when I get around to it, it won't be pretty.

"In the end, the same sheep who love their kings for the comfortable lies he tells are the first to stab his back when the truth comes clear. Why should prophets manage better? My father the great king taught me long ago, speak the truth, feed the people and kill your enemies. I will never be that coward."

He paused to look carefully at his councilor. "Of course you would never kill anyone, would you, Daniel? Do you even own a weapon? I personally have hundreds. You may borrow any of mine you like."

"Weapon, O king?" Daniel said. "I have in my care a sacred scroll, words from the prophet Isaiah."

"Well, I say get yourself a dagger," Nebuchadnezzar said. "Vengeance can be tremendously renewing. My course is clear, right? It is even ordained. I shall, some day, finish Jerusalem once and for all."

"I doubt that," Daniel said, "God has made eternal promises to his people."

"Well, a king can't be too concerned about eternity, my man. It clouds current events."

"Then, maybe it will interest you, O king, to hear a prophecy a bit more timely," Daniel said, "concerning this lasting conflict between Babylon and Judah."

"Jeremiah said more?"

Daniel closed his eyes and recited...

> *It will come to pass, when seventy years are accomplished, that I will punish the king of Babylon, and that nation, says the Lord, for their iniquity, and the land of the Chaldeans, and will make it perpetual desolations.*

"Perpetual desolations?" Nebuchadnezzar repeated. "That doesn't seem fair at all." He rose from his chair and groaned with discomfort, frowning. "I will most certainly be dead, counting seventy years from the time when this bad business started," he said, "so that's a plus. But you know, Daniel, we are discussing my beloved country here, mighty Akkad!"

Daniel nodded but said nothing.

"I respect your god, of course," the king added, "knowing firsthand what he can do with outlandish dreams but understand, Daniel, if any other man beside you or Jeremiah had mentioned such a contemptible prediction..." He stopped, shaking and unable to speak.

"All earthly things shall pass, O king," Daniel said. "Does the revelation that there will be an eventual end to Babylon truly surprise you?"

"Surprise me?" Nebuchadnezzar shouted. "It offends my very soul. It insults, disgusts and enrages me. How's that? The land of the Chaldees has existed as a distinct and mostly mighty nation since the mists first drifted across the great plateau. Under my father we only began to restore our rightful status, our art, our natural language, our traditions..."

"Even so, O king, dynasties have come and gone in Akkad."

"Yes, but that's my point!" Nebuchadnezzar shouted. "They always come back, greater than ever. But this ugly phrase of your god's, perpetual desolations, sounds final to me. It sounds unlikely as well but I have learned too much about your god's power to simply ignore it. You tell me, Belteshazzar, how can Babylon at one time be an extension of his will and at the next the object of his fury, marked for destruction?"

"Perfect justice, I'm sure," Daniel shrugged, "though it seems a mystery."

"Well it's too much," Nebuchadnezzar said. "I'll tell you this, though, warning or none, prophecy or none, I will not stand by while Judah's weak-kneed liar king, Zedekiah, the ingrate who I myself placed on the throne, robs me blind and plots behind my back. If your god must eventually punish Babylon for doing his will, who am I to contend? Who is any man to dare oppose a god? Though you are brilliant, Belteshazzar, you cannot debate that issue with me."

"We both seem to know our roles in this drama, O king," Daniel said, rising to leave. "Yet neither of us fully grasps the why of it." He stopped on his way out and added, "May I ask, then, O king, what will prompt you to move decisively against Judah again?"

"The instant I receive hard proof that Zedekiah has climbed into bed with Pharaoh," the king said, "I will have no choice but to absolutely, finally and forever demolish Jerusalem and end its existence as a seat of power for all time. I swear it will be no more."

Daniel bowed and left the citadel, forgiving the king for his fuzzy thinking. Poor Nebuchadnezzar knew nothing of God's boundless mercy, Judah's promised restoration and Israel's eternal covenant with the Lord.

*

Hard proof of Judah's latest adultery was not long in coming. Nebuchadnezzar's spies established that poor dumb Zedekiah, after years on the throne as Babylon's puppet, had done the unthinkable and tried to cut a secret deal with Pharaoh. The spies provided witnesses and documents. Seeing them, Nebuchadnezzar lost his patience a final time.

"Zedekiah," he shouted at the meeting that day, "will be Judah's last king!"

Nobody said a word.

"I'll lay siege again," the king swore, "but this time every stone in Jerusalem will fall. I'll tear up her streets. I'll raze every home. I'll burn crops. I'll separate husbands and wives, children and parents; I'll… I'll…" He stood and pointed heavenward. "I'll grind that stiff-necked, double-dealing nation into dust."

"And the temple?" Mishael asked.

"Dust!" the king shouted.

Philosir the Phoenician, the boys' old nemesis from the captive school years earlier, had by then worked his way up from obscure administrative duties in a remote district to full membership on the royal board. He had immediately become Daniel's enemy just as Suusaandar had predicted. Hearing the king's outburst the Phoenician stroked his beard and smiled. "And what if this means war with Pharaoh?" Philosir asked. "Are you ready, O king, to confront Egypt again?"

The king rolled his eyes. "When has Egypt ever lifted a finger to help the Jews?" he asked. He looked at Daniel sadly. "Pharaoh will do nothing. Nothing! I shall level Jerusalem at my leisure. The entire Hatti-land is watching too, make no mistake. Will Judah skate free with her treachery, they wonder, so that they might feel safe to do the same? That's been Egypt's game all along. But I will send a clear message. Jerusalem's fate will chill the bones of every king in the Hatti. It will be remembered for thousands of years. No one will dare challenge Babylon after the pain that she shall cause."

*

Without the king's Hebrews, the council voted in favor of another campaign against Jerusalem but nothing happened right away. The sky remained free of omens. The earth never shook. The captives already in Babylon continued to prosper. And so Hananiah asked Daniel one day if he might take hope from the king's lack of action and all those good signs.

"No, not from that," Daniel said, "but a recent exile in Nippur named Ezekiel has delivered a word of hope from the banks of the Kebar River. *'For I will gather you up from all nations,'*" Daniel recited…

> *…and bring you home again to your land. Then I will sprinkle you and you will be clean. Your filth will be washed away and you will no longer worship idols. And I will give you a new heart with new and right desires and I will put a new spirit in you.*

"Beautiful," Mishael said, "I wonder, will we live to see it?"

"Not our generation or scores more to come," Daniel said. "I believe this applies to a much more distant time."

His friends looked at him, confused.

"There is no quick cure for people Israel," Daniel told them plainly. "As for us, let's embrace God's eventual mercy and go forward in faith."

They of course asked more questions but Daniel stayed mum.

*

The final blow to Nebuchadnezzar's patience came when his spies reported that Zedekiah had jailed Jeremiah once again for his public support of Babylon. Believing Egypt would back him, Zedekiah had bragged publicly about cutting a deal with Pharaoh.

"It's a new kind of stupid, on a celestial scale," Nebuchadnezzar said, speaking so evenly and calmly that all who heard his voice knew the Jews were finished. "Preparations are complete. The season is good for war. Mark this as the final time that this obscene people will betray me or anyone else."

Enshunu and Philosir applauded. Within the month Nebuchadnezzar led a huge force to Jerusalem and two and a half years later Judah fell to Babylon for the third time in nineteen years. Not long after it ended, Enshunu stood before the council and read a draft of the official record…

> *"During the ninth year of Zedekiah's reign,"* Enshunu began…

> *…King Nebuchadnezzar of Babylon led his entire army against Jerusalem…Jerusalem was kept under siege until the eleventh year of Zedekiah's reign…Then a section of the city wall was broken down and all the enemy soldiers made plans to escape…*

"The coward tried to run at night," Nebuchadnezzar interrupted. "But we caught him at Jericho and hauled him to Riblah where sentence was passed."

"May I go on," Enshunu asked.

Nebuchadnezzar nodded.

"The King of Babylon made Zedekiah watch as all his sons were killed."

Hananiah dropped his head.

Then they gouged out Zedekiah's eyes, bound him up in bronze chains, and led him away to Babylon.

"He's here now," Nebuchadnezzar said, "under guard, still in chains and blind as a bat." He looked right at his Hebrews as if daring them to speak. "Now that ingrate has no nation to betray, no family or children to put at risk. May he soon die and rot."

Daniel had folded his hands and listened quietly, looking neither left nor right. "But your rage did not stop there, O king, did it?" he said.

"No," Nebuchadnezzar sniffed, "it did not. I charged Nebuzaradan, my captain who replaced old Arioch, to go back to Jerusalem and mark the complete destruction of the temple, the royal palace, all the big homes and every last one of the city's important buildings." He tapped the table. "Then, still following my orders, my captain broke the city walls, burnt everything that would burn with fire, and destroyed every chip, sconce and vessel in the entire temple that he did not bring home to Babylon with him."

Daniel nodded solemnly but Azariah shook with rage.

The king read Azariah's eyes and smiled. "Those that escaped the sword that day we brought here," he said. "They are all my servants now, lowly servants, a multitude of new eunuchs among them, bound to me their new king for the rest of their lives. I allowed most of the poor to remain in the land. Jerusalem is a beautiful place, really. Those we left behind will care for the fields and vines. Meanwhile, Nebuzaradan broke the temple pillars, removed the water carts and big bronze bowl at the entrance and carried it all here to add to my treasure. All that remains of the kingdom of Judah now..." He paused to smile even more broadly. "...is dust, as I swore would be so."

"The end for all time, then," Enshunu said, "of the noxious race of the Jews."

All but four men at the council table clapped their hands.

*

As details emerged it became clear that Babylon's latest assault on Jerusalem was even worse than Nebuchadnezzar had said. Hananiah stood in the shadow of the Ishtar Gate as the last treasure taken from the temple arrived in Babylon on groaning, ox-drawn carts. When the bronze sea, an enormous basin cast in Solomon's time according to God's instruction, passed into the city, Hananiah and his friends cried like kids. Then they heard from a spy's report what Jeremiah had written about poor Jerusalem's suffering…

> *Their skin has shriveled on their bones…*
>
> *it has become dry as wood.*
>
> *Happier were those pierced by the sword*
>
> *than those pierced by hunger,*
>
> *whose life drains away, deprived*
>
> *of the produce of the field.*
>
> *The hands of compassionate women*
>
> *have boiled their own children;*
>
> *they became their food*
>
> *in the destruction of my people.*

"The house of Judah now, like Israel over a hundred years before, is no more," Daniel said, "a humbled captive in Babylon having disobeyed our God. But he is just we know with all our hearts and souls. Therefore let us look forward to what the God of Israel has promised beyond this shroud of tears."

"But how can we possibly be redeemed?" Hananiah asked. "It seems to me that nothing remains for our people in Babylon but to grow old and die of loneliness."

Then Daniel, as he often did at the oddest times, curled his lips deftly upward in an unfathomable smile. He knew something important and contrary, of course, but just what that might be, as was his custom, he refused to say.

III. The Furnace

13. Two sticks

AZARIAH KNEW WHAT he knew, Jerusalem was dead and the Jews were finished forever, but Daniel did not agree. "Read Isaiah," he said. "Consider our friend, Ezekiel!"

They had come to know Ezekiel well after he arrived in Babylon with thousands of others following Nebuchadnezzar's second siege. Ezekiel had studied to become a priest in Jerusalem but, after settling in Nippur as an exile, he had become a mighty prophet instead. Like all prophets Ezekiel often said strange things. One sunny afternoon while chatting with his friends he pointed toward heaven and said, "The houses of Judah and Ephraim will one day be restored."

That was insane. The ten tribes of the northern kingdom, Ephraim, they were sometimes called, had been overrun and dispersed by Assyria more than 140 years earlier. They did not exist. The remaining tribes, Judah and Benjamin, were now captives. How could these two peoples ever be restored? But throughout history it had been the uncanny knack of the prophets, Jeremiah and Ezekiel most recently, to upset ordinary people by proclaiming the impossible then calmly folding their arms and leaving them to figure it out for themselves.

Azariah made a powerful case against Ezekiel's vision but prophets have little use for logic. Ordinarily a sweet, humble man, Ezekiel smiled at Azariah condescendingly and refused to explain further. But not long afterward, in Nippur, he followed up his odd notion by revealing more detail. *Thus said the Lord God to Ezekiel…*

> *I am going to take the stick of Joseph—which is in the hand of Ephraim—and of the tribes of Israel associated with him and I will place the stick of Judah upon it and make them into one stick; they shall be joined in my hand.*
>
> *You shall hold up before their eyes the sticks…and you shall declare to them: Thus said the Lord God: I am going to take the Israelite people from among the nations they have gone to and gather them from every quarter and bring them into their own land. I will make them a single nation in the land on the hills of Israel and one king shall be king of them all…*

"So," Daniel said, seeming both pleased and relieved after hearing the news, "at the ends of the earth, God will find all his scattered chosen one day and he will call us all back."

"Back to what?" Azariah nearly shouted (because Daniel's optimism sometimes wore him out). "And to where? Our king, Nebuchadnezzar, has, as he swore, turned us into dust."

Ezekiel and Daniel smiled smugly at one another as if they were members of an elite club. Of course they were. O, these prophets of the Lord. Nobody ever liked Jeremiah. Habakkuk was impossible to bear. Daniel had been odd and exasperating even as a child and suddenly Azariah's new friend, Ezekiel, with his dreamlike reports of a glorious restoration (that no sane man could begin to imagine) had become equally difficult.

"You pose excellent questions, my friend," Daniel told Azariah, "for it will require more than one miracle to restore Israel as a nation; yet I see it as nothing for the creator of the universe to accomplish, albeit in his time. But there lies a bigger mystery in our brother, Ezekiel's, revelation that you seemed to have overlooked."

Azariah blinked at Daniel stupidly.

"What of his mention of the king?" Daniel asked.

"Obviously it is our Messiah," Mishael said. "Messiah will rule the new Israel."

"From the line of David," Hananiah said, "and what a day that shall be."

Azariah threw his hands up. Messiah? Jews had anticipated the coming of Messiah for centuries—Azariah's own mother had mentioned him—but Messiah never came. It was a story too good to be true.

"There's a child born in my district to whom the Lord already speaks," Ezekiel beamed. "Yes, a budding prophet, Zechariah is his name. I suspect he'll have much to say about that glorious day to come. You boys should keep an eye on him."

"Like you, I would like to believe in a future," Azariah said. "The restoration of our nation and our people, the advent of Messiah, a light to the world, the proof of the goodness and truth of our one God, but Daniel, Ezekiel, my good friends, stop to think. We Jews are on the back slope of extinction. How many promises, declarations, visions and reports…"

"Exactly as many as needed," Daniel cut him off. "It is a joy and a wonder that we with a little faith know, of a certainty thanks to our brothers, Ezekiel, Isaiah, Jeremiah…"

"And Amos, Hosea, Micah, Zephaniah, Habakkuk…" Mishael added.

"Yes!" Daniel said. "All these men have prophesied that it shall be so. God will manifest his will regarding undeserving Israel and restore her, someday."

Azariah knew better than to press. He had to admit that a day never passed in Babylon when Daniel's faith and hopefulness did not help him fight on. Changing the subject, Daniel teased Mishael, Hananiah and Azariah again about "something glorious to come in which you yourselves will play an amazing role."

"You keep saying that," Azariah told him, "but you never say more."

"Yes," Daniel said, as if resolving everything, "I know."

*

Back when the boys had entered the king's service, after Daniel had interpreted Nebuchadnezzar's dream and saved the lives of Babylon's wizards and academics, Daniel became instantly famous in Babylon, known to be wise, powerful and perpetually joyful. But Daniels' friends knew, despite his constant smile, that he could be stubborn too. For example, Daniel had ignored Jeremiah's advice to marry. He never mixed with women and never sought their company, though he did not expect the same from his friends.

"Find women, marry, build homes," he advised other exiles. "Obey the word of the Lord."

"What about you?" Azariah challenged one day.

Daniel smiled as if he had hoped to be asked. "It is not disobedient to be set apart," he said. "We may marry, build and prosper. It's good in God's eyes. But it's also possible to not do those things and amply serve the Lord."

His friends tried to change his mind. Why not grab a little comfort under this veil of tears? they asked. Marriage would not have been difficult for Daniel. Women seemed to think that he was handsome. He was also a man of means, politically connected and a noted personality in town. Crowds gathered wherever Daniel went. Strangers called out his name (Belteshazzar) as his chariot passed in the streets. Everyone thrilled at his famous smile.

"There's not a nubile Hebrew girl in all Babylon," Azariah said, "who would not gladly take your hand."

"The Nippur women are especially attractive," Hananiah added. "Most are orphaned so you would have no mother-in-law to feed."

That seemed nice.

But Daniel remained alone. His days passed simply; prayer and work filled his time. His first and only debt, he explained to his friends, was to the God of Israel, who had mercifully preserved him.

Azariah married an exile from Jerusalem in the spring following the destruction of the city, after living over twenty years in Babylon with only his brothers as friends. Hananiah and Mishael soon found good women too, grabbing a little comfort, as they had recommended to Daniel, under their personal veils of tears. And during all this time Babylon had grown in influence and splendor. The boys marveled at its achievements (to which they, in no small measure, had contributed). But Daniel warned, "This epoch is near an end."

"An end to Babylon?" Azariah said, his heart leaping. "Will it be soon?"

Daniel answered only, "A corner has been turned."

What did that mean? But even a small, God-induced setback to that evil nation's course would be wonderful in Azariah's eyes though he had no idea how it might occur. Then, at a council meeting not long afterward, he got his first clue.

14. The envy of the world

"Counselors," Nebuchadnezzar addressed his advisors one morning, "have you beheld the magnitude of my reserves?" All the king's lackeys nodded on a bright and windblown day. Nebuchadnezzar's council had met in many venues over the years but none as light and airy as the palace boardroom down the hall from the royal living quarters. Like the king's bedchamber, this room had a spectacular view of Amytis's lush hanging gardens, by then complete. As sunlight sifted through the wind-tossed palms beyond an open window, the king began to boast. "Tribute from the Hatti overflows," he said. "I've accumulated enough gold to pave the road from here to Riblah then buy Egypt with the change!"

Nearly everyone laughed. Not Daniel, though he smiled, and not Philosir his bitter rival who, in the years Azariah had known him had never smiled or laughed at anything. Enshunu, the high priest, now tottering old, was there too with his big mouth. "Marduk has certainly blessed you," he told the king. "Gifts flow in abundance through Babylon's minions to you, mighty Nebuchadnezzar, our leader and the sacred bull's prized son."

Applause followed Enshunu's little, kiss-up speech except from the Jews.

Typically, Nebuchadnezzar ignored base appeals to his vanity but he was, on that day, so energetically full of himself that he basked in the old man's praise. He pushed back from the table, strode to the window and looked out. "Behold!" he said, raising his jaw a notch with pride. "My queen longed for bushes, vines, shrubs and flowers more like those of her Median home and here they are!"

"A staggering marvel," Enshunu said. "You are the envy of the world, a hero to your bride."

Nebuchadnezzar actually blushed. Enshunu paused to let his fawning ripen then added, "Let's mint a new ensign for Marduk atop Esagila, O king! A gold icon, pure gold, crafted by commissioned artisans, cast in our sacred bull's honor, delivered to the top of the ziggurat by you, O king, for placement in Marduk's holy shrine."

"A celebratory ceremony in the square," someone suggested.

"Music, fools, virgins, festivities and gifts!" Enshunu added.

Philosir artfully cleared his throat. Everyone turned to listen. Over time, in his consistent but clever opposition to the king's Hebrews, Philosir had proven to be opportunistic, unrelenting, and shrewd. He had opposed Daniel's every suggestion while on the board yet always managed to quickly abandon a clearly lost cause without once losing face. Neither the king nor his Akkadian peers had ever questioned Philosir's motives.

"Clearly, Marduk, Nabu and the rest are well-pleased," Philosir said, his thin lips only hinting at a smile. "But perhaps the magnificent windfall would best serve the nation in the form of a monument to you, O king, and your deity?"

"The gold belongs in the temple atop Esagila," Enshunu snapped.

"In your care, Enshunu?" Philosir asked. "What glory, then, to our magnificent king?"

"Philosir, you make good sense," Nebuchadnezzar said.

"There are already tons of gold, silver and copper atop Esagila," Philosir said. "Why not bless the people with a brilliant likeness of your majesty, O king? It would command well-deserved respect. The entire nation would be obliged to bow before it."

"Belteshazzar would never bow..." Enshunu began, but then he seemed to catch on.

"Yes, Belteshazzar," Nebuchadnezzar said, turning to face Daniel, "what say you?"

"No man is more deserving of praise than you, O king," Daniel said, recognizing Philosir's potential snare but also aware that pride had his king literally bouncing on his toes, "but while it is true that you are without equal on earth as a man, you are, finally, only a man subject to God's..."

"The gods," Enshunu interrupted.

"Subject to God's justice and judgment. Such a show of pride, in my opinion, would be unwise."

"He speaks of Yah?" Philosir asked. "How dare this Jew, no matter how accomplished, flaunt the conquered Hebrew god at this table in mighty Babylon? Belteshazzar is nothing more…" Philosir stopped to point at Daniel and his friends. "These Jews are still slaves, after all."

The king narrowed his eyes, seeming to carefully consider the Phoenician's words.

"I too am a vassal, O master," Philosir continued, "but one who knows his place."

"Praise mighty Nebuchadnezzar, restorer of the glory of Babylon," Enshunu said.

All at the table applauded but the children of the God of Israel.

"They're right," the king told Daniel. "A golden ensign of my deity would be a blessing to the entire nation." He spread his hands and began to expand the vision. "It'll be huge," he said, "gold, stem to stern, as bright as the sun."

"Brighter!" Enshunu said.

Then Philosir sprang his trap. "And we'll enact a law," he said, "requiring all the king's subjects to bow down before the thing."

"I love it!" Nebuchadnezzar gushed. "Queen Amytis will love it too."

Over only four dissenting voices the motion passed and the king said, "I will make it so."

Within just months Nebuchadnezzar had directed the design, fabrication and erection of a ninety foot high, nine foot wide icon of nearly pure gold to set upon the plain of Dura not far outside Babylon's walls. When it was finished, a special ad hoc committee invited satraps, prefects, governors, celebrities, advisors, treasurers, judges, magistrates and all other provincial officials to come to a dedication.

There would be oration, delicacies, trained animals and minstrels.

The decree, crafted with the assistance of the Phoenician, Philosir, read in part…

> *O peoples, nations of men of every language: As soon as you hear the sound of the horn, flute, zither, lyre, harp, pipes and all kinds of music, you must fall down and worship the image of gold that King Nebuchadnezzar has set up. Whosoever does not fall down and worship will immediately be thrown into a blazing furnace.*

"How can we attend the awful dedication and stay true to our faith?" Hananiah asked. They discussed the problem for hours but Daniel had little to say. Much unlike him, he offered only occasional encouragement; no suggestions, no pep talks, no advice.

*

Azariah and friends rode to Dura to see for themselves only days before the colossus was due to be completed. The king's towering icon was not hard to find. The grossly elongated likeness loomed over the countryside, its blank metal eyes peering south toward Egypt, Babylon's hated rival. Rain had washed it clean earlier in the day so its every feature glinted with blinding light. "Like an evil beacon," Hananiah said.

Mishael hugged himself. "Let's just send regrets and stay away."

But Daniel said, no. "Our being present at the dedication is part of God's plan."

That seemed to settle it. Dedication day arrived and the four friends attended a spectacular outdoor party. The statue had been wrapped in an immense shroud for an unveiling. Scores of celebrities milled about its base, squinting up. Army officers, puffed-up dignitaries and prominent holy men grinned ear-to-ear as they stood by, eager to worship the work of men's hands. Thousands of ordinary citizens from town picnicked with their families on the nearby hills. Grandstands had been erected all around. Azariah sat with his friends, their wives had stayed home, in the most distant of the stands behind the monument, content not to be seen.

From there they spied familiar faces. Queen Amytis with her little children, Amel-Marduk and Kaššaya, had come, sitting beside the king. Amytis wore a brilliant red robe, sparkling jewelry and a white, feathered plume. In a smaller grandstand to the left, Amytis' oldest daughter, Nitocris, sat with her husband, a common man named Nabonidus, and their toddling boy, Belshazzar. Enshunu and a flock of splendidly dressed priests, all Marduk men, sat near them.

Azariah spotted filthy Nebuzaradan, the captain who had destroyed Jerusalem and gouged Zedekiah's eyes sitting in a nearby bleacher. "He will die soon," Daniel mentioned casually, with no more weight to his words than if predicting rain. (And, when Nebuzaradan died later that same week, Azariah was not surprised.)

Enshunu recited a meaningless prayer. Speeches began and ended. Trumpets introduced a herald who announced, "From this moment forward all will bow down when the music plays or they will die by fire." The music played, the shroud dropped, people gasped as they set their eyes upon the towering golden monstrosity for the first time. Even those watching at a distance in the hills were undone. Of course everyone fell to their knees when music played except Azariah and his friends.

"No one noticed today," Daniel said afterward, "but we're in an ugly spot."

"What shall we do," Mishael asked, "when it happens again?"

"Obey only the commandments of the Lord." Daniel said.

"And be burned alive?"

"Possibly," Daniel answered, "but I think not." Then Daniel told his friends that he was leaving town. Azariah was crushed. Daniel had never turned his back on them before.

*

After the dedication Daniel returned home to pray. Mishael, Hananiah and Azariah lived in homes in their districts with big trees and friendly neighbors, many of them Jews recently displaced from Jerusalem, but Daniel chose to live within Babylon's walls. Being close to his work made it easier to handle the whims of the king. Shortly after his appointment to the council, Daniel bought a two-story house not far from the palace. It had an enclosed court-yard, a small cottage in the back and a garden that seemed always to be in bloom. Unlike the showy homes around it, Daniel's new place had a small, practical courtyard with no showy fountains or pools. There was no family mausoleum beneath the structure. Its exterior walls and perimeter fence were not glazed but whitewashed. Daniel loved the upper floor where he kneeled to pray several times each day beside a big open window that looked out toward Jerusalem, above a shaded street.

A Hebrew widow, Pnina, of the house of Hagabah, lived with Daniel in the cottage on his property. Pnina's family had been murdered by Nebuzaradan in Jerusalem during Babylon's final siege. She had been beautiful at the time and so, though much older than most, Babylon took her captive for her looks. But poor Pnina had arrived in Babylon wrecked by her loss and the rugged march; too weathered to sell as a concubine, too weak to sell as a slave. It was common practice to allow the unmarketable captives to die of exposure en route but, after Pnina somehow survived the march, a king's man took pity and dropped her in a settlement near Borsippa to fend for herself. It was, he had explained to her, the best he could do.

One day not long after, Daniel found Pnina alone and starving in Borsippa on the street. He invited her to come to Babylon and work for him and live in his cottage. She accepted, desperate yet cautious at first, but when she realized that Daniel's motives were pure she grew to love him like a brother. As a brother cares for a sister, Daniel grew to love Pnina too. So, naturally, given their strong common affection, Pnina felt free to criticize Daniel after he revealed his plans to leave town.

"Why do you run now when your friends need you most?" she asked. She had laid out fresh clothes for his trip and prepared a plain broth for his meal. "Did you not say that the king's golden idol and the new law demanding its worship threaten us all?"

"You're in no danger," Daniel said, "only Shadrach, Meshach and Abednego."

Pnina stood muttering while Daniel blew to cool his soup. When he failed to notice her theatrics she cleared her throat and spoke again. "And now you use their pagan names?" she asked. "Why so? How dare you?"

"Because, Miss Pnina," Daniel said, "that's who they are right now. Please don't worry. They shall make it on their own. That's my prayer."

"Your prayer? Who shall save them if not you?"

"The God of Israel saves," Daniel said. "That's part of what this is all about."

"Explain then, Belteshazzar," Pnina spat, using Daniel's pagan name to demonstrate her displeasure, "how exactly they might survive when they seem so perfectly trapped?"

"I have no idea," Daniel admitted. "God has not been clear to me on that point."

"You do know!" Pnina snapped. "You see things, admit it, sir, and you refuse to say. It is not an attractive habit, prophet, to treat an old lady this way." She raised her arms overhead and pleaded with the ceiling, "Why does he keep things from me when I've proven again and again that I can be completely trusted?"

Daniel laughed. "I do know that I must return from my trip only after they are tested," he said. "I know in my heart that they will not bow to the idol on the plain. They will stand their ground. I will counsel them beforehand."

"Then all will be well?"

"That would require some amazing faith," Daniel said.

Pnina glared at him.

"I love them too," Daniel said, "but this is not my call." He looked around and asked, "Do we, by chance, have any bread? If so could you bring me some?"

Pnina returned from the kitchen with a crumbly crust, dropped it just out of Daniel's reach and left the room, muttering about his insensitivity.

*

Since his appointment to high office Daniel had served Babylon and her king faithfully every day. His motivation to do so was simple. God, through Jeremiah, had instructed him to willingly take on the yoke of Nebuchadnezzar. Daniel obeyed the Word, not always understanding but ever striving to be obedient, bound in his soul to remain so no matter what. Still, leaving Babylon while his lifelong friends faced mortal danger was the most difficult thing he had yet been called to do.

Daniel first headed north to visit the families of Adin and Yorah, recent exiles from Jerusalem whom he had discovered while studying a transit list. Their names seemed familiar. Shortly after they met and he had introduced himself, Daniel asked them what they knew about the merchant, Ahiel, his family and of course his daughter, Ya'el.

Adin reported that Ahiel had died of starvation during the third siege just before the city walls were breached. His home had been destroyed and its contents reduced to ash. Tearfully, Yorah described the old merchant's house in flames. But neither Adin nor Yorah knew anything regarding the fates of Ya'el, her sisters or her mother.

"So they may have survived," Yorah said.

Daniel prayed with them, spoke of better days to come and moved on to visit Ezekiel near Nippur, where he discussed the king's golden statue with the already notable prophet, and the wicked decree that threatened the lives of their friends.

"We'll fast for them," Ezekiel said, "as they dangle on the thread of their faith."

"They feel I've abandoned them," Daniel sighed.

"My spirit tells me, Daniel, that they will soon understand your absence as the gift that it is," Ezekiel said, "and they'll treasure your obedience for the rest of their days. But for now there's no way around the matter, Shadrach, Meshach and Abednego will be condemned to die by fire."

15. Proper reverence

FOR OVER TWO decades the Lord's protective wings had held back the evil-intentioned Phoenician, Philosir, and left him impotent against Azariah and his friends. Now, it seemed, for reasons unknown, God's protection had been withdrawn. Philosir had run Daniel out of town and sprung a lawful trap that would end in three deaths.

The executive director of the king's council was a mousy, Ammonite slave named Kurri. With Daniel gone, Philosir had lobbied Kurri to schedule the next council meeting at the weaponry depot on the plain of Dura which stood virtually in the shadow of the king's enormous idol. It was impossible to get to that meeting place without passing the thing. Unlike Daniel, whose position and title allowed him to do as he pleased, Azariah and friends could not simply choose to miss a council meeting. They were required to attend.

"But if we do attend," Hananiah said, "music will certainly play. Philosir will see to that. And when we don't bow down to worship Nebuchadnezzar's likeness they will kill us."

"In a furnace," Mishael sighed, "but there's nothing we can do."

"No, we can run away like Daniel did," Azariah said, "and never come back."

Mishael began to pray. Hananiah joined him. Azariah groaned soon afterward and kneeled beside them. "I do not understand," he muttered, "what makes you two so eager to burn alive."

Hananiah draped an arm around him. "Not eager, but willing," he said. "In truth you are braver than either of us."

Maybe they were right. Mishael and Hananiah had so much more faith than Azariah they also suffered less from fear. "I'm in," Azariah sighed afterward, "but when we get to Dura we will be condemned. And then what?"

None of them knew.

*

Meeting day arrived. Azariah, Mishael and Hananiah joined the other king's councilors at the citadel's west gate and from there continued south, under escort, toward the armory. At Dura, as they passed under the shadow of the outrageous golden idol, music played. Councilmen and guardsmen dismounted and fell to their knees, bowing deeply, eyes shut tight until it stopped. But Azariah and friends remained upright.

When the meeting began soon after—Kurri held the gavel in the absence of Daniel and the king—Philosir rose and called for a point of order. "We have a law on our books, do we not," he said, "concerning the proper reverence to show the king's icon on the plain?"

Kurri, as did everyone, nodded.

"And did not these Jews, Shadrach, Meshach and Abednego, ignore that law?"

"I saw it all," Enshunu said, "a shocking and flagrant display of disrespect."

"Sergeant at arms," Philosir shouted, "come forward, arrest these Jews, find a big, lit furnace and throw them in it according to our sovereign law."

Azariah knew the soldier who served as sergeant at arms that day, a distinguished military man and loyal servant of Nebuchadnezzar and, before him, his father. The sergeant stepped to the front of the room before speaking. "These men," he said, "are well known to me, to the king and to all Babylon."

"So, what?" Philosir asked, trembling with excitement.

"So, sir," the sergeant answered, "prudence demands that I dare not consider their execution without first confirming it with the king."

"Then arrest them," Philosir said. "Hold them in chains until the king returns."

"I will not," the sergeant said, smiling a little, "for I truly value my head."

"But they broke the law," Philosir snarled like a dog. "We all saw it. We all know the new ordinance and its punishment." He snapped his fingers at another guard. "You arrest them."

The sergeant raised his hand and the second man stopped cold. Every man at the council table other than Philosir sat quietly, staring at his hands.

"Not one of you on this council has the fortitude to defend the honor of our king?" Philosir asked.

"Let the record show," Enshunu said, "that I too favor the Jews' immediate execution."

Philosir, as always, knew when to fold. "You're pretty sure of yourself, Sergeant," he said.

"Sir, I am sure of my king," he answered.

A discussion followed about whether Azariah and his friends should be allowed to vote that day given their pending criminal status. That too was resolved in their favor, for every man at the table feared the volatility of the king, and the meeting ran normally from there.

"Do you think we skated free?" Mishael asked afterward in town.

"No," Azariah said. "You know the law as well as I. We're doomed."

"Barring a miracle," Hananiah said, "he's right. Nebuchadnezzar hates surprises. I wonder what he'll say."

*

The king returned to town in the midst of making preparations for yet another war. Since no activity exhilarated Nebuchadnezzar more than combat, he arrived back in town in a wonderful mood until learning that Enshunu and Philosir had requested an urgent meeting, "to air a grave complaint."

"I have to remind you guys," the king said before they started, "war is imminent again in the Hatti. You know that always gets my juices flowing. A whining session with my advisors is the last thing I have time for just now."

"We understand completely, O king," Enshunu said, "and would never trouble you except for this most important matter. O king, your servants are here today to report a sin against yourself and the state. Your council met at Dura, the music sounded and all bowed down to your image on the plain except Shadrach, Meshach and Abednego."

Nebuchadnezzar said nothing.

"The act was clearly criminal, O king," Enshunu said, "but your sergeant defied a direct order to arrest them and burn them alive. He remains unpunished and the Jews remain free."

"And you are suggesting...?"

"Four executions, O king."

Nebuchadnezzar shut his eyes. "I've made you all rich," he said. "Rich, respected, powerful... Yet you come to me, at war time, with the pettiness of jealous girls?"

"We come about the law, Majesty," Enshunu said.

"And the desire to also punish my loyal sergeant at arms?"

"Is Babylon under your sovereign decree, O king, or is it not?"

"Watch your mouth, priest," Nebuchadnezzar shot back. "Even holy leverage has limits in this town when dealing with the king of the land."

Enshunu lowered his head.

"I've heard your complaint," the king said, "now say again what you would have me do."

"Only justice," Philosir said. "Burn the three, hang the sergeant or whatever. We seek punishment according to Babylon's sacred law."

"Incinerate the Jews?" the king said. "Hang my sergeant?"

Philosir and Enshunu nodded.

"There's no case to be made against my man at arms," the king said. "Forget that."

"Yes, Sire," Enshunu said, "but the three..."

"Did you consider that they simply didn't hear?"

"As you know, O king," Enshunu said, "Jews never honor gods other than their precious God of Israel. Their disobedience was blatant, highly insulting and flew in the faces of witnesses."

"A score of unimpeachable witnesses," Philosir said, "the king's own council!"

Nebuchadnezzar shut his eyes. It became clear to him then that he had grown a little vain, as Daniel had warned and, by approving the construction of his likeness at Dura, he had allowed himself to be tricked. "You fellows knew this would happen," he said, "and don't say differently."

"Your decrees are inviolate, O king, is this not so?"

"True enough," Nebuchadnezzar sighed. "My great father taught me when I was but a boy, even kings must appear to play by the rules for the good of the nation."

Philosir and Enshunu smiled.

"But I am amazed," he said, "that you fellows have the brass to sit here, all self-satisfied, after clearly setting a trap against my favorite... against my finest advisors."

"We mean only to honor your legacy," Philosir said. "Shadrach, Meshach and Abednego must die by fire for the good of the nation."

"A well-framed argument," Nebuchadnezzar said. "I will investigate. You two will remain silent about this while I do so, understand? But do not worry, I will observe the law."

*

A week passed and Nebuchadnezzar did nothing. No one complained and the king dared hope that the matter might die. But several astrologers soon came to him with the identical grievance of his advisors, Enshunu and Philosir, having been goaded into action, the king suspected, by them.

"O king, live forever!" their leader said. "You have issued a decree, O king, that everyone who hears music in the presence of your sacred golden image must fall down and worship that image of gold, and that whoever does not fall down and worship will be thrown into a blazing furnace."

"Yes," the king said.

"But the whole nation knows that Shadrach, Meshach and Abednego, your servants and counselors from Judah, neither serve our gods nor worship your golden image. Will you allow your decree to be mocked by slaves? Will you ignore our thousand-year traditions for these three men's sake?"

"They're good Jews!" Nebuchadnezzar yelled. "Good Jews don't bow to idols. You fellows ought to understand that by now. Idol worship and disobedience is what started them down their road to destruction."

"Nevertheless..." an astrologer began.

"Nevertheless?" Nebuchadnezzar barked. "Do you really feel it is wise to be nevertheless-ing your king, just now, with me in a spiteful mood?"

The man bowed deeply and stepped back.

"Where on earth is Belteshazzar?" Nebuchadnezzar bellowed.

An attendant, a highly regarded general of the army, stepped close and whispered at the king's ear. "He has been traveling, Sire, and is rumored due back in town from Nippur very soon. But as for this matter, as distasteful and costly as losing your Hebrews may be, your word remains sacrosanct in Babylon only because we enforce it. Letting such behavior pass without punishment would be a dangerous precedent that would surely weaken you."

Servants in the halls heard the king break things and curse for hours afterward. Still later, Nebuchadnezzar issued an order summoning Shadrach, Meshach and Abednego to a special session of the royal court.

16. Five homeless Jews in a huddle

ANIEL RETURNED FROM Nippur on the day before his friends' trial. Azariah had gotten word of the prophet's plans so he, Mishael and Hananiah were waiting in his garden when Daniel arrived at home. The prophet dismounted, stepped past them into the house without speaking then washed his hands before offering a smile.

"How are you my dear friends?" he asked. "Frightened, Mishael? Disillusioned, Hananiah?" He turned to Azariah. "And you, of course, are angry."

Despite their anxiety, Daniel's accuracy made his friends laugh. Daniel looked each in the eye before continuing. "My brothers," he said, "can we set aside hurt feelings for a moment and simply agree that you three are in a perilous spot?" He waited until each nodded. "Good, now of a mind, let's use the speck of time available to us to discuss how you might handle your problem."

Azariah had come to accuse Daniel, not to be charmed, but the prophet had disarmed him. He followed the others to the dining room and sat with them at the table. Pnina served hot broth. While at it, the old women opened her mouth to speak but Daniel lifted a finger in an unmistakable sign, refusing to hear a word.

"If the king really wished to kill us," Azariah began, "he would have had us arrested immediately, thrown us into a furnace and moved on."

"Obviously, he wants to talk," Mishael said, "and that must be a good sign."

"Yes, and no," Daniel said. "Philosir has set a keen trap. The king may truly wish to wiggle out from under this but he has absolutely no leeway under the law. I'm afraid you men will need to make a choice."

They stared at him, waiting.

"Dishonor God," Daniel said, "or die."

"That's it?" Azariah asked. "Not even a pep talk today from our good friend, the prophet? All we get after you run away and hide is a fatal choice and best wishes?"

"Correct," Daniel said. "What are you going to do?"

"What do you recommend, O wise one?" Azariah asked.

"It's not my choice," Daniel said, "but, if asked, I would advise you to select the fire."

Azariah began to shake with anger, he couldn't help it. During all their years together Daniel had been the good, the strong, the upright fellow. Never had he flinched or run from danger. "You advise us," he asked, "to allow ourselves to be killed?"

"It would happen at the big new brick, monument and institutional paver plant east of town," Daniel said, "the only one with an opening large enough to accommodate the bodies of fully grown men."

"The one that fired the new lion statues?" Mishael asked. "Those that flank the pagan temple stairs?"

"The same," Daniel said. "It's quite an appliance."

"Stop this foolish talk!" Azariah said. "Brother," he said, "I can understand Mishael's boyish meandering but how can you, Daniel, be so casual about our end?"

They listened to birds chirping outside, in the garden, for quite a while before Daniel cleared his throat to speak. "You have to mind," he said, whispering, "that none of this is real."

His friends went blank. Pnina grumbled from her listening post in the kitchen, having stooped and hidden from sight behind the open door.

"God abides in heaven," Daniel said. "We pray to him. His Spirit comforts us when we are deserving yet we do not see him. Only the Spirit may teach us the true meaning of an event in its hour."

"That makes no sense," Hananiah sighed.

"Just tell us, Daniel," Azariah said, "will we live or die?"

"Time is not, as it seems, an arrow in flight," Daniel answered, "but a static thing that can, on occasions, be manipulated back to front, front to back, as it suits God's will."

"All my life I have prayed nearly as often and fervently as you, Daniel," Hananiah said, "and yet I have no idea what any of that means."

Daniel sat peacefully and waited.

"You are not suggesting..." Azariah's voice dropped to a whisper. "...that we might... survive?"

"We stand on a ship's bow," Daniel said, "plowing through the apparent turbulent sea of time. But through faith and supplication we begin to realize that the ship stands still and the ocean only appears to fly by! We are not trapped on that ship nor bound to travel its course."

"You see the future?" Mishael asked. "Our future?"

"Some is accessible," Daniel said. "I do not completely understand."

"You truly, truly are a prophet then?" Azariah whispered.

Hananiah stood. "What became of our mothers and fathers?" he demanded.

"I don't know," Daniel said, looking away.

"Please," Hananiah pleaded.

Daniel's eyes welled with tears. "They're long dead," he whispered, "murdered all."

They stood beside the dining table and hugged in a sad exilic huddle while Pnina sobbed softly in the kitchen. Then Azariah pushed back. "Must every Jew die to satisfy the Lord?"

"No," Daniel said brightly, "he has promised some will not."

"Some? Some is not nearly enough, Daniel," Azariah answered, heading for the door. "I will not be sacrificed to a golden caricature erected in honor of a madman. I'm running."

"He led us out of Egypt," Daniel said. "The Lord marched before us in the desert and also served as our rear guard. He favored us, protected us, loved us, fashioned a covenant, magnified us and gave us his living Word."

"So?" Azariah challenged.

"So, all he ever asked in return from us, his chosen people, was that we would revere and obey him only. But we desecrated the Sabbath. We worshiped the work of our hands. We murdered babies, short-changed widows, abused orphans and consorted with whores."

"I never did any of that," Azariah said.

"Yet every Jew pays, according to a mystery," Daniel surprised them by shouting, "as he warned us through Moses we would."

"I am through paying and praying," Azariah said. "I'll run to Egypt, to Moab, I don't care. Babylon can kill me when they catch me but

I will not lie down for the butcher king who murdered my family. Think, friends! Nebuchadnezzar murdered all our families and we sit and serve his interests like fools. I will not let him incinerate me like so much trash." He stood at the door and asked, "Mishael and Hananiah, are you coming?"

They stood still.

"You're not considering submitting?" he said.

"Submitting to our God," Daniel said, "not to the king of Babylon."

"Come with me, my friends," Azariah moaned. "We'll fight them and die like men."

"What will happen tomorrow, Daniel," Hananiah asked, "if we appear before the king?"

"He doesn't know everything!" Azariah shouted. "Why does he always ask about Ahiel's little daughter if he understood anything except blind faith in God, who seems amused at best that we've suffered so on his behalf."

"Truly, I do not know Ya'el's fate," Daniel admitted, "nor do I know what will happen to you, dear friends, if you oppose the king." He continued with clenched fists. "But I do know that the God of Israel lives. I know that without him none of this fraud called life makes sense. All is a mystery. All is in his hands. Sweet Ya'el may yet live and you too, brothers, in his merciful hands, may also survive, even in a fire."

Azariah fell to his knees. "Who in this cold universe has that kind of faith?" he pleaded.

"You do, my friend," Daniel said.

That seemed to stun everyone, especially Azariah.

"Though we are at constant war with him," Daniel began again, much more softly, "Satan is helpless in the end. Our fates abide in God's mind. They have resided so, securely, since before the beginning of time. We prove nothing to God by our choices. We simply discover who we are."

"Oh, dear God," Azariah moaned. "Please, Daniel, how can you expect us to test physics itself?"

"I'm afraid it is the Lord, God, who expects it," Daniel said, "not I."

It was too much. Azariah rose again and opened the door. This time Hananiah and Mishael joined him. "Better to die by Nebuchadnezzar's arrows then allow him to burn us alive," Azariah said. But they paused at the threshold not quite able to go.

"I love you, brothers," Daniel said, waving goodbye.

"Come with us," Azariah pleaded from the threshold, "before they kill you too."

Daniel, full of peace, remained where he stood.

Mishael began to sob. Hananiah joined him. Then Azariah and Daniel wept with them as the three stepped back inside, hugged one another and dropped to the floor to pray again most desperately. Pnina hurried in from her eavesdropping post in the kitchen and joined them on the floor, groaning as she fell to her knees.

Five homeless Jews in a huddle, sobbing.

"O God," Daniel prayed, "O dear God in heaven, though none of us are worthy, give us peace and please, O please, save all your people from the fire."

*

Daniel could not pierce the veil. He could not guarantee his friends' safety. It was clear to Azariah that, in his heart, Daniel truly believed that their best course of action was to submit to test Nebuchadnezzar's furnace's flames. But Azariah could not imagine such courage. As cold evening air spilled in through Daniel's open windows and crossed the floor to where the five of them had remained all afternoon on their knees, praying, the house grew darker.

"Tell us what to do now, brother," Azariah sighed, much too drained by then to fear what Daniel might say. "Just say it and it shall be."

"Only you can say," Daniel said.

Azariah frowned, but Mishael chuckled so oddly that his friends turned to peer at him in the failing light.

"Our course is clear as can be," he said with a big, stupid grin.

Pnina felt his forehead, checking for fever.

"We shall go to the king," Mishael said, "and joyfully refuse to bow to his filthy idol." He smiled again, no hint of concern on his sweet round face, and added, "It's as simple as that."

"You are giddy," Azariah said. "Maybe something to eat?"

"Can't you see it?" Hananiah said. "He's not unhinged at all, he's...brave."

Mishael was a coward.

"You must expect that we'll avoid our fates somehow," Azariah said.

"Nope," Mishael said, "into the furnace we'll go."

"The Comforter has found him," Daniel whispered.

"I too see a miracle in his eyes," Pnina added.

"Wonderful," Azariah said. "Mishael will be at ease when we burst into flames."

"My spirit says we'll survive," Mishael countered, jumping to his feet all enthused. "My spirit says that God himself will perform a shocking, mighty miracle for our protection and the Lord's glory. But let's burn, brothers... Let's go up in smoke together if that should be his will. Let's rejoice in obedience rather than bow to that filthy abomination on the plain."

Azariah's shoulders sagged. His eyes filled with tears. Mishael's courage had shamed him. Pnina struggled to her feet and stepped so close to Mishael that their noses nearly touched. "Something has definitely changed in there," she whispered, peering into his eyes.

"We will all be changed soon, sister," Mishael said, startling old Pnina with a hug.

*

They set off to meet the king for judgment on a cloudless day. People waved to them on the streets as they passed. "What wonderful times we had as small boys in Jerusalem," Hananiah said as they neared the citadel. "It rained at the proper times, Josiah ruled fairly and we lived in safe, warm homes."

"The whole world seemed bright then," Mishael added.

"Indeed," Azariah said, "those were some wonderful months."

"Do you enjoy being sour?" Hananiah asked. "Do you wish even to die bitterly?"

"We're not going to die," Mishael chirped, but he was still flushed with faith.

At the palace, servants assisted while they washed then led them to the king. "I have cleared this chamber for your trial," Nebuchadnezzar said. "No one will observe us or hear what we say."

"A good sign!" Mishael whispered. Azariah patted his head.

Sitting in a plush, cushioned judgment seat in the middle of a windowless hall, the king got right to business. "You're the best advisors I've ever had short of Belteshazzar," he said, "and I'd like you to reconsider." He stood and began to pace, adding emphasis with his hands. "Consider, gentlemen, with a simple gesture on your part we can get past this worship matter and everyone will win. So..." He frowned for a moment, thinking. "I'll make a show for the council by agreeing with Philosir and the priest that, of course, no problem, I'm on board. But then I will point out that you boys have the lawful right to be tested. It's on the books. I checked. Are you with me so far?"

The boys waited, saying nothing.

"So business calls you to Dura," the king said, "and the music plays and everybody turns to see if you guys will bow. And you do! That's your test, but you hardly bow at all. The gesture I have in mind for you fellows would not even qualify as a curtsy, much less a supplication. You see?" He bent a notch at the knee to demonstrate the recommended move then he smiled like a child.

"I'll be there, prearranged. You flex, I nod then say loudly, that looks very good to me." He straightened and glared at them to demonstrate his most threatening king's eye. "Who in Babylon would have the bladder to challenge me?"

"That's it?" Azariah asked. "That's all we do?"

"Yes," the king said, "and this unpleasantness is finished for all time! Surely your god won't mind a wink and a nod to save your skins?" He grinned again. "There'll be no need to even avert your eyes! You just twitch, like this..." He acted out a ridiculous scene, walking, stopping and then pretending to hear music play. With one hand behind an ear he quick-dipped at the knee. "Even if you don't tilt a mite but just turn your heads," he laughed, "I will say that you did! How's that? Enshunu and his hacks can complain but what can they do? Not a thing; the truth will be what I shall say it is. Does my offer not meet you boys more than half way?"

It sounded great to Azariah but Mishael spoke a truth that shamed him.

"O Nebuchadnezzar," Mishael said, "if we are thrown into the blazing furnace, the God we serve is able to save us from it and he will rescue us from your hand. But even if he does not we want you to know, O king, that we will not serve your gods or worship the image of gold you set up."

How had frightened little Mishael become such a man?

Of course the king exploded. He cursed them in Aramaic and the coastal tongue then finished them off in Akkadian using words they had never heard before after all their training. "You boys are ungrateful, unpatriotic, dangerous, irresponsible, ill-bred and despicable in my eyes," he finished.

But something about the king's tantrum lifted Azariah's spirits. The mounting rant quickly became so comical that Azariah avoided peeking at his friends for fear he might laugh in his face. Midway through the tirade the queen stepped into the chamber and, hearing him, applauded.

"I say," Queen Amytis said, "quit talking and burn them now."

Amytis had never been a fan.

Nebuchadnezzar called his guards.

"Take these ingrates to the new furnace outside the east gate," he said.

Mishael smiled, pleased that Daniel had been right about the venue.

"Have the master stoke it seven times hotter than normal. When I arrive we'll pitch them in but don't dare start without me. I want to watch them fry."

Technically, in the absence of cooking oil, they were to be broiled or baked.

Guards grabbed them at once. On their way out, the king's younger daughter, little Kasšaya, ran past them barefoot in the hall, her hair falling in tight black curls aside her creamy child's cheeks. A small, jewel-encrusted cylinder seal bounced against her chest as she hopped in place. "Where are you taking Daddy's Hebrews?" she asked. Then she ran off, calling out to her brother, "Amel, Amel, Abednego and Daddy's other Jews are in trouble. Come see."

*

The guards hustled them down the palace steps to the citadel gates and onto waiting chariots. As they sped toward the brickyard the boys were amazingly calm. A gift from God, Azariah's spirit had soared after making his choice; faith before Babylon. When they arrived at the site they were led straight to the oven. Several yardmen were already at work beside it erecting a gangplank for their execution. The yard boss labored hard at boosting the fire but the specter of roaring flames only heightened Azariah's growing sense of peace.

"How can you be certain it will be exactly seven times hotter?" he asked playfully. The furnace master turned and spit at Azariah's feet. "What if it's nine times hotter or only three?" Azariah pried on. "Could that amount to an issue between you and the king?"

"I've no time for this foolishness, Jew," the master muttered. "He should off your heads, plant them on pikes and be done with you. Hot or cold he'll expect a full quota of pavers from me, not a brick less today, though he's gobbled up half the day and will waste tons of fuel for this show. That's royalty for you."

"Quiet, there," a king's man snarled but the yard master spit at his feet too.

"I've brought seven times the normal charge to feed the flames," the old man told Azariah, "and enlisted witnesses to note that this big can—he pointed toward the furnace—is blazing hot. If that won't satisfy the king he can make his own arrangements. He's done so before."

None of that mattered. Not only were Azariah and his friends unafraid, they were cloaked in a kind of sweet-smelling ecstasy, prepared, even anxious to die for their faith. The brighter side of moving on, Azariah figured, was the certainty that his family would be well-cared for and that, after his loved ones, he stood only to lose Babylon, an unholy heap of idolaters, sensualists, murderers, short-changers, false witnesses and thieves.

Not much unlike Judah at the end.

"But we are not going to die," Mishael insisted.

Soon the heat from the flames forced everyone back. Mishael and Hananiah seemed so eager to burn it disturbed the guards. The king had not yet arrived so the soldiers led them back to a cooler spot, beside weathered bins where the air reeked of sharp chemicals, stacks of baked bricks, mounds of colored sand, mud, reeds, chalks, crystals and salts. Up front, workers set the incline in place at the furnace mouth while the master shouted oaths and stoked the fire more.

"Seven times hotter," they heard him complain. "How, by Marduk, would I know?"

While he worked the flames grew brighter, hotter and even louder, like a howling desert wind. Azariah began to worry that he might lose his nerve. "Pitch us in now, fellows?" he asked, but the guards refused.

"The king," one told him, "really wants to see this."

17. Smoking

NEBUCHADNEZZAR ARRIVED, TOOK a long look at the roiling furnace fire then smiled. "Wrap these ingrates in thick rope," he shouted, pointing to Azariah, Hananiah and Mishael, clearly sick about their failed negotiation but immensely angry too. His servants had spit on his magnificent gesture, he told them as he stepped past. "And so, here we are."

A detachment of Nebuchadnezzar's elite personal guard had accompanied him from the palace to the yard, big brutes all. He handpicked six of those on the spot to do the deed. "On my signal but not before," he told his anxious guards, "run these ingrates up that walk and hurl their thankless carcasses inside."

His men turned to look at the ramp. Its builders had shored it with stacked bricks along its length in order to align it perfectly with the opening of the furnace, a little below it so the soldiers would not have to stoop to throw the bodies in. But though the ramp had been fashioned from stout square timbers it quickly grew so hot that its bracing nearest the flames had already warped, turned black and begun to spit smoke. Without being ordered, several yardmen, fearing the thing might burst into flame, had formed a bucket brigade and begun to pitch water along its length. But, close to the mouth of the oven, most of the liquid turned to steam in the air. Even as they labored, the planking continued to twist, cup and groan.

"O king," the furnace master said, "you had best act now if you hope to finish this."

But Nebuchadnezzar only folded his arms.

Azariah peeked at his friends. Mishael seemed to be enjoying himself, spooled up in hemp like a fool. Hananiah winked and smiled! By then the fire had raised a towering black coil into an otherwise cloudless sky, straight upward hundreds of yards then flattened by a high wind, pointing west toward the horizon over the plain.

The neighborhood about the yard was filled with the homes of exiled Jews. Many of these by then, made curious by the smoke, stood shoulder to shoulder along the roadway, craning their necks to see what was going on.

"The king himself is here," Azariah heard one shout. "Someone is in trouble for sure."

Why had that made him smile?

A huge crowd of exiles had gathered to watch from the periphery before it became obvious why the king continued to wait. Here came Enshunu, Philosir and several of their friends into the brickyard at a royal pace upon decorated, lumbering chariots. Philosir bounced on his toes with anticipation as he approached. Enshunu seemed thrilled too. After his wagon stopped the fat old priest nearly jogged to the pit, huffing, puffing and grinning as only an enemy might, overjoyed by the prospect of his rivals' deaths.

"The fire is hot," the king said, "witnesses are present and discussion's done." He glanced at his three doomed servants, a shadow of sadness crossing his features, then quickly turned away. "Pitch them in," Nebuchadnezzar shouted over the fire's roar. "Let this be a lesson to all who refuse to compromise with their king."

But by then, despite the work of the bucket brigade, the ramp had burst completely into flame, white-hot in spots and groaning as with a voice. Tongues of flames licked up and out of the mouth of the firebox, shifting in hue before their amazed eyes, red, orange, violet, blue. Nebuchadnezzar's six selected guards failed to move forward as ordered and stood their ground. The furnace master clasped his hands and pleaded, "Sire, we've waited too long. The thing's gotten much too hot."

Nebuchadnezzar drew his sword. "Do it now," he told his men, "or you boys will return home tonight without feet, hands and tongues."

Two guards grabbed Mishael, one at each arm, and started up the ramp with his head pointing toward oblivion like the tip of a ram; the same then for Hananiah and Azariah.

"O God of Israel," Azariah cried out, "preserve us!"

Well before Mishael reached the furnace mouth, Azariah saw with open eyes (though they should have been scorched shut) the clothing of all six of their would-be executioners burst into flame as they charged forward, pair after pair ignited in an instant. But the soldiers' fear of their king (or their toughness, discipline, loyalty, who knew?)

carried each forward several more paces and they somehow managed to toss the boys in.

As the last to be launched, Azariah saw Mishael's and Hananiah's bearers fly off the ramp to the side as flames devoured their uniforms and charred their flesh. Managing somehow to glance back, the last thing Azariah saw before going airborne into the furnace was the king of Babylon, the furnace master and even old Enshunu standing open-mouthed as they watched. Once inside, Azariah was shaken by a thunderclap then hammered by silence.

It was horrifying, sailing into that fire. Then it was sublime.

*

As his bearers took their last living steps Azariah had blurted words from a new prayer he remembered suddenly...

> *Happy shall he be that rewards you as you have served us.*
> *Happy shall he be that takes and dashes your little ones against the stones.*

A bad choice, he realized later, to select verses focusing on revenge, but he had remembered only the happy part as he was launched. But what irony! Those who had tried to kill Azariah died themselves.

In the fire, much seemed to happen at first then nothing happened at all. After Azariah's would-be happy prayer stuck in his throat he switched, in midair, to the first phrase of a blessing... *I thank you, living and eternal King...* expecting those words to be his last.

But they were not.

There stood Hananiah beside him smiling like Daniel; Mishael too, in fine shape. How could that be? Azariah's rope wrap had burned completely away so he was able to reach for his friends but he found nothing to grab... So he danced.

Exactly as Daniel had advised, the three of them cut joyous steps amid the flames as if in God's own arms...*We thank you living and eternal King...* understanding nothing, trusting all. "Thank you, thank you," Azariah mouthed again and again. Then, without words, Hananiah somehow suggested that they might be dead. It seemed reasonable. Mortal men cannot have fun in a fire. Then Mishael pointed at something beside them. No, he pointed at someone.

A fourth fellow had joined them in the blaze. They moved in step with him as he danced too. Azariah had no idea how long they had been at it—a minute, a month, he had no sense of time at all—before the three stopped, stepped to the portal and peered out. Just beyond the furnace mouth he found multiple pairs of eyes, well back, peering into the blaze in utter disbelief, none revealing more awe than those of the king of Babylon. Nebuchadnezzar had fallen to his knees but then leaped up as Azariah and friends approached the rim.

The king asked, "Weren't there three men that we tied up and threw into the fire?"

"Certainly, O king," Azariah heard someone say.

"Look! I see four men walking around in the fire, unbound and unharmed, and the fourth looks like the son of God."

With his arms up as a shield against the shocking heat, Nebuchadnezzar stepped forward and yelled, "Shadrach, Meshach and Abednego, servants of the Most High God, come out! Come here!"

They laughed at the king, they felt so secure in the flames. The four joined hands (somehow) and danced again. Danced! If Azariah had ever dreamed such joy were possible under the shadow of God's wings he would have thrown himself into an inferno years earlier. How joyous it was to be assured that God lives. How grand to know that miracles were his to grant as he pleased. How humbling to understand with certainty, despite all, that people Israel had not been abandoned and never would be.

Because Israel's God keeps his word and he is just.

*

The stranger who had joined the boys in the furnace left as suddenly as he had come. It became clear to Azariah, sadly, it was time to rejoin the world. The boys easily hurdled over the furnace's white-hot rim, setting their bare hands upon it pain free. The gangplank had burned down to a path of charred chunks.

Azariah felt absolutely nothing until his feet hit the ground. Thump, thump, thump and they stood shoulder-to-shoulder before the king and witnesses, fully clothed and cool to the touch with not a wrinkle, crease or spot on their clothing. The breeze smelled fresh, birds chirped madly, as if celebrating, and the earth felt firm underfoot.

Cheers from their fellow exiles rang in their ears from the crowd at the perimeter road. The boys examined one another, poking, prodding, laughing, hugging...

Enshunu and Philosir hugged each other also but at a distance, like terrified women. When the boys stepped toward them over the lifeless bodies of six of the king's elite guards, Nebuchadnezzar's councilors ran like frightened hounds.

"Cowards!" the king shouted over his shoulder before falling to his knees, raising his eyes skyward and proclaiming for all to hear, "Praise be to the God of Shadrach, Meshach and Abednego who sent his angel and rescued his servants! They trusted in him and defied the king's command and were willing to give up their lives rather than serve or worship any god except their own God. Therefore I decree..."

The king stopped, interrupted. Someone was coming. When the brickyard had been designed, Nebuchadnezzar's royal landscapers had dotted the expansive industrial plot with shrubs and grass to improve its look and hold down dust, but a great cloud of dust swirled behind a surging chariot as it rumbled inward through its gate, the cart's wheels off the ground again and again as it careened toward them.

"Whoa, ho!" Daniel shouted after nearly tipping his rig in a sideslide stop. "Praise God and your wondrous faith!" he called out, running so fast that his sandals flew away. His hair fell loose to his shoulders as he sprinted toward his friends, never slowing, to first knock down Azariah with a headlong hug. They fell together laughing but the Lord's own prophet quickly jumped up and punched him hard in the arm. Then he pushed Hananiah and flicked Mishael's ear. By then Philosir had found the courage to creep closer. Enshunu followed not far behind. Neither had managed to close his mouth. The boys formed a circle, joined hands, and hopped together first left, then right, singing a song they knew not, grinning like loons through their tears.

Amein! Amein, amein, amein, amein!

"Therefore I decree," the king began again when they had finished, "that the people of any nation or language who say anything against the God of Shadrach, Meshach and Abednego be cut into pieces and their houses turned into piles of rubble, for no other god can save in this way."

All seemed forgiven.

"I'm no fool," Nebuchadnezzar said, beaming. "Your god is superior to most."

Azariah sighed; it seemed the king was a fool; a brilliant, talented fool who seemed unable to sniff the truth. Poor man, after witnessing a miracle of unsurpassed mercy the king was only able to promote the god of the Hebrews toward the top of his list of deities then vow to butcher all those who spoke against him. How better to define a fool than one who cannot discern the infinite, all-loving and merciful when it pokes him in both eyes?

*

While the dust still hung in the air from Daniel's wild entry, several of the onlooking exiles cautiously crossed the road to peek into the blistering oven. Speaking in hushed tones, they examined the charred corpses beside the hotbox on the ground. Then, very warily, they approached Azariah, Mishael and Hananiah to prod at them with fingers to be certain they were real.

"I was so wrong," Azariah confessed tearfully.

"I told you," Mishael said. "We all told you."

They had.

Daniel kneeled and offered a blessing over those who died.

"Why bother?" Nebuchadnezzar sniffed, overhearing, "the cowards did their duty only after I threatened them."

"You are a great king," Daniel began, "but…"

Nebuchadnezzar stopped him from saying more—kings hated to be wrong even more than people—and he said, "Okay, I'll see that they are buried with honors at Esagila, how's that? Their survivors will be set apart as heirs of heroes of Babylon." That resolved, Nebuchadnezzar faced Philosir and Enshunu. "Well then, you scheming lavender lads, things didn't work out so well for you today."

"Marduk," Enshunu stammered, "surely managed this all."

"Out of my sight," the king hissed at them. "I ought to replace you both."

They left at once, still speechless, but Azariah knew that the king would not replace them on his board; Philosir was too gifted and the wily old priest was too well-connected in town owing to decades of passing privileged information and granting favors to the old-line families in Babylon who dared to rival the royal line of the king.

While the boys watched, some of the neighborhood exiles taunted the furnace by dancing near its flaming mouth and shouting insults. Others sang songs praising the God of Israel and mocking the adversary for failing to kill the three boys. Several delivered loud, impromptu narratives honoring God for the amazing intercession that saved Shadrach, Meshach and Abednego from destruction.

The king wrapped his brutish arms about his suddenly forgiven heroes and repeated his previous misguided praise (and corresponding threats) concerning the creator of the universe. It was heartbreaking how dumb that brilliant man could be.

*

The king promoted Azariah, Hananiah and Mishael on the spot to even higher stations in his empire; more authority, privileges and pay. Then he summoned his chariot, called out My Hebrews! and waved goodbye as he and his guards that had survived raced off.

"My Hebrews," Daniel repeated, both mocking and praising the king.

Days later Azariah tried to discuss their experience with his friends without breaking into tears. "What really happened in that furnace?" he was finally able to ask.

"And who," Hananiah added softly, "joined us in the fire?"

Mishael, a new man by virtue of his encounter with the Spirit, shrugged off the question as unimportant. "It's God's mystery," he said, "to be explained in his time. I know all I need in my soul."

"I suppose," Azariah sighed, "although we lack understanding it's enough for us to simply remember God always, observe his ordinances and always give thanks for his mercy."

"None of this would have happened," Hananiah sighed, "if Daniel had fought our battle."

They asked his forgiveness.

"Don't be hard on yourselves, my good friends," Daniel smiled. "These are difficult times."

18. An overpowering rebuttal

THE ACCOUNT OF the boys' survival spread from the brick-yard, into town and throughout the provinces even before the furnace cooled down. Babylonians were a cynical lot but the multiple, breathless, first-hand reports of the miracle would not stop. By week's end the story had crossed the Hatti-lands, rendered by then in several different dialects and tongues. Nothing was added, so rich was the tale; three exiled Jews in Nebuchadnezzar's service had defied the king to remain true to their faith and were thrown in a furnace full of flames; and they had lived!

Among those living in the Hatti, nearly as entertaining as the account of the miracle itself was the added delightful impact of heavy-handed Nebuchadnezzar's defeat. The God of Israel had proven to be the king's better. People begun to praise God's name again to the coast of the Western Sea.

No nation was more superstitious than Babylon, so some in Akkad insisted that Shadrach, Meshach and Abednego were gods too. The three boys rose to an unhealthy level of regard in the public eye. After they survived the furnace crowds formed and followed them wher-ever they went. Enshunu's rivals tried to enlist their political support against the aging high priest. Ordinary citizens, even military men, began to wear amulets and charms upon which their names were inscribed. Daniel, already a legend in the land, rose even more in esteem because all Babylon credited him for having orchestrated everything. But the miracle in the furnace prompted many to ask a much more accurate question...

Just who is this God of the Jews?

For a few, the tangible God of Israel suddenly stood as an over-powering rebuttal of the trappings of superstition and idolatry. Sadly, most Babylonians only added the living God to their pantheon, one of many beside the great bull, Marduk, Nabu, Sin, Tammuz, Enki and countless planets, comets, vapors, serpents, mice and minor deities.

"Should we spread the Truth?" Azariah asked.

"It has been made plain enough to those who would search their hearts," Daniel said. "Thanks to your faithfulness, friends, and God's immeasurable mercy, the doorway to understanding has cracked open just a bit in this dark-leaning wasteland."

"I will also give thee for a light to the Gentiles..." Azariah began.

"That you may be my salvation unto the ends of the earth," Daniel finished for him, knowing his Isaiah cold. "But though Nebuchadnezzar is truly God's inscrutable instrument, be certain, my brothers, this nation's cruelty to Jerusalem and our people will not go unpunished."

That suited Azariah fine. He was prepared to move on cheerfully, in fact reborn, but Daniel suddenly grew grim. "I'm afraid," he began again in a voice so soft they could barely hear him, "the promises we've just recited refer to a distant time."

Daniel never shared much with his friends of what he knew, what God had begun to show him in visions about the Last Days, but Azariah knew that the Lord had allowed Daniel to see much more than Daniel had been willing to reveal. But one day, sensing his friend's frustration, Daniel threw Azariah a bone.

"The God of Israel chose the line of Abraham, Isaac and Jacob because of Abraham's faith, his ability to look beyond the mists, moon and stars to honor the Creator himself, not his works. But, despite his choosing us, we abandoned him. He will not utterly destroy us, that much we know from his Word, and he will someday make good on every promise."

"Jerusalem restored?" Hananiah asked. "Messiah delivered?"

"As clearly promised, yes."

"But when will he come?" they asked.

Daniel said nothing.

"Whenever it may be," Mishael said, "on that day we shall once again be his people."

"And he," Daniel added, "shall be our God."

*

Azariah wondered, stepping back from the glory of the fire to the mire of everyday life, Will I ever feel the same? Yes, he worked with the same energy after the miracle as he had before, serving his district as a reluctant celebrity. But fame meant nothing to him. The blaze had been real, life was a dream. Even more than losing his parents, Jerusalem's fall and the torturous pain of exile, leaving the furnace to reenter the world had been Azariah's most difficult trial.

"So this is it?" he asked one evening after another of the king's sessions. "Faith found, miracles witnessed and now we wait to die?"

"We'll grow old in service, I suppose," Hananiah said, "then other exiles will continue where we stopped. Then a day will come…" But his voice trailed off.

Daniel waited for a while before speaking. "I've been allowed to see that even greater misery, generation upon generation, is yet to befall our people before all is fulfilled," he said. "Please pray for each other, our people and for me."

*

What Nebuchadnezzar had witnessed in the brickyard clearly changed the king but, because he was a king, not forever. For a while after the miracle he was more inclined to cheerfulness and less given to rage. "My Hebrews!" he would call out whenever Azariah and his friends stepped into the council chamber or when they passed in the citadel halls.

Enshunu, however, grew to hate the sons of Judah even more. He had also come to openly despise Philosir, whose failed attempt to destroy the Jews had left a fortune in gold sitting in Dura and not under Enshunu's loving care in the temple atop Esagila. Nebuchadnezzar himself had become a serious god to some because of fascination surrounding the statue on the plain, and therefore become a rival to Enshunu's bull. Worst of all, Enshunu's enemies, Shadrach, Meshach and Abednego had become folk heroes.

So nothing sat well with the fat old priest.

But these were glory days in Babylon. Nebuchadnezzar ignored the growing discord on his council and the nation flourished just the same; best ruler, advisors, resources, law, science and military in the world after all. No nation had ever been more powerful, no dynasty ever so great.

"Another way to look at high water," Daniel told his friends one day, "is as the beginning of decline."

Azariah argued at the time; it seemed to him like nothing could stop Babylon. But sure enough, at the moment Babylon seemed poised to rule unchallenged forever, mighty Nebuchadnezzar fell in love with himself and went completely mad.

It was no accident, it came with ample warning and it lasted seven years.

IV. Madness

19. Never impugn the divine

NOT VERY LONG after the miracle of the furnace, King Nebuchadnezzar did something even those who knew him well would not have guessed. He began to buy into the long-standing myth of the Babylonian deity-king. One day at a council meeting he admitted that he thought he might be godlike. "Or very nearly so," he told his advisors, "like the one who stood with my Hebrews in the fire."

"You're only a man," Daniel reminded him later, "and you should be mindful, O king, not to impugn the divine."

"Am I not the head of fine gold?" the king asked, reminding Daniel of the dream he had interpreted under duress years before. "Truly, I am. You said so yourself."

"It was symbolic," Daniel said. "You are, O king, but a man."

Nebuchadnezzar sniffed, unconvinced. After decades of working with the gifted ruler Azariah had become fond of him though the general-king had wrecked theirs and countless other lives. Nebuchadnezzar was unbelievably energetic, talented and courageous with uncanny perception and superb organizational, engineering and leadership skills.

But he was no god.

His Hebrews had prayed for years that Nebuchadnezzar might one day shed superstition and discover the Light, but as time passed and success followed success, the king's unhealthy self-opinion grew without bounds. He believed, for example, that the adulation that had accrued to Azariah, Mishael and Hananiah from their furnace adventure had cast an even greater aura upon him. "Without me," the king explained, "none of it would have happened."

"You attempted to kill your three finest advisors," Daniel said, "and instead murdered six of your most loyal guards."

"No one is perfect," the king came back.

"O king," Daniel said, "you've seen miracles with your own eyes that should have shattered your enormous pride long ago. But nothing has changed you. Even the disgusting idol at Dura remains. Every day, music plays and fools hasten to bow before it when you know in your soul that your decree is an unholy sham."

"I've made room for your beliefs," the king answered, "why do you ridicule mine?"

It was hopeless. Despite everything Daniel had tried to teach the king about the God of Israel, Nebuchadnezzar insisted upon measuring the creator of the universe as a sort of gifted peer. "And," the king said, "I have commanded all Babylon to regard your god highly."

"Threatening to cut people to pieces," Daniel said, "and turning their homes to rubble is no way to honor the One who has preserved you against your enemies and allowed you to rule the world."

"Think, Daniel," Nebuchadnezzar came back, "can you truly imagine a nation as splendid as Babylon relying on but one god?"

"Ridiculous," Queen Amytis agreed. She had become less the hater after Shadrach, Meshach and Abednego survived the furnace but only marginally so. Her children, the prince and princess, Amel-Marduk and Kasšaya, were also present for the discussion. They laughed at Daniel's notion too. The Hebrew god had proven excellent at dreams and fires, their mother told them, "but there is no god like Marduk when it comes to war."

Both of them nodded eagerly; pagan royalty to be.

"Each god has his place," Nebuchadnezzar explained. "The God of Israel excels at saving, kindness, justice and mercy, all good things in their season, but he could never lead Babylon in gory battle as well as our mighty bull. Surely you can see that?"

Daniel reminded the king of how, over a century earlier, the Lord had humbled Sennacherib's army at Jerusalem. "Not too long before that day," Daniel said, "that same Assyrian ruler had whipped Babylon's king in battle and taken him captive to Nineveh."

"Sennacherib was a lice-infested monster," Nebuchadnezzar said. "I curse his name."

"The God of Israel sent an angel and wiped out a hundred eighty-five-thousand of his men."

"One hundred eighty-five thousand?"

"Camped outside the city, found dead overnight."

"And Jerusalem survived?" the king asked.

"Sennacherib ran away."

"Then he was a fool," Nebuchadnezzar said. "A good leader would never lose an army that size and also honors many gods."

But it became clear as time passed that Nebuchadnezzar had begun to honor only himself. There was no talking to him. Daniel told him to his royal face that it would come to no good. "This kind of self-adulation will be the end of you," he had said.

Nebuchadnezzar smiled condescendingly and answered, "I hardly believe that."

*

Despite the king's self-enchantment everything went well for several years while he kept busy with his favorite pursuits; building things (an immense passion at which he had no equal) and planning, preparing for and making war (a pastime Nebuchadnezzar approached like a competitive sport).

"Gentlemen, I am going after Tyre," he announced to his council one day, his eyes gleaming like a child's up to mischief. "I will bring that prideful city down within five years, seven tops. Babylon will rule the jewel of the western sea."

Of course Enshunu, Philosir and the king's other pagan sweethearts on the council (less the military, who were no fools) applauded the announcement. The high priest and his self-absorbed allies knew nothing about Tyre except that its riches were legendary and its location sublime, lying like a pearl upon the distant, sunswept coast. Not only would the city be a terrific asset to Babylon once conquered, they agreed, but it would also serve as a grand place to visit with their families at summertime. But Azariah had read much about Tyre beginning with the reports Suusaandar had once handed to him while in the captive school. The king's best spies had strongly warned of the city's prodigious military might and the ample natural protection of that famed center of commerce and trade. So Azariah cleared his throat to gain the king's attention.

"Abednego!" the king said, "what have you to say?"

"O king," Azariah said, "the land you design to conquer is well-known by the sons of Judah. Long ago, Hiram, king of Tyre, assisted mighty King Solomon in Jerusalem as he built the magnificent temple of the God of Israel."

"That would be the same temple that Babylon recently leveled," Philosir said.

Enshunu chuckled.

"There exists a long and complex history between Judah and Tyre, O king," Daniel said, "a record that has turned quite dark. Be certain that a righteous burden of debt to Judah hangs over Tyre to this day. But I suspect that your servant, Abednego, is about to offer you an insightful, current caution."

The king showed instant irritation. Everyone knew that Nebuchadnezzar loved to be advised but hated advice itself. "Tell me your caution, then," he said in his well-known, make-this-quick, tone.

"Sire," Azariah answered, "they are a clever and industrious people."

"Phoenicians all," Philosir added proudly, "inventors of navigation who taught mankind to brave tempests and torrents at sea on nothing but frail barks. Tyre, queen of the sea, her great port serves the world."

"I know all that," the king said. "She is quite the prize. That's why I aim to conquer her."

Azariah rarely had the nerve to challenge the king but he too had changed having survived Nebuchadnezzar's best efforts to murder him. He stood and said forcefully, "O king. Even if Babylon is able to take the adjacent mainland at Tyre, your own sources report that the city's inhabitants may easily retreat to the rocky, fortified island half a mile off shore. From there they will still have their ships, they will command easy access to food and the materials necessary to both wage effective war and survive a lengthy siege."

Nebuchadnezzar began to strum the tabletop with his fingers.

"The island's walls facing the mainland are over 150 feet high," Azariah said. "They stand nearly perpendicular to where they meet the sea. The fortifications are built to withstand any ram yet devised. The channel between the mainland and her coastline is over twenty feet deep. It's swept with powerful currents, turbulent winds, change-able weather and…"

"Enough!" Nebuchadnezzar shouted, fists clenched on the table and his eyes shut tight. "That is quite enough. I am Nebuchadnezzar the second, son of Nabopolassar, king of Akkad, ruler of the known world, favorite of the gods. I am the gleam in Marduk's eye, lord over millions..." He stopped, breathing heavily, as if he had jogged a great distance.

"And even so, O king," Daniel said softly, "Tyre remains a mighty, imposing fortress."

Enshunu cleared his throat to speak but Nebuchadnezzar stopped him with a raised hand. "I'm finished with you fellows today," he said. He pointed at Philosir. "We'll see how well your storied inventors of navigation fare against my siege machines."

"Sire," a military man spoke up, "regarding that defensive wall at the island that Abednego just mentioned, there is no known device or system capable of assaulting it."

"Then we will design and build better machines!" Nebuchadnezzar yelled again. "What, by Marduk, is wrong with you people?" He stood, turned in a circle and announced, "Every one of you gutless wonders get out of my sight now." But as his advisors began to file out the king said, in a softer voice to Azariah and friends, "Of course, I don't mean you four."

When the room emptied the king said, "Tell me what you know about Tyre. I want to hear it but, understand, nothing you can say will change my mind. Tyre will fall and Babylon will command her port."

"Agreed," Daniel said.

Nebuchadnezzar did a double take. "What happened to, Caution, O king?"

"Jeremiah is not the only prophet alive today," Daniel said, "though it is Jeremiah whom you know best."

"You mean yourself, of course, my Belteshazzar, my Daniel," the king said, big smile. "I've known of your elite status among your people for quite some time now."

"Among the thousands you have ripped from their homes in Jerusalem," Daniel said, "lives the mighty prophet, Ezekiel, now your subject living in exile near the Kebar, in Nippur."

"A full-blown man of your word, you say?" Nebuchadnezzar asked.

"Full-blown," Daniel said, "and he has revealed much about this very day."

Daniel and his friends told the king all that Ezekiel had recently revealed while in the Spirit regarding the future, Nebuchadnezzar and Tyre.

For thus says the Lord God, Behold, I will bring upon Tyre from the north Nebuchadnezzar king of Babylon...

"That truly sounds inspired," the king said.

Daniel continued...

He will slay your daughters on the mainland with the sword and he will make siege walls against you, cast up a mound against you, and raise up a large shield against you. And the blow of his battering rams he will direct against your walls...

"That's exactly what I've been thinking," Nebuchadnezzar smiled.

...and with his axes he will break down your towers. Because of the multitude of his horses, the dust raised by them will cover you. Your walls will shake at the noise of cavalry and wagons and chariots, when he enters your gates as men enter a city that is breached.

"Hi, ho!" the king said. "Even your god is on my side."

Daniel ignored the king's frequent interruptions and read much more.

"I will win, then," Nebuchadnezzar said when Daniel had finished, "this settles it."

"The prophecy speaks of you and Babylon, O king," Daniel said, "as well as other nations."

"Meaning what?"

"Meaning that, clearly, Babylon will defeat the mainland city..."

"But what of the island?" the king interrupted. "That shall fall too, by my hand. I am sure I remember hearing something about the island and me."

"Perhaps so, perhaps not," Daniel said. "Ezekiel says for sure only that, the island shall eventually fall."

"To whom if not to me?" Nebuchadnezzar asked. "I am the great-est general, am I not, having assembled the greatest army the earth has known?"

It was obvious that Ezekiel's words had puffed-up Nebuchadnezzar even more. After hearing them, he dismissed his advisors' cautions and began planning his campaign against Tyre.

*

Well before Nebuchadnezzar revealed his designs on Tyre, every-one in the city, merchants to nobility, whispered and worried about their king's growing conceit; no small reaction amongst a people who still bowed before the same man's golden image on the plain of Dura. Azariah had never dreamed a human being could become so self-absorbed.

He stared at his own reflection, had predicted that posterity would judge his queen the most fortunate woman of her time for having married him and, though he knew better, had begun to encourage Azariah and friends to bow to him as a deity, taking offense each time they refused.

"He has gone completely over the top," Hananiah said. "He insists that the cuneiform refer to him only and always as, I quote, that great king, son of a great king, beloved of Nabu. He has threatened to dismiss Enshunu and serve as both Babylon's king and high priest. A rumor circulates that his concubines are no longer allowed to look directly at him, that when the king visits them..."

"Enough, don't you think?" Daniel asked. "True enough, something will certainly take the wind out of Nebuchadnezzar's sails. No man can avoid judgment while so inclined to his flesh."

"So what will happen to him?" Mishael asked.

That question hung in the air until springtime. When the weather turned favorable Nebuchadnezzar led an army east to Tyre after he had personally designed and built several magnificent new siege machines and rams for challenges his army would face at Tyre's rocky coast. But first Babylon had to conquer the mainland fortress.

The campaign began with mild expectations. Tyre, Nebuchadnezzar told his staff, would fall only after five to seven years of protracted battle. And it might have happened exactly as the king predicted if only he had taken a personal warning to heart; one that came to him directly from the Lord in the form of a vision.

*

One morning, after Babylon's siege at Tyre had slogged on for nearly four years, King Nebuchadnezzar revived from a troubling dream feeling exactly as he had decades earlier. He roared an oath and ordered Amytis and the children out of the royal bedchamber, saying, "I've had a baffling vision. Send for my wise men, enchanters, Chaldeans and diviners!"

"Think back, O king," the queen said. "We have done this before. Why not summon your servant Belteshazzar to start?" She began dressing quickly to leave. "Though stubborn and a Jew he remains the only man who has ever been able to calm you."

"I have a thousand seers on the payroll," Nebuchadnezzar snapped back. He stepped to the doorway and shouted, "I say I've had a disturbing dream and I want to know what it means."

The queen stepped into the hallway and posed the kings' complaint as a command. The palace help went scurrying. King's men were alerted and couriers dispatched. Soon scores of bone readers and astrologers including the High Priest of Marduk arrived. By then, fat Enshunu could not walk without the aid of an exquisite jeweled staff. He had difficulty hearing, too, but neither ailment stopped him from trying to take charge.

"What is your pleasure, O marvelous son of Marduk," he asked.

"I had a dream, priest. It disturbs me. I want to know its drift."

Enshunu bowed at the waist "Time past, Sire," he said, "you had a similar need and I nearly lost my head. I pray on this occasion, Excellency, do honor me with a recitation."

That seemed fair. Nebuchadnezzar remembered the mess he had caused years before when he insisted that everyone guess. He told Enshunu and the others all that he remembered about his dream. But even then, after they had heard it, Enshunu stood blinking like a barn owl before him. "That's it?" he asked.

Nebuchadnezzar looked around the room. "I have here assembled the cream of my mystical crop, do I not? Was anything I said just now confusing, contradictory or unclear?"

Enshunu snapped his fingers. Three of his assistants pushed a small wheeled cart forward bearing a weighty set of engraved tablets and a tall, etched cylinder. "A catalogue, Majesty," Enshunu said, "of the most reliable indices of spells and mumblings known to man, an extensive piece of work bearing profound omenology, oven fired to last forever."

"Wonderful research tool, surely," Nebuchadnezzar said. "And the answer is?"

"Patience, please, Majesty," Enshunu said. He and his helpers began to page through the brittle plates and rotate the cylinder, pointing and murmuring at excerpts for quite a while, sometimes nodding in agreement, sometimes bickering among themselves, until the high priest sighed and turned again to face his king. "Master," he said, "along with a wealth of traditional wisdom we've searched the wisdom of Sumer and Nineveh too, notes extracted from the surviving tomes from her great library!"

"I am no fan of Nineveh."

"Of course, Sire. But fan or no, I'm afraid, so far, there seems to be no mention..." Enshunu stopped to wipe his brow with the sleeve of his robe. "There is nothing in these annals, O king, which as you know rely heavily on the advent of certain creatures, the lie of cast bones, the thrusts of tides, apparitions, innards and phases of the moon..." He stopped again. "Please, Majesty, humor me; was there perhaps somewhere within your vision say, a striped fox, a white bat or a one-legged crow?"

Nebuchadnezzar shut his eyes.

"Please do not make light of these things, Majesty, for these mysteries are..."

"Garbage!" the king shouted. "You are phonies, freeloaders, inbred first cousins and carrot eating clowns. I despise you all and I want you out of my sight this instant." He pointed at Enshunu's jewel-encrusted walking stick as his high priest waddled away. "I could equip a thousand troops, you old fake, for the cost of that fancy cane of yours!"

The chamber doors shut with a thud and they were gone.

Amytis returned soon after, smiling in the king's face as only the queen of the land might dare. "Your rich, fat priests have failed you as always," she said. She studied her reflection in a polished piece of obsidian while running her fingers through her hair. "They mock you behind your back; did you know that, Nezzy? They take your best wine for themselves as they bless it, and I'll bet you a bag of silver that while at it they spit in our food."

"I never considered that," Nebuchadnezzar said.

"Please, mighty king," Amytis said, "call Belteshazzar and tell him your dream."

Nebuchadnezzar sometimes feared Amytis so he occasionally told half-truths. "I am not as dependent on him as you might think," he said. "However, I do plan to hold a business dinner with my Hebrews very soon during which we shall discuss Egypt."

The queen laughed. "I do not like those people in our home," she said. "They belittle our customs and hold that their god is superior. But I admit that Belteshazzar has established his great power through the workings of his god, though I fail to understand how it works. If the Jewish god is as powerful as he seems, why are all his people slaves?"

"I have wondered the same myself more than once," Nebuchadnezzar said. "Belteshazzar claims their misery is their own fault. The nation was warned."

"Go, arrange your business dinner," Amytis sighed. "Get your dream unwound and be done with it; but I swear, if I hear you call those men My Hebrews again I'll scream."

*

The king greeted Belteshazzar, Shadrach, Meshach and Abednego in an anteroom after they washed downstairs, My Hebrews! and led them to a private dining room in the citadel. Slaves served brown beer, red meat, a cold porridge, fish from the royal lakes and coarse-grained bread. Though Nebuchadnezzar promised that the food had not been tainted by pagan priests or their prayers, Belteshazzar drank only water, sipped clear broth and ate pulse. After dinner Nebuchadnezzar dismissed the help and locked the door behind them using a clever plaque and peg system he had invented himself. But Belteshazzar looked him directly in the eye before he could speak and said, "It's time, O king, for your servants Shadrach, Meshach and Abednego to leave us. What you have to say does not concern them and the hour grows late."

Nebuchadnezzar never ceded control to anyone, it was awful form for a king, but he sighed and sent the others away. There was no sense in trying to bully Belteshazzar, it never worked, and he desperately wanted to unravel his latest mystery. "I had another dream," he told Daniel after the others had left. "I gave Enshunu and his buffoons a chance to reveal the thing but they failed. Again. It didn't feature crippled bats or crows, you see." He shook his head. "The queen said I should have called you first but lately politics have been trying."

"I understand," Daniel said. "You did not want to create discord."

"No, who cares?" Nebuchadnezzar said. "A few palace goiters getting upset has never bothered me. It's just that lately I've been strongly tempted to kill them. That impulse getting the best of me, while fun to consider, would really cause a stir. But I hoped, if I gave them a chance at this challenge, you know, to please me…" His voice trailed off. ·

Belteshazzar said, "Enshunu will die soon."

"And power struggles have already begun!" Nebuchadnezzar came back. "When that crusty old frog croaks there'll be backstabbing among the priests, the old dynastic families will get their ambitious juices up… I'm afraid not even a great king like me can prevent scheming and ambition."

"So you invited them all…?"

"To tell me my dream and they failed. I cursed them of course but I'll hold back on how I really feel until the infighting winds down. Why let everyone know my thoughts?"

Belteshazzar nodded.

The king told his dream.

Belteshazzar spent a moment in prayer after which he opened his eyes and said, "My lord, if only the dream applied to your enemies and its meaning to your adversaries."

Nebuchadnezzar bowed his neck. "I'm the most powerful man in the world," he said. "Just say it. I fear neither man nor gods."

"Have you already forgotten the miracle of the furnace?" Daniel cautioned.

"Not altogether," Nebuchadnezzar said, but that sort of lecturing was exactly why he sometimes hated chatting with Belteshazzar. The miracle had haunted him, so much so that he sometimes tried to block it from memory. But only this Hebrew slave had the nerve to throw it in his face time and again. "You do your job, Daniel, okay?" he said. "Let me worry about divinity and the rest."

"But your failure to understand the divine, O king, is your problem."

"Noted," Nebuchadnezzar said. "I've heard your opinion. You've heard my dream. Now interpret."

Belteshazzar nodded.

Nebuchadnezzar braced himself for whatever.

20. Running half-naked in the hills

DANIEL PAUSED BEFORE revealing the meaning of Nebuchadnezzar's dream to him, neither to contend nor to make him angry, but because Daniel hoped, through prayer, to be able to say exactly what God intended.

"Are we ready now, you think?" Nebuchadnezzar asked after much fidgeting.

"The tree you saw," Daniel began, "which grew large and strong with its top touching the sky, visible to the whole earth, with beautiful leaves and abundant fruit, providing food for all, giving shelter to the beasts of the field and having nesting places in its branches for the birds of the air, you, O king, are that tree. You have become great and strong; your greatness has grown until it reaches the sky, and your dominion extends to distant parts of the earth."

"Just as I have believed!" Nebuchadnezzar smiled. "What's so bad about that?"

"You, O king, saw a messenger, a holy one, coming down from heaven and saying…

Cut down the tree and destroy it, but leave the stump, bound with iron and bronze…

Nebuchadnezzar pounded the table. "Why must you always do this?" he shouted. "I do not need a recap. I, myself, told you these things and I certainly don't need to hear them again. Just tell me the meaning now or I'll…" He stopped, mid-sentence.

Daniel waited patiently. They had played this scene out before.

"Do as you please, then," the king sniffed, "but it's taking much too long."

Daniel finished the interpretation at his pace. Nebuchadnezzar listened poised at the brink of an explosion until the end, when he learned that his vision pointed to an extended time, not too distant from that moment, when he would lose his mind.

"Mad, you say?"

"But you can avoid it, O king," Daniel said, "if you repent and admit that heaven rules."

Nebuchadnezzar looked up at the ceiling.

"Seven times," Daniel said, "will pass until you acknowledge that the Most High is sovereign over the kingdoms of men."

"What, exactly, is a time?"

"O king," Daniel said, "do what's right in God's eye. Renounce your pride, do justice and be merciful to the oppressed. Then you may be spared."

"But how can a professional oppressor be kind to the oppressed?" Nebuchadnezzar asked. "You see my point, correct? No one should understand this better than you, Belteshazzar, one of my victims. I conquer. I punish. I expand Babylon's horizons no matter who gets trampled. I derive joy from trampling, in fact. If I forswore oppression then I simply wouldn't be doing my job as a great king, you see?"

Now Daniel looked up at the ceiling. "O king," he said, "Which do you think might work more favorably for you; to change your prideful ways now or to chew cud on all fours for several years in the future?"

"You make it sound like an either-or," Nebuchadnezzar said. "I'm not at all sure you've got that right. Certainly there must be subtleties to consider, options I might pursue to appease your god toward an end not so drastic, the negation of the essential me, mighty Nebuchadnezzar, son of Nabopolassar, a born ruler, general, king and yes, in many cases, oppressor extraordinaire?"

"The meaning of your dream is clear, O king."

"Well, we will just have to agree to disagree," Nebuchadnezzar said. "Either way, the stump in my dream was saved, right? That's me, the stump? No matter what I may do, according to my dream, your god indicates by what he has revealed that I shall be preserved."

"There is a hard way, O king, and an easy one," Daniel said.

"There's also my way," Nebuchadnezzar said, "the way of the mighty, handsome, righteous, beloved king of Babylon." He stood and stretched. "Go home, Belteshazzar. I feel fine. I feel magnificent. It's not that I don't believe you but what you've just revealed actually testifies to my amazing stature. You admitted yourself I'll endure."

Daniel left without trying to persuade the king further. The result was foreordained. For a year following their meeting Nebuchadnezzar ruled as splendidly as ever. Vassal states paid tribute. Foreign nobles bowed. His successes in engineering, construction and war were inscribed on monuments, etched on tablets, glorified in poems, baked into bricks and set to music in popular songs.

Then, just as God had promised, the king went mad.

*

When the howling, paranoia and incontinence began, Nebuchadnezzar had ruled Babylon for twenty-three years. During this time he had ended Assyria forever and sacked Jerusalem three times. He had overrun the Hatti and brought all her kings in line. The siege of mighty Tyre, by then in its fifth year, was going well.

"Tyre will fall in less than a year," Nebuchadnezzar reported to his council. "The island fortress will be next. Morale, logistics, supply and our newly designed rams and ramps are working superbly."

Enshunu praised the king then took credit for himself. "I have constantly implored Marduk on your behalf, O king, for your safety and success," the priest said, "and the great bull has therefore smiled upon you. He shall surely grant continued victory."

Enshunu could barely walk by then even with his fancy cane. But he had another, more serious, problem. The Marduk cult was no longer the rage it had once been in Babylon not only because of its high priest's growing senility and ensuing loss of clout, but also due to the substantial blow to Marduk's stature dealt by persistent testimony regarding the sons of Judah who had survived the king's fire.

The telling and retelling of Shadrach, Meshach and Abednego and the fourth presence dancing in the fiery furnace had not diminished as time passed but had been enhanced and amplified throughout Babylon and beyond, though, most often, in whispers. And so, naturally, some Babylonians had begun to question the ability of trinkets, planets, reptiles, livestock and spurious virgins to improve their lives.

Even Philosir had made discrete inquiries regarding the Hebrew god after witnessing the miracle of the furnace. Ezekiel amused his friends one day with an account of the big Phoenician's accosting Jews at random on the streets of Nippur, asking them how, to whom and why they prayed.

"What is there to say?" one exile from Jerusalem told him. "God loves to bless his people but he also demands that we abide by our covenant, or..."

The old man paused.

"Or what?" Philosir asked. "What could... What would the God of Israel do?"

The man extended his arms. "Or this," he said, gesturing in the direction of Babylon. "We have been torn away from our land into exile."

Philosir began away.

"I kept a vineyard near Jerusalem," the man shouted after him. "I had a good woman, land, three chaste daughters, four sons and a sturdy home. But my oldest son built an altar to Baal to please his wicked wife. They performed pagan rites in a grove and ignored our prophets' warnings. Now I have nothing, the house of Judah retains less than nothing; no dignity, no nation, no temple. That's what the God of Israel will do."

*

During a break at the fateful council meeting the king took Daniel aside. "It's been a year since you heard my dream," he said, "remember? But I've not humbled myself one whit and my success abounds." He scratched his beard with the backs of his nails, smiled wickedly and said, "Consider, just this once, Belteshazzar, that you and your god were flat wrong. I am no prouder than a man of my mettle should be."

"I am just a man, O king," Daniel said, "but the Lord is never wrong."

"Follow me," Nebuchadnezzar said wide-eyed, and he led his Hebrews up a private staircase and onto the citadel roof where he pointed toward Babylon's magnificent skyline and asked, "Is this not the glorious nation that I've built by my power and majesty?"

"This boastful spirit cannot serve you well, O king," Daniel warned.

"I forgive your mistake," the king said. "Go back to the council and wind up. I'll stand here in the sun and revel a bit in this refreshing breeze."

As they left the rooftop, Azariah saw the king cut a little dance step and snap off a wink. Daniel reconvened the meeting downstairs.

Philosir began a presentation concerning lines of supply to Tyre. Then everyone heard a voice from the sky…

> *"This is what is decreed for you, King Nebuchadnezzar: Your royal authority has been taken from you. You will be driven away from people and will live with wild animals: you will eat grass like cattle. Seven times will pass by for you until you acknowledge that the Most High is sovereign over the kingdoms of men and gives them to anyone he wishes."*

Azariah heard that voice in Hebrew. Enshunu later claimed that the words struck his ears in the Akkadian tongue. Philosir heard Aramaic. Before anyone could discuss it they all heard a desperate bellow from the roof.

"Daniel!" (not Belteshazzar) the king cried out.

And that was the poor man's last intelligible utterance for seven full years.

*

The king tumbled down the stairwell into the meeting room bent at the waist and rocking like an ape. He had lost his crown and befouled himself. His eyeballs failed to track. His tongue lolled from his mouth. Queen Amytis heard the commotion and came running with Kassaya, her daughter, who had married by then, carrying her child, the first royal grandson, Labaši-Marduk, on her hip. When the small boy saw his grandfather he screamed.

Nebuchadnezzar smiled at the toddler then vomited.

The women ran. Philosir and the other councilmen followed them out—even feeble Enshunu showed surprising speed—except for the king's Hebrews who stayed with the king. While curious servants watched from a distance they led Nebuchadnezzar staggering into the hallway.

"Let's take him to his chamber and try to calm him," Azariah said.

"No," Daniel said, "he's in God's hands now."

They led the king downstairs to ground level along a remote wing of the castle where stone tablets, old furniture and memorabilia were stored, to a small foyer beneath a seldom-used staircase. From there, a narrow, web-covered doorway led outdoors to a sunlit court. They hurried under several vine-covered trellises to a rusted gate which opened onto a quiet, tree-lined lane. They were no longer in the citadel.

"Shortcut," Daniel smiled when they stopped to pause for breath.

They walked along back streets unobserved until they arrived at a large lane feeding into the plaza near the main gate at Processional Way. When they began across the king began to bellow. A crowd recognized Nebuchadnezzar, who seemed in great distress, and so encircled the boys and called for help.

"The king has lost his mind," Daniel told a mounted soldier who rushed up (not a king's man, a regular troop). "God demanded it."

The horseman dismounted and approached the king, trying to look into his eyes. "Is what these men say true, Majesty?" he asked.

"You expect the king of Babylon to confirm that he's gone mad?" a mate asked. While the two men huddled to consider the likelihood, Nebuchadnezzar broke away and bucked through the crowd to the Ishtar Gate then through it. Once outside he stopped to catch his breath, leaning on the city's outer wall.

By then, hundreds of citizens had recognized Nebuchadnezzar and followed him. When they called his name the king seemed to hear and try to answer but he could only slobber and hiss in return. When Daniel joined him again, the king wrapped him in a sloppy hug and everyone—shocked by the staggering spectacle their once dashing ruler had become—fell silent. "Our king has defied God, himself," Daniel said in a powerful voice, "and now he's thoroughly mad. He can no longer be comforted or spared humiliation but he will return to serve Babylon as king again in God's time, wiser and chastened."

No one knew quite what to make of that. As citizens and several armed soldiers weighed Daniel's words, their sovereign swayed from side to side drooling like a mastiff. After a moment he raised his arms as if to sing but brayed like an ass and passed gas. Women began to sob.

"O king," the lead guard shouted, "do you require our assistance in any way?"

Nebuchadnezzar dropped his drawers, flashed his buttocks then ran away, across the perimeter road onto the same bridge that Azariah and friends had crossed years earlier when they had become slaves.

"Thank you, Sire," the guard said. "We'll be returning to our posts, then."

Knowing nothing better to do, everyone dispersed. The king's Hebrews helped Nebuchadnezzar cross the span to the west bank of the Euphrates. From there they stood and watched as Nebuchadnezzar loped west on all fours then north toward the foothills, barking now and then until no longer visible. It took official Babylon several days to come to terms with the truth. Their king had gone mad and deserted them. The condition did not seem temporary. Someone else would have to take charge.

*

Nebuchadnezzar reappeared near the city's main gate and in town from time to time, his clothes foul, his hair matted and his dark eyes stuck open and wild. After a few years passed every farmer in the district seemed to have a tale to tell about their once great leader yipping at the moon, running naked amid thorns or eating fescue on all fours beside cattle. Queen Amytis was sometimes inconsolable, sometimes full of rage. The king's council blamed the God of Israel for Nebuchadnezzar's madness.

"Credit is due, not blame," Daniel answered their charge. "The creator of the universe did exactly as he promised but do not be concerned. When the king humbles himself he will be restored. Babylon will be far better for it."

"I move all Jews be put to death for placing a curse on the king," Philosir said. "Further, Belteshazzar, Meshach, Shadrach and Abednego should not be allowed to vote on this matter due to serious a conflict of interest."

"And if, in time," a Sepharite at the table who served in the treasury asked, "the king regains his senses as Belteshazzar has promised, and if he finds we have murdered his Hebrews in his absence...what then?"

"Why in the name of Nabu," old Enshunu demanded, "does this cowardly board, in this our glorious nation of multiple, splendid gods, none so powerful as Marduk, insist on showing the invisible Hebrew deity and his followers such respect?"

No one answered.

"Will you dare second the motion then, Enshunu?" the same Sepharite asked.

"No," he said, turning to look out a window, "it's beneath me."

So another of Philosir's attempts to kill his enemies died in its tracks. And so, almost, did Babylon. While her king grazed in the hills the nation stumbled. The siege at Tyre went sour overnight. Without Nebuchadnezzar's leadership the campaign, once nearly won, collapsed and stumbled on. Again, from beyond Elam and the Great Plateau, reports continued to surface regarding a threatening emerging nation. But no one seemed to care.

"It is called Persia," a spy reported. Azariah had heard that name before. "And even now she stretches from the great gulf up into the basin, menacing the plain to our east and Media and Lydia northwest."

"Surely, Belteshazzar," Philosir said, "you do not imagine these upstarts are a threat to Babylon?"

"A threat to some," Daniel said, "and a century-old promise to others."

Philosir blew off Daniel's comment, knowing nothing of the accuracy of prophets.

*

Enshunu died while the king ran wild in the hills. Some said the priest was poisoned by rivals, others pointed to his age. In either case no one missed him. But everyone missed Nebuchadnezzar. The nation was governed in his absence by his council and occasionally, when Amytis felt like asserting herself, the queen. Daniel's reputation was so stout that everyone believed his prediction that the king would return to power sane and strong after seven times, whatever that might mean.

But while Nebuchadnezzar was incapacitated, morale sagged in the military, construction slumped in the districts and revenues lagged in the treasury. Babylon's vassal states were again charmed by Egypt, circling like a vulture from afar, so revolt and bloodshed ran rampant in the Hatti.

Reports continued of royal sightings. Nebuchadnezzar's body, it was said, was drenched with the dew of heaven. His hair grew like the feathers of eagles, his nails like the claws of birds. Babylon accepted Nebuchadnezzar's downfall as the work of the well-respected Hebrew God and so, as the seventh year of his madness approached the nation dared to become anxious for the king's return. And sure enough, exactly seven years from its onset, counting by the moon, the king's insanity ceased.

*

Nebuchadnezzar reappeared at the appointed time whole, clean, fully clothed and upright at the Ishtar gate. Later he told his Hebrews that he had found his robes in a ravine and repaired them after stealing needle and flax from a farm. He combed his hair for the first time in years after scrubbing in a stream. "I simply woke up," he told them, "that's the entire story, no rhyme nor reason."

"You know better than that," Daniel said, and the king nodded with an exciting new hint of humility.

He returned to Babylon on a sunny day. Commerce buzzed outside the city walls as always when, without warning, Babylon's immensely popular ruler came striding and smiling across the Euphrates Bridge, straight through the Ishtar gate and into town along Processional Way, his eyes burning with their familiar fire. Spotting him at once, the people chanted his name. A thousand hands reached to touch him as he jogged into town toward the square. Once there he bounded to the top of Esagila as powerfully as he had over thirty years earlier on his first day as king. Anxious men, wide-eyed children and joyful women flooded into the square trembling with emotion. Atop the tower their renewed potentate led cheers for half an hour then raised his arms and kept them up until the thousands fell still.

"Praise and glorify the Lord!" the king thundered so loudly it echoed off the walls.

Everyone went wild, assuming he meant Marduk.

"His dominion is an eternal dominion. His kingdom endures from generation to generation. All the peoples of the earth are regarded as nothing. He does as he pleases with the powers of heaven and the peoples of the earth. No one can hold back his hand or say to him, What have you done?"

The square exploded with cheers again when Nebuchadnezzar announced that he would resume immediate control of the kingdom. Bonfires, music and dancing followed that same evening and lasted for days.

After three successive candidates to replace Enshunu had been assassinated in a matter of months, a young cleric named Hasdrubal (who, lacking both influence and enemies, had survived) rose to the post of Marduk's High Priest. Enshunu's death had dictated wild times not just for Hasdrubal, but for the entire priestly caste in Akkad. Some of the new priest's peers, minding devilish omens and fearing change, had packed up their incense, spells, virgins, treasure and theology to relocate far west to lands even beyond Nineveh, to Ephesus and Pergamum, great cities said to lie near a rocky, fog-shrouded coastline well north of the Western Sea.

Priestly pressure on Hasdrubal remained great. He had no choice but to credit the state's top god with the miracle of Nebuchadnezzar's return. So he did. Yet, when the bonfires died and the music stopped, the real story lived in whispers. The God of Israel had cursed the king for his arrogance. He, not some planet, goddess or cow had removed that curse as promised after seven years. The Jewish exile, Belteshazzar, had said it and it was so!

Once again Babylonians were forced to ask, Who is this Belteshazzar? Who are these Jews? Why had their god, as powerful as he seemed, allowed his people to be conquered, humiliated and carried away as slaves?

And why had he blessed them afterward while in captivity?

"Because that's exactly what he promised," Daniel told all who would listen.

And many in Babylon considered Daniel's explanation and believed.

*

Did the king learn his lesson after scampering on all fours for seven years? The short answer was no. For a while after he was restored to office Nebuchadnezzar strutted a bit less around the citadel. He seemed to listen to others more patiently at meetings. The king no longer seemed as inclined to shout as he had been in years past. He threw far fewer fits. Sometimes he went months without ordering a beheading. Royal decrees for death by drowning had gone down. So, for a time, it was undeniable that Nebuchadnezzar had become a milder man. But as revenues recovered, as abundant rain resumed all across the fertile valley and as Babylon's magnificent army began to stack up victories again, the king grew prouder still.

Most in Babylon praised Nebuchadnezzar as a god with the king's complete approval. Daniel feared that he might remain an idol worshiper to the end of his days.

21. Sometimes, you can't kill everyone

VICTORY AT THE coast came shortly after Nebuchadnezzar recovered from his madness. When the mainland city of Tyre fell Babylon rejoiced as if they had conquered the world. They almost had. Praises were sung in the streets. Monuments marking the most recent victory were built in parks and squares, one of them on the plain at Dura in the very shadow of the hideous icon that honored the king as a god.

But Nebuchadnezzar assembled his advisors shortly after Tyre fell and threw a fit. "I disappear for a spell," the king began, "and Akkad grinds to a complete halt without me? That's woeful leadership on your part, men, and gross incompetence too."

Daniel smiled and asked, "What is it that really disturbs you today, O king?"

Azariah, Mishael and Hananiah literally gasped. Not even Daniel had leeway to so boldly challenge the king, especially while he was fuming.

"It doesn't strike you as bad, Belteshazzar," Nebuchadnezzar said, "that it took thirteen stinking years to do a six-year job? Over double the time required, at great cost to the treasury not to mention the loss of life, all to defeat some sailors, tinkerers and dye makers who lived at the beach? And after all that we never took their stinking island?"

"And what of Egypt?" Daniel asked.

"This is an outrage," Philosir said. "Why do you tolerate such insolence, O king?"

Strictly speaking, Philosir was correct. Not even Queen Amytis could legally address Nebuchadnezzar without first bowing a bit then wrapping her words in something like your majesty, Sire, or O king, and it was never good practice to look directly into his eyes, especially his angry eyes, but Daniel had broken all those rules.

"What do you suggest I do, Philosir?" Nebuchadnezzar asked the big Phoenician.

"Punish him, Sire!" Philosir said. "Set a royal example."

No one spoke. The king's other councilors turned and coughed in their hands for it quickly became clear by the king's amused look that Philosir, for once, had miscalculated.

Nebuchadnezzar surprised everyone by smiling. "This is the Hebrew prophet, Daniel," he said, pointing Daniel's way. "Everybody in Akkad knows him by that name as well as the Akkadian name we gave him at the slave school. Do you remember hearing, Philosir, the story I've told a million times about how Daniel and I first met?"

"Yes, Sire," Philosir said.

"So then, Philosir, if, as a beardless boy, this Daniel virtually dared me to split him in two without blinking an eye, if his friends here…" He stopped and pointed at Azariah, Hananiah and Mishael. "If these three men cheerfully defied my law then scared the living Marduk out of the entire nation by taunting me from inside a really big, hot fire… Just how do you suggest I set out to intimidate them today?"

Hasdrubal, the new high priest, looked left and right at the others seeming unable to choose a side. Philosir and two other Phoenicians rose to leave the room.

"Stay where you are, everyone," Nebuchadnezzar snapped, "and hear this out."

The Phoenicians obeyed, quite unhappily, but the clash between the king and Daniel had not ended. Nebuchadnezzar refocused quickly and asked in his darkest voice, "Tell me, Daniel, what of Egypt, then?"

Daniel grinned and did not bother to answer. It was too much. The king jumped to his feet, to his very toes and looked about to explode. By that stage of his life Azariah had grown to humbly think of himself as fearless—he had, after all, once danced in white-hot flames—but Daniel's courage at that moment completely dazzled him. Azariah was suddenly a child again standing breathlessly beside his friend in Jerusalem, in the plaza, as General Nebuchadnezzar held his sword high over Daniel's head and Daniel refused to blink.

At the moment of his choosing, Daniel answered the king. "Pharaoh Necho died, O king, while you…"

"Yes!" Nebuchadnezzar bellowed. "While I ran berserk and half-naked in the hills. Don't you think I know that?"

"Your last opportunity to defeat your lifelong nemesis has passed."

Azariah's best guess regarding what might follow next involved the big vein that throbbed on the king's forehead but Nebuchadnezzar breathed deep then addressed his council calmly. "Belteshazzar's surmise is correct," he said. He lowered his head and looked about to cry. "The effeminate water rat, Pharaoh Necho II, ruler of inbred Egypt, has died, may worms eat him, and because of my runaway pride and punishment at the hand of Belteshazzar's god, I have forfeited forever my chance to grind up that incestuous snail and his overrated army."

He looked droop-eyed at Hasdrubal and confessed, "And that had been my dream."

Poor fellow. Sometimes even kings lack the time and power to kill every man they wish. Nebuchadnezzar sat again, mumbling in his big cushioned chair at the head of the council table. No one dared speak until Daniel added, "But you will yet conquer Egypt, O king."

"Really, Daniel?" Nebuchadnezzar said.

"That, O king," Daniel answered, "is the word from the Lord."

*

Daniel explained later that Ezekiel had recently prophesied in Nippur…

> *the land of Egypt unto Nebuchadnezzar king of Babylon and he shall take her multitude and take her spoil and take her prey and it shall be wages for his army.*

Nebuchadnezzar remained delighted but Azariah was confused. "Why did Ezekiel even speak it?" he asked. "What has Egypt's fall got to do with us Jews?"

Daniel explained that Ezekiel's word concerned all those Jews still in Judah who intended to flee to Egypt against God's instruction. Jeremiah had warned them…"

> *…O ye remnant of Judah; Go ye not into Egypt: know that I have admonished you this day… If ye wholly set your faces to enter into Egypt…then it shall come to pass that the sword which ye feared shall overtake you there…you shall be an execration and an astonishment and a curse and a reproach and ye shall see this place no more.*

"Throughout time," Daniel sighed, "Egypt has intoxicated Jews like strong drink. Beginning in Moses' time and lasting to this day, Egypt remains a dark symbol to those who hide from their heritage and their God."

"Few men would choose to be Jews, I think," Mishael said, "if they had their choice."

"So it appears I have no choice," Azariah said, "but to accept that Nebuchadnezzar will continue to lead a loud, comfortable life pounding the Hatti, plaguing Egypt and enslaving Jews according to some mysterious purpose while we, God's people, suffer."

"Afterward," Daniel said, "Babylon shall pay mightily for her sins."

"And what about Nebuchadnezzar?" Azariah asked. "Will he be punished too?"

Daniel refused to say more. Azariah suspected that he simply didn't know.

*

Egypt fell like a rock. The re-energized Babylonian army, brimming with confidence from its eventual success at mainland Tyre and using the splendid new war machines invented by their king, swept south, routed Pharaoh and set the nation by the Nile on her ear. To avoid execution at Babylon's hand, Pharaoh Amasis, one of Necho's successors, abandoned his homeland and escaped to an island in the Western Sea. After Hasdrubal read aloud the official record of the campaign for the cuneiform account, Nebuchadnezzar added, "I would have kicked old Necho all the way to Cypress too, had that coward only lived."

Azariah believed it was true. Nebuchadnezzar always seemed to win.

22. It seems that God doubts us

NEBUCHADNEZZAR DIED AT age sixty-eight, forty-three years after he had assumed his father's throne. While he lay in state thousands visited his bier. No one mourned his passing more than Daniel and his friends, having worked with him daily for four decades. Queen Amytis, true to her distaste for Jews, ignored condolences from his Hebrews but Daniel looked past her slight, regretting only that the king never seemed to have come to know God. "Though the almighty had directed his life from the start," Daniel sighed, "the king of Babylon never seemed aware."

Before Nebuchadnezzar's memorial, Azariah and friends held a private wake for him at Daniel's house. The four old exiles drank natural juices and ate pulse—Daniel had never learned how to throw a party—and they called one another my Hebrew! as they shared anecdotes about the king.

For example; Nebuchadnezzar's last great civil project was a 16-mile long, earth-filled dam in the north, near Media, which he had lined with monographed brick fired in the same furnace in which he had tried to roast three of them alive. The dam flooded an entire valley between the Tigris and Euphrates and its reservoir became a blessing to its district. The brickwork was bound with an amazing elastic mortar invented by the king himself, really something to see, but what problems they had encountered in its construction.

They laughed and cried over dam stories for hours.

What better testimony to a man's greatness than his memory garnering honor among those whom he had orphaned and tried to kill?

"May God, if it be his will," Daniel sighed as the long day ended, "rest mighty Nebuchadnezzar's soul."

*

The nation threw a magnificent state funeral. Azariah cringed at the thought of attending another pagan rite. The memorial would go Marduk this, Nebo that and they had all long since tired of that nonsense. But then they learned that the king's will demanded the reading of a special prayer he had composed himself.

"Nebuchadnezzar composed a prayer?" Azariah asked. "What might that be like?"

They attended his service to find out. A horde of teary-eyed mourners packed the sunny quadrangle at Esagila while Amytis read aloud from the ziggurat steps. "*O eternal ruler, Lord of the Universe!*" it began...

> *Grant that the name of the king whom you love,*
>
> *Whose name you have mentioned, may flourish as seems good to you.*
>
> *Guide him on the right path.*
>
> *I am the ruler who obeys you, the creation of your hand.*
>
> *It is you who has created me,*
>
> *And you have entrusted to me sovereignty over mankind.*
>
> *According to your mercy, O Lord, which you bestow upon all,*
>
> *Cause me to love your supreme rule.*
>
> *Implant the fear of your divinity in my heart.*
>
> *Grant me whatever may seem good before you,*
>
> *Since it is you that controls my life.*

"*And you who guides us all, afterward,*" the queen finished, sobbing.

There wasn't a dry eye in the square. Only the cult priests seemed unmoved. The king's petition was no pagan riff. How, then, had Nebuchadnezzar spent his entire public life wrapped up in fake gods, bogus omens, smoke, signs and fire? Days passed before Daniel remembered that the queen's reading at the funeral was precisely the recitation that he and his friends had heard four decades earlier, their first day in Babylon, "When Nebuchadnezzar ran up the ziggurat steps to assume the throne. He said the exact same words, anything but pagan, I am sure of it."

"How did we miss it then?" Mishael asked.

"There was a lot going on," Daniel said. "We have rushed past demons and curses for decades," Daniel said, "altars, shrines, amulets and idols everywhere."

"But this prayer of the king's," Hananiah whispered, "honors the one true God."

They looked at one another stupidly.

"Who could have anticipated such humility from a man who once built a ninety-foot tall monument to himself," Azariah said, "and plaited it with gold?"

"Perhaps he secretly read our scrolls?" Mishael said.

"Maybe, as he aged, the old king sensed the truth of things in the depths of his soul," Daniel said, "and felt compelled to honor the real God at the last."

"Hedging his bets?" Azariah asked.

"No, sincere," Daniel said. They blinked at one another. Nebuchadnezzar, never a subtle man, may have put one past both his Hebrews and his people. "It's even possible that Nebuchadnezzar discovered the truth long ago."

"And then laughed at us privately for years?" Azariah asked.

No one knew. After the service they returned to Daniel's house but this time they mourned the king's loss and rejoiced in his possible salvation. There is nothing like a funeral to force one to think of eternity. They remembered their parents, recalled the destruction of the temple in Jerusalem and speculated about the end of Babylon now that its great soul had died.

"It's the beginning of the end of the beginning for Babylon," Daniel said.

"You say," Azariah countered, "but it's all the same to me in Babylon, Jerusalem, everywhere; misery and heartache without end despite our constant prayers. Is this the best that God can do?"

"Do you doubt him?" Daniel asked.

"It seems that God doubts us," Azariah said. "I say only, I see what I see."

"And what did you see in the fire?"

Hananiah and Mishael teared up at Daniel's mention of the furnace but Azariah, exceptionally bitter that day, kept on. "So that is life," he asked, "a succession of horrors and loss during which we may occasionally be allowed a glimmer?"

"Of his glory and promise?" Daniel said. "I say yes, most definitely. Horrors are what we manufacture in the absence of faith. We cannot lose what we never owned."

Sometimes life in Babylon was simply too much to bear.

*

While in Nebuchadnezzar's service, Azariah had witnessed victory upon victory and success upon success. He wondered how a nation as rich and powerful as Babylon could ever fail in the world.

"Nebuchadnezzar has no equal in Babylon, perhaps in all creation," Daniel said. "Surely in the absence of his brilliance and the presence of so much discord among this nation's fractious priests, Babylon will stumble toward oblivion."

"Jeremiah prophesied that our exile will last seventy years," Azariah said. "So, depending on when we begin to count, we are promised something like thirty more years until it ends. But I see no way that Babylon could collapse in such short time."

"You quote Jeremiah, revere Isaiah and hang on Ezekiel's every word," Mishael said, "yet you argue constantly with our personal prophet, Daniel."

Azariah hung his head. Mishael had a point. But it was difficult to hold in proper regard, no matter how brilliant, someone whom he had consistently beaten in foot races as a child. "Daniel hasn't always been right," he muttered.

"Not always," Hananiah laughed, "only completely so for four decades."

And Daniel proved right again. Babylon began to disintegrate before Azariah's eyes exactly as his friend had said. After the king passed, his Hebrews were removed from their seats at the council table and replaced by younger men. Drought reappeared across the valley in short order. Rumblings of revolt spread across the Hatti, Persia grew ever stronger and Egypt continued provocative games. Factions developed and the captive school failed.

Even the queen's gardens began to look shabby, but the most disturbing event that followed Nebuchadnezzar's death had nothing to do with the weather, plant life or affairs of state. A recent triumph of God's goodness and mercy had tragically turned to defeat. Azariah and his friends watched helplessly when the widow Pnina made a decision that broke Daniel's heart.

23. A difficult town in which to reminisce

WHILE SHE WAS still young and living in Jerusalem, Daniel's helper, Pnina, had a son named Asher who also lived in the city and served as an officer in the service of Zedekiah, the king. Mother and son were separated during the last days of Babylon's third siege. Pnina had assumed that Asher had been killed when the city fell. None of Zedekiah's personal guard were said to have survived. But Asher had lived!

At a small celebration held at Daniel's house, Asher told the story of their miraculous reunion after spending more than twenty years apart.

"The king decided to run away," Asher told the other guests. "It seemed cowardly to me. I chose to stay though my commander warned that I would die. I would sooner die defending Jerusalem, I told him, than live after running away."

"Oh, my," Pnina gasped, "what did your commander say?"

"He drew his sword," Asher said. "I should kill you now for calling us cowards, he said, but he did nothing. That night, the king and the rest of our detachment slipped through a breach in the wall and abandoned Jerusalem."

"They were captured just the same," Hananiah said.

"Yes," Mishael said. "Zedekiah lost his sons then his eyes."

Everyone sighed. Babylon was a difficult town in which to reminisce. After the meal Pnina lit candles, brought wine (for all but Daniel) and reclined upon a cushion, smiling through her tears as her son continued his story.

"I stayed behind with a handful of others," Asher told them. "The enemy broke in and we were quickly overcome. I was run through, navel to ribs." He showed everyone a long, ghastly scar. "They left me for dead but on the next morning, much as like in a bad dream, I remember being thrown onto a cart heaped with bodies."

Pnina shut her eyes.

"Later, I suppose, someone heard me groan and tossed me out."

"God bless that someone," Pnina said, "for he surely saved my son."

"For a long time I lay helpless in a corridor in the city. Sometime after dark a woman found me lying in a pool of my own blood. It was dangerous to be about, troops were everywhere, but the woman dragged me, somehow, to safety."

"She must have been very brave," Pnina said, "and quite strong."

Asher nodded. "She was called Ya'el," he said.

The room fell silent. Everyone looked at Daniel.

"Dark eyes," Azariah asked, "sweet smile and very beautiful?"

"Yes, very."

"Ahiel's daughter," Mishael said. "I know it."

"Many go by that name," Daniel sighed, but his fingers moved to the small stone he had carried from Jerusalem and polished every day, now strung around his neck.

Asher went on. Ya'el cleaned his wounds then prayed, entreating the God of Israel to provide comfort. "Comfort," Asher repeated, "not life. I responded to her prayers by surviving the night. She offered to stay with me but I insisted that she run and hide."

Ya'el left Asher with a crust of bread, a chipped urn half full of dirty water and a last desperate prayer. He lay hidden under debris for days while Babylon continued the systematic destruction of the city. "Under Nebuchadnezzar's captain, Nebuzaradan."

They all remembered that name.

"The soldiers never found me," Asher said, "but with the stench of death so heavy in my nostrils, with the sounds of suffering so clear in my ears, I really didn't care whether I lived or died."

"But the God of Israel honored precious Ya'el's prayers and preserved you," Pnina smiled.

Babylon left Jerusalem in a shambles; thousands from Jerusalem were led into exile leaving her walls, homes, the palace and the temple utterly destroyed. A family from the hills found Asher afterward, carried him outside the city and, over time, nursed him back to health. "I cried like a child," Asher whispered when Pnina moved beside him and hugged his neck, "over Judah's demise."

*

Nearly a year passed before Asher could walk again with the help of a cane. He eventually made his way back to Jerusalem, questioned several survivors and learned that his father had been murdered and their home had been leveled. (Pnina barely blinked. She had known these things in her soul for several years.)

"But no one knew what had happened to you, Mother," Asher said.

"Don't ask," was all Pnina would say.

"I worked in an olive grove east of the city beyond the Valley of Judgment," Asher said. "One day, while on my way into Jerusalem for supplies, I met a neighbor who had recently returned from Egypt after escaping Babylon's siege. Your mother was carried to Babylon, he said. I heard it on good word."

It took Asher two years to cover the distance that Azariah and friends had marched in six weeks. "Of course there was no sign of her," Asher said. "But my wounds had cost me permanent weight and strength. I stayed here in Babylon and made a life."

"Then yesterday," Pnina said, "while at market over two decades after the fall, I heard his voice." She shuddered with tears. "I turned and saw these eyes, my own son's eyes, his precious eyes and I knew it was my Asher."

Mother and son embraced. Azariah, so often weak in faith, fell to his knees with the others and praised God for their miraculous reunion. But then Asher and Pnina's story, like so many others fashioned by the God of Israel's willful people, turned ugly.

*

On ordinary days Pnina preferred to stand to the side at mealtimes, her hands folded at her waist. There she would wait to serve food or refill Daniel's cup. But on the evening she was reunited with Asher she reclined with the others at the table as they ate.

"My son, my son," she murmured repeatedly, for there is no love quite like a Jewish mother's. Sadly, Azariah learned, there is also no corner in the cosmos as cold and dark as the heart of that same mother who has taken offense. "What exactly did you do in Babylon all that time," she asked Asher, "while you were not looking for me?"

"I met a wonderful woman," he said. "Zakiti is her name."

Azariah felt an instant chill in the room. Pnina raised her chin a notch and, hand upon her heart she asked, "Zakiti? What kind of name...?"

"She's Chaldean, Mother," Asher said, "a lovely widow from the southern district with a sweet, tender soul."

Pnina made a show of catching her breath. "A lovely Chaldean widow?" she asked. "Is that what my ears have heard?"

"A constant comfort as I've struggled with my health," Asher said. "I love her. As you know, Mother, Jeremiah himself has advised exiles to marry. Soon we will."

"The prophet never said to marry goyim," Pnina spat. "There are thousands of women here from Jerusalem. Are you too good to marry one of them?"

Azariah peeked at Daniel. Here was a side of Pnina that neither of them had seen.

"She is learning our ways," Asher said, "and I have hopes..."

"We're a ruined people," Pnina interrupted, "uprooted and lost and you have hopes?"

"We will all return to Jerusalem one day, Mother, the prophet says."

"Return to what?" Pnina said. "With what? As what? We are Jews, not half-breeds, not Chaldeans." She raised her arms to plead with the ceiling. "Better I had died yesterday, O Lord," she cried out, "than to suffer this knife to my heart."

"Please calm yourself, sister," Daniel said. "When we were children, you may remember that King Josiah's priests found Moshe's Book of the Law."

"In the temple," Pnina moaned. "What has that got to do with my son and his goy?"

"*Keep therefore the words of this covenant...*" Daniel recited from memory.

...and do them that you may prosper in all that you do."

"Those words were spoken to captains, elders, officers, little ones, wives, and for the stranger that is in your camp."

Pnina tilted her head, confused.

"We are the covenant people," Daniel explained, "but God's promise extends to all."

"Her blood," Pnina said, "is the very blood that butchered us. That's all I know."

"Who's more of a Jew, Mother?" Asher asked, "a pig-eating Samarian priest or someone who embraces…"

"I despise them all," Pnina raised her voice. "You know what they did. Do you want I should make distinctions regarding my deep disgust? How could you…? How could you? I cannot understand how you could do this…to me."

"Only hours ago, Mother, I feared you were dead."

"Alive, dead," Pnina shrugged, "what does it matter? My life is nothing now."

"But I am teaching her our faith."

"Wonderful!" Pnina said. "Teach your precious Zakiti. O, my shame!" She pointed a finger. "You cannot teach blood. Pagan blood can never be cleansed. They killed your father. They raped us and carried us away." She stopped and turned to Daniel. "Never mind. I no longer care. Tell this man he is not welcome in this house."

"Your son…" Daniel began.

"I have no son."

"Your son, my brother, a defender of Jerusalem and partner in the covenant… He, as well as his future wife, will always be welcome in this home."

Pnina looked at Daniel as if he had stabbed her. "Do as you please, then," she muttered. "I'm no ingrate. I'll always respect you, prophet, but please tell that man…" She stopped to point again. "…that I have no son," and with that she left the room.

Asher wept.

"Go to her in the garden cottage," Daniel said, "and knock upon her door."

Asher went out and knocked but Pnina refused to answer. The door remained shut while her only son begged for kindness at her threshold, beyond which she had mourned his loss each night for many years.

*

Pnina died not long afterward. Once aware that the end was near she had asked Daniel to summon Asher to her side. Asher came quickly but arrived too late. They never reconciled.

Is not poor Pnina's story also people Israel's?

Longing, repenting, entreating, studying, observing, reciting…but never humbling? Cherishing common blood but not a common spirit; rejecting brothers, sisters, sons, daughters and truth itself to avenge imagined affronts and sate their stiff-necked pride?

"Is there a Jew on this planet with ears to hear and eyes to see?" Azariah moaned on the day Pnina died. "Shall God's judgment on Jerusalem pass in vain?"

"Time must pass," Daniel said. "Then more time and more pain."

"The last days?"

"As Amos revealed long ago, the Lord shall not utterly destroy the house of Jacob."

"Though Jacob," Azariah said, "sometimes seems intent upon destroying itself."

V. The Writing on the Wall

24. Soon, a marvelous voice

I T IS NOT always clear at the end of things that things are about to end. Things, in this case, were the Babylonian Empire, the Hebrew captivity in Babylon and Azariah himself, a short but impressive list except for the last.

Thanks to King Nebuchadnezzar's insight, inventions and innovations the nation's military remained strong. Also due to the genius of the departed king, construction and engineering in Babylon remained the most sophisticated in the world. But that was it. When Amel-Marduk, Nebuchadnezzar's only legitimate son, ascended to the throne, that once loud-mouthed little boy quickly proved to have no talent for leadership. The cost of his incompetence became obvious at once; Babylon collapsed in stature throughout the region under growing clouds of confusion.

"I once watched that brat, Amel, fight with his sister in the palace halls," Azariah told his friends and the prophet, Ezekiel, one day in Nippur. "Even then the boy seemed a coward. Now that he has failed as king the collapse that Daniel predicted seems much more likely."

"We Jews understand better than most that nations fail," Daniel said. "These proud and painted Akkadians have known nothing but comfort and safety all their lives. Ruined by decades of good fortune they cannot conceive of their decline, much less complete collapse."

"They shop, celebrate and play mindless games," Mishael said. "Meanwhile poor King Amel takes counsel from malcontents, liars and hangers-on. His generals treat him disrespectfully. The minor cult priests pursue traitorous alliances while Amel's own sister and her husband plot against his life."

"Yet the boy is unaware."

"And we sit here off to the side as has-beens," Azariah said. "God has finished with us. There is nothing more to do."

Ezekiel and Daniel began to laugh.

"I find your smugness irritating," Azariah told the two prophets but, like all those in their line of work, Ezekiel and Daniel were impossible to coax, intimidate or embarrass. They never bothered to explain anything to anyone unless God himself ordered it. And on those rare occasions when they were kind enough to provide a bit of detail, Azariah always felt so guilty afterward (about his impatience and glaring faults) he regretted being alive.

Even so, Daniel and Ezekiel were right again, at least about each other. As the years passed the two amazing men added to their chronicles of wisdom, visions and revelation. Over and over again they were caught up in the Spirit of the Lord.

"What an important time this must be for our people," Mishael said, "since there are by my count four living prophets today!"

"Five," Ezekiel said.

"No," Azariah shot back, happy to point out the prophet's mistake. He spoke slowly in order to enjoy the moment. "I count you and our brother Daniel in Babylon and Jeremiah and Habakkuk still alive in Jerusalem. Therefore, we have four."

"Zechariah makes five," Daniel said.

Azariah, Mishael and Hananiah went blank.

"Surely you remember my mentioning him to you years ago?" Ezekiel said. "Born here in Babylon? Even today he is not much older than you four were when snatched out of Judah."

"And he's a prophet at that young age?" Azariah asked.

"Yes," Daniel said, "and no. We will hear his marvelous voice soon."

If they were right, and Daniel and Ezekiel always were, the Lord had anointed five Hebrew prophets to comfort Israel through her most difficult time. This additional proof of God's kindness brought tears to Azariah's old, undeserving eyes.

For the moment, as Babylon wobbled like a spent top, Daniel and Ezekiel carried the banners of hope and faith in the land of the Chaldees. What amazing things they offered up again and again in the Spirit; visions, dreams, mysteries, inspiration, prayers, predictions, promises… But none of their utterances were more shocking, exciting or uplifting than Ezekiel's revelation concerning a valley of dry bones.

*

After Nebuchadnezzar's death and their forced retirements, Daniel, Mishael, Hananiah and Azariah visited Ezekiel much more often in Nippur. Azariah had grown to love that man as he loved Daniel. Ezekiel was an older, amazingly thoughtful man who always managed to be upbeat no matter how much sadness God showed him. And though he rarely dwelled upon the past (good policy for a Jew), he did, from time to time, consent to share a little about himself.

"I was studying for the priesthood," Ezekiel said, "when, four years after Josiah died, I remember the end of the first siege, Babylon breaking through the outer wall, storming the ramparts and carrying people and treasures away. You fellows, I now know, were among them." He looked up at the clouds and seemed to forget what he was about to say.

They waited patiently. It was a gorgeous day. Ezekiel lived in the city not far from Azariah but their favorite place to meet and talk was in the shade upon the banks of the river Kebar, downstream from a breezy bend. Azariah watched the afternoon light glint here and there about a snag in the river until the prophet spoke again.

"Of course you were just children then," Ezekiel said.

"We spent that first evening after the attack camped just outside the wall," Mishael said, "some of what we heard that evening…"

Ezekiel raised his hand and Mishael stopped. "There is no benefit to recalling it," he said, "but I will share with you something quite important, something quite thrilling, uplifting yet strange, a word that came to me in the Spirit at this very spot not long ago."

Ezekiel cleared his throat and they all moved closer. "You'll recall my sharing," he said, "that someday God will find those tribes of Israel who were scattered by Assyria almost two hundred years ago. He will cleanse them and reunite them, so says the Lord, with Judah and Benjamin who lie captive here now."

"The two sticks," Hananiah said. "We remember but I, at least, do not understand."

The prophet's hands began to tremble. Plainly, he was upset. "On the day I heard that word," Ezekiel said, "I had gone out by the Spirit and he set me down in the valley."

"Which valley?" Mishael asked.

"A valley full of bones," Ezekiel said. "The Lord led me all around them, countless spread over the valley and they were very dry. The Lord said to me, O mortal, can these bones live again? I replied, O Lord God, only you know. And he said to me, Prophesy over these bones and say to them, O dry bones, hear the word of the Lord!"

"Did you do it?" Azariah asked.

Ezekiel closed his eyes. Over the rush of the wind in the willows at the river's edge, his friends moved closer to hear him speak. "*Thus said the Lord God to these bones,*" Ezekiel said...

> *I will cause spirit to enter you and you shall live again. I will lay sinews upon you and cover you with flesh and form skin over you. And I will put spirit into you and you shall live again. And you shall know that I am the Lord.*

"And what did you do?" Mishael asked.

"*I prophesied as I had been commanded. And while I was prophesying there was tumultuous rattling... And the bones came together!*"

"No."

"*Bone to matching bone,*" Ezekiel said. "*I looked and there were sinews on them and flesh had grown and skin had formed over them; but there was no spirit in them.*"

"But how could there be?"

"*Then the Lord said to me...*

> *Prophesy to the spirit, prophesy, O mortal! Say to the spirit: Thus said the Lord God: Come, O spirit, from the four winds, and breathe into these slain so that they might live again. Again I prophesied as he commanded me. The spirit entered them and they came to life and stood up on their feet a vast multitude. And he said to me, O mortal, these bones are the whole house of Israel.*

"Hallelujah!" Hananiah cried.

> *They say, 'Our bones are dried up, our hope is gone; we are doomed.' Prophesy therefore and say to them: Thus said the Lord God: I am going to open your graves and lift you out of the graves, O my people, and bring you to the land of Israel.*

It was too much. They all began to sob, to cling to each other sobbing, holding on to one another as though they were clutching the Lord himself. Maybe they were.

"You shall know, O my people, that I am the Lord..." Ezekiel said.

> *...when I have opened your graves. I will put my spirit into you and you shall live again and I will set you on your own soil. Then you shall know that I the Lord have spoken and have acted, declares the Lord."*

With the exception of his experience in the fire, hearing Ezekiel speak those words was the most exhilarating moment in Azariah's life.

*

Ezekiel's revelation of the restoration of Israel filled them all with longing. At about that same time Daniel filled them with wonder after he had spoken with the angel Gabriel himself! They all listened carefully to his account but none of them, not even Ezekiel, could make sense of their conversation. Worn out by his efforts, Daniel languished unable to function for many days. "I was dismayed by the vision," he told them, "and no one can explain it."

Yet one thing was certain, Azariah and friends were living at a pivotal moment in history, the high or low juncture (depending on one's faith) for all Jews. Daniel had mentioned Babylon's turning of a corner before Nebuchadnezzar had gone mad, even before Azariah and his friends had been thrown into the fire. But, because it seemed so unlikely, not until well after Nebuchadnezzar had died did Azariah truly grasp that the nation's end was near. The time for God's justice was at hand.

"But as weak as she is," Hananiah said, "who can challenge Babylon? Egypt is an inbred wreck, Assyria is long forgotten and the Hatti is a pasture of slaves."

"Persia," Daniel said plainly, pointing to the Isaiah scroll he had held for decades. They had all read it many times.

"But who exactly is Koresh?" Mishael asked.

They were forced to wait a season to find out while the parade of incompetent leadership in Babylon continued, laughable, if not a matter for tears. After about two years as king, clueless little Amel

the writing on the wall

was accused by the Marduk priests of governing in an impure manner, a setup to open the door for his sister's husband, Neriglissar, to assassinate him and assume the throne. After four years, Neriglissar failed miserably. He was replaced by his son, who lasted even less time.

Incompetence at the citadel led to chaos in the streets. Rumors spread regarding the alarming, and suddenly threatening emergence of Persia. Then everyone knew Koresh's name.

25. Nuggets of joy

TWENTY-THREE YEARS AFTER Nebuchadnezzar died, every principle upon which Babylon had depended to be excellent—its law, leadership, army, science and engineering—had played out. There seemed to be nothing more to do but to brace for a death blow. Proof of its end was everywhere; fairness had vanished from the markets and courts, trade had collapsed, crops had failed, corruption bloomed in government and debt mounted without end. But in the universities, at the bazaars and along her shaded streets, even as Babylon tottered, Azariah continued to hear, "We are the greatest nation in the world!"

How so?

All those who had made Babylon great were dead. Effort, accountability and excellence had died with them. The nation had remained upright only by imposing higher taxes on the wealthy and increasing levies on slave states. Failure was everywhere but no one seemed to notice, much less care. Consumption, whoring, violence, lasciviousness, silly pastimes and gross self-indulgence had become driving public concerns. He who spoke out for virtue, accountability or restraint was branded backward or mean-spirited. How long could that last?

"Babylon praises its glorious past," Mishael complained. "People hope to rekindle old glory by devising change but at no cost to them. They bicker. The courts have no regard for justice but are advocates for the powerful. If these fools would only pull together..."

"Still nothing would change," Hananiah said. "Man can never know true security without reliance on the Lord."

"But in the time of Solomon..."

"Israel relied on God," Hananiah interrupted again, "and Israel flourished until the great king and his people turned their backs." He smiled at Mishael. "Surely you understand by now, brother, though a nation may thrive for a season, without divine protection it must fail."

Insult to injury, Daniel nodded and said, "Hananiah is right."

Hananiah chuckled, "Who will unify Babylon, Belshazzar, the fool?"

It did not seem likely. The boys had last seen Babylon's latest ruler, the regent, Belshazzar, as a child at the unveiling of the king's idle on the plain at Dura years before.

"He seemed stupid even then," Azariah sighed.

Belshazzar's rise to power had been an odd one. Nabonidus, his father, had married Nebuchadnezzar's oldest daughter, Nitocris, and owing to his wife's royal blood became king. The people disliked Nabonidus at once, believing he was descended from the hated Assyrians. Nabonidus fed the rumor by rejecting their top god, Marduk, in favor of the moon goddess, Sin. Then he appointed Belshazzar as his regent and moved to the desert to live in a temple dedicated to Sin and was rarely heard from afterward.

Belshazzar had become Babylon's fifth ruler in only seventeen years while Nebuchadnezzar, his grandfather, had ruled for forty-three.

Azariah had, by then, grown quite ill, but he was not too old or feeble to thrill at hearing ever more frequent reports that Koresh of Persia had amassed an army of millions to the east and begun to advance toward the sea. Persia's path to the sea included Babylon.

"He's conquered Lydia and has coerced Media," Daniel said. "They are now combined."

"Akkad will follow," Azariah said, pleased about it. "Everyone expects it."

*

Mishael died shortly after the Persian rumors began to bloom, full of faith and anxious to move on. Within weeks, Hananiah passed too. But Daniel had skipped past his eightieth year in shining health. "Thanks to all that pulse you have eaten," Azariah joked, and they laughed together for a while.

Though Azariah remained alive he had begun to struggle to walk. Daniel visited his sick bed often. Ezekiel visited too whenever able. Despite Babylon's grim outlook and both prophets' startling dreams and visions, Daniel and Ezekiel remained upbeat about their people's future. Of course, it was their job to take the long view.

"Is your optimism appropriate," Azariah asked Daniel, "given what's in the wind?"

"Sift through these sour things," Daniel told him, "and you'll find nuggets of joy."

Nuggets. The Word foretold of more suffering yet God's own prophets glowed with health and grinned like carefree boys, speaking of joy.

"We will know, understand, say and do everything when necessary and not a moment before," both Daniel and Ezekiel assured him, "because the God of Israel is in control."

26. Full circle

FOR A LONG time Azariah lay in bed not quite living, not quite dead, wondering why the Lord had chosen to string out his days. "Why do you think?" Daniel asked while sitting beside him one day.

Azariah smiled in his bed a little wickedly. "I must confess, my brother, though I know that vengeance is the Lord's only, I have prayed since I was a child to someday see Babylon fail."

Daniel patted his shoulder and rose to leave. "Persia has nearly arrived."

"So I will, then?" Azariah asked. "I'll see it?"

"God loves you, forgives you and is perfectly just," was all Daniel would say.

That was so him. Azariah was well-accustomed to his friend's odd answers but hallelujah! just the same. Persia threatened Babylon's gates and Azariah grew encouraged. He watched fascinated from his sickroom window as his neighbors grew more frightened every day. Riots broke out in the city as the end finally became clear. Mobs at Esagila lashed out at the regent, the priests and the army, charging treason, which was true. The price of barley had tripled. Lawlessness had spread. Minor priests had formed secret alliances with the enemy. Earthquakes shook homes and the absence of rain had left a dull layer of dust over Babylon's once bright bricks.

Yet, amid all these dark omens, the young regent, Belshazzar, had announced plans to organize a party, an orgy, an extravagant feast. No one understood why.

"The nation mourns the loss of what she once was," Azariah said aloud, alone in his room, "understands what she has become and trembles over what she will soon be, spent, sapped and defeated on her feet."

Panic continued for days just beyond Azariah's window then everything grew quiet.

*

Daniel's chariot service had long been terminated by the state but one day, as fear gripped the city and neither man nor horse could be seen, the smiling face of a king's man appeared over Daniel's garden gate. Out of nowhere the mysterious soldier offered Daniel a ride.

"To the outskirts of Nippur?" the driver suggested.

"How wonderful is the God of Israel!" Daniel said, clapping his hands, for Azariah had been on his mind. "Many have fled to the desert or the Hatti," Daniel sighed as he and his escort clattered down Babylon's abandoned lanes toward Nippur. "Look at these barricaded homes."

"Yet, rumor is," the driver said, "that our regent plans a celebration this very night."

Daniel nodded. He had known. The driver brought Daniel to Azariah's door without asking. They eyed one another pleasantly for a while. "The king's service, you say?" Daniel asked.

"I did not say," the soldier laughed, "but yes, precisely."

"So, I expect..."

"I'll be back exactly," the soldier said, "when it's time for you to return."

*

Azariah would die soon, Daniel knew, but he found his friend's bedroom as fresh, bright and airy as his mood. "Greetings, prophet," Azariah said just as a kiss of bright afternoon air wafted through an open window (free of the fine dust that covered everything else). "I knew I'd see your white beard and cherub's face before long."

"Do you suppose, good friend," Daniel asked, "that today is the day?"

"For two wonderful events, yes!" Azariah said.

Daniel sat beside him. "What a time we've had, my brother."

"Four boys not old enough to spit," Azariah said, "ripped away from our homes..."

"Yet preserved."

"...orphaned at a tender age..."

"Yet cared for."

"...threatened constantly with death..."

"Yet blessed by one another and the comfort of God's Holy Spirit."

"I give up," Azariah said, beginning to laugh. "To hear you tell it, prophet, our time here has been but a dip in a mountain stream."

"Clean water," Daniel said softly.

Soon they were both laughing, holding their sides then holding one another shedding tears of remembrance, endurance and love. "Oh, my," Azariah sighed as he dried his eyes, "how pleased little Mishael would be to see us two old mules sniffling like schoolgirls." He fell back upon his pillow and said, "So, prophet, tell me about the crisis in the city."

"Belshazzar," Daniel said, "will host a party this evening."

"While the Persian host crosses the frontier."

"He will serve his guests upon the gold and silver plates, goblets and trays that Nebuchadnezzar lifted from the holy temple in Jerusalem when we were boys."

Full circle. They prayed together and, when finished, Azariah spoke in a manner Daniel had never heard. "Your passion, friend, to serve our God," Azariah said, "puts me to shame."

Daniel put a finger to his lips but Azariah went on.

"You pray every day on your knees by your window from which you can clearly be seen, not to be seen, but for the light and air. And I thank you," he said.

"Please," Daniel said, "you praise me too much."

"Now I've personally heard Jeremiah, Habakkuk and Ezekiel entreating the Lord," Azariah said, "and crafty Nebuchadnezzar could also lift a mighty pleading in his day, but none was ever so inspiring on his knees as you, my good and faithful friend."

Daniel looked outside. Not a soul could be seen on the street. The sun, nearly set by then, had tinted the sky's rim crimson and streaked the earth's edge gray.

"The horde approaches," Azariah said.

"Look, goes the Word. Disaster is spreading from nation to nation. A mighty storm is rising from the ends of the earth."

"The cup filled with the wine of the Lord's wrath," Daniel sighed.

"Praise almighty God," Azariah sighed, "this very evening Babylon will begin to pay for her abuse of God's people. Our people, Daniel.

Persia begins a new part of his plan." He watched his friend, Daniel the prophet, standing quietly at the window awash in fading light. Daniel's smile had left him; a rare thing indeed. "What troubles you, my old friend?" Azariah asked.

"I must leave you now," Daniel sighed, "as difficult a thing as I've ever had to do."

"I'm the grim one, remember?" Azariah said. "Go, my brother. Our separation will last but a little while. I hear your chariot on the street."

*

On their way back to Daniel's home the charioteer stopped in the plaza of the great ziggurat in the square. Night had fallen by then and a bonfire blazed as ever up top though the quadrangle was strewn with litter and not a soul walked about. "Esagila," Daniel said, "center of the pagan world, core of darkness, bottomless font of sin." He pointed across the square to a far wall. "As a child I stood over there, driver, and I heard the wildest cheers... I can still see young Nebuchadnezzar racing up those steps, mark it over sixty years ago."

The driver said, "You haven't asked who I am."

"And would you tell me?" Daniel asked.

The two men laughed.

"Tonight is the night, Daniel," the driver said.

And Daniel answered, "I know."

*

Azariah lay breathing with difficulty, aware that Persia's most direct path to the city lay along the broad lane just outside his door. Here, he knew, two armies would soon pass. The days-long silence first broke when several companies of Babylon's once elite and invincible home guard ran by in disarray, fleeing the frontier. Azariah rolled out of bed and somehow staggered to the street. His neighbors appeared alongside; fathers carrying rakes, knives and axes; mothers with children clinging to their skirts. Azariah knew this scene. He had lived it as a child. If only he, so many years ago, could have hugged his mother a final time.

"To your homes," came a clear voice, "you are in no danger here."

There stood the prophet Ezekiel speaking softly yet heard by all. And the crowd disbursed! Azariah's jaw dropped as Ezekiel approached him, thinking, No one sees more pain than these men of God yet their faces reflect such joy.

"I came to visit," Ezekiel said, "though certainly not expecting to find you on your feet." He helped Azariah back to his home and into bed. "Tonight is momentous both in man's history and in people-Israel's future," Ezekiel said.

"Babylon will fall this evening," Azariah said, "and you've come to provide me details."

"No, son," Ezekiel said, "I've come to administer a blessing before your death."

Azariah smiled.

"Our friend Daniel cannot be with you tonight," Ezekiel explained, "though he would give anything to do so. But he'll be engaged in a work at the palace that will echo for millennia."

So the drama would continue for thousands of years! Azariah's thoughts turned to his weaknesses. There was so little he understood. The smell of scented candles, perhaps fresh flowers, filled the air. He began to tremble. Ezekiel produced a vial of oil, prayed over it and then anointed him. "Pray for Daniel all this evening," the prophet added before leaving. "He shall face amazing challenges."

"And after all this," Azariah asked, "will my brother be called home too?"

"Not even then," Ezekiel said, laughing a little. "Daniel has much, much more to do."

Azariah's eyes widened.

"Oh, yes, my friend," Ezekiel said, "The God of Israel has only begun to use that man."

27. Only a king could do this

DANIEL'S CHARIOTEER STOPPED before the garden gate exactly where they had met earlier. He cupped a hand behind an ear and said, "Listen, the regent's party has begun." Daniel looked over the rooftops. The sky flared with firelight in the direction of the castle.

"They drink from the Lord's vessels," Daniel said, "and they eat defiled food from his plates, praising gods of gold and silver, of bronze, iron, wood and stone."

The men shook hands, goodbye.

"I'll not see you again in this sphere," Daniel said.

"Go, prophet," his driver answered. "Prepare yourself and pray."

*

In the midst of the hanging gloom about the citadel, jugglers performed before bonfires at the palace gates. Musicians played, magicians performed and minstrels, with bawdy jokes and clever songs, enticed hundreds from hiding in their homes to feast at the citadel from Jerusalem's captured dinnerware.

"But why?" Daniel's neighbors asked him in the shadows, wringing their hands as they listened to the echoes of the groundless celebration. "We remember the fiery furnace though it was very long ago. We recall when your god struck the great king mad. Why then, when we surely need a miracle to save the nation, does the regent choose to provoke your god?"

"I cannot tell you," Daniel answered. "I simply know that it must be."

Some thought Belshazzar was crazy, others guessed he hoped to assert his independence or boost the nation's morale, but most supposed he was simply a young fool who liked orgies.

But what sweet irony, Daniel thought, that the God of Israel had arranged for both the beginning and end of Babylon's dominion over Jerusalem to be marked by that nations' lust for her temple treasures.

*

Belshazzar's mother, Nitocris, knew that Babylon's end was near and understood that she risked her life by remaining in town. But she preferred that risk to hiding in the desert with her husband, the cowardly king. She looked from her chamber window in the direction from which she had heard Persia would come. The battle for Babylon, if it ever came to that, would not last long. Neither her husband nor her son owned a backbone.

When the party began downstairs Nitocris watched as a storm formed in the north, but when the noise from Belshazzar's celebration grew louder than the distant thunder, the regent's mother rushed to the great hall to protest and found a disgusting scene.

"This disgrace has only begun," she told Belshazzar, "and these fools you call guests are already half-naked and staggering drunk. Send them home now, son, I beg you, for the preservation of your honor. Just this once, act like a king."

"I am a king, Mother," Belshazzar said. "Look around. Only a king could do this."

Nitocris' gaze rested upon several linen covered tables across the hall where sat stacked the gold and silver goblets, trays and platters that her father, Nebuchadnezzar, had lifted from the temple in Jerusalem. Nitocris had inherited neither her mother's distaste for Jews nor her father's belief in their superiority but she knew what she knew. "This is wrong," she told her son. "These vessels are not simply dinnerware. They are holy items taken by your grandfather to teach Judah a lesson. He demanded that they were always kept locked up, safe and clean."

"Over thirty gold dishes," Belshazzar said, reciting from a list, "a thousand silver dishes, twenty-nine silver pans, thirty golden bowls, four hundred and ten matching silver bowls and thousands of other pieces. Well over five thousand articles in all!" He winked at his mom. "I've reserved all gold for our table."

"Have you not yet learned, son," Nitocris said, "not to trifle with the Jews or their god?" She turned to leave but Belshazzar grabbed her hand.

"Since I was a boy," Belshazzar hissed, "I've heard fables about those noxious people. I do not fear them or their god. I do not believe the stories about three Hebrew children dancing in a fire."

"Your grandfather saw the thing!" Nitocris said. "I saw his eyes that same day. He was the bravest of men, a coward like you could not imagine, but he was undone—shaking with fear and apprehension for days—after those boys stepped out of that inferno unharmed."

"Then he could not have been as brave as you say," Belshazzar answered her smugly, sipping wine. "Tell the musicians to play louder," he ordered a servant, "and let the meal begin."

The regent insisted that his mother sit beside him at the main table as his nobles, consorts and concubines continued their revel but, when the food was served, Nitocris refused to touch or even look at the golden plates. All the while the guests ate and drank and danced to increasingly wilder music. Some fell to the floor breathless, wasted by wine, but their peers simply stepped over or around them until they too began to stagger. From time to time, as the rowdiness continued, guardsmen approached the regent to whisper in his ear.

"What are they saying?" Nitocris asked.

Belshazzar gulped wine from a golden chalice then wiped his chin with a sleeve. "What's left of the army has run away, Mother. Are you happy? Are you thrilled to be right? It appears our traitorous priests have met with the enemy and cut a deal."

"And so?"

"And so Persia is upon us, Mommy," he laughed, but only briefly. "I asked the captain to protect us. He promised he would."

Nitocris opened her mouth to respond but stopped short. Had her hearing failed? Had the music in the crowded hall really faded to a murmur? Though her head seemed clear it appeared that the guests dancing nearest the royal table had begun to move slowly, as in a dream. Belshazzar grabbed his mother's hand.

"You see this too?"

Before her son could answer, a band of purple light spread across the hall. The musicians stopped playing. The chamber grew dark beneath the violet haze. Nitocris tried to scream but could not. Her son's terrified eyes had fixed upon something behind her. It took all her will to turn. There, a human hand—nothing but a hand—hovered in the air for several seconds, writing with one finger on the wall.

*

Nitocris had fainted but Belshazzar, after too much to eat and drink, only fell back in his chair, his insides rolling painfully. The joints of his loins were loosed and his knees knocked together as the glowing apparition of the hand stroked ordinary figures upon the plaster…

מנא מנא תקל ופרסין

…then disappeared. The hall brightened instantly after. Those guests who had remained upright stared at what the floating hand had left behind. Belshazzar moved his lips as he tried to read but the words made no sense.

"Can anyone explain them?" he asked.

No one answered.

Nitocris tried to revive but seemed to be trapped in a stubborn trance. The regent called several of his magicians and diviners forward and said, "Any of you able to read this writing and tell me its meaning shall wear purple and the gold collar around his neck as third in the kingdom."

"What benefit in that," one answered, "if Babylon won't survive the night?"

"Arrest him," Belshazzar shouted, but no one moved.

Most of the guests who were able ran from the room but some stayed put and began to argue. What had they really seen? What could the writing mean?

"Can any of you interpret this?" Belshazzar asked again.

His seers remained silent, staring blankly at the wall.

Nitocris's eyes snapped open. "You have fouled yourself," she hissed, after looking at her son. "Wash at once then return when you are able."

"I'm in charge here, Mother," Belshazzar said, but he left quickly, covered in filth and so grateful that his guests were too drunk or frightened to be entertained by his shame. When he returned no one had moved. Belshazzar had never wanted to be regent. Now all eyes were on his mother for direction and he was relieved.

"O king, live forever!" Nitocris said aloud, encouraging her son to stand straighter with a subtle gesture. "Let your thoughts not alarm you nor darken your face. There is a man in your kingdom who has the spirit of the holy god in him; in your grandfather's time, illumination, understanding and wisdom like that of the gods were found of him, and your grandfather, King Nebuchadnezzar, appointed him chief of the magicians, exorcists, Chaldeans and diviners. Seeing that there is to be found in Daniel (whom the king called Belteshazzar) extraordinary spirit, knowledge and understanding to interpret dreams, to explain riddles and solve problems, let Daniel now be called to tell the meaning of this writing."

"Does anyone here remember him?" Nitocris asked, when finished,

"Belteshazzar, the great seer, still lives in town not far from here," someone said.

"We'll solve this then," Nitocris said. "Let us summon Daniel now."

*

After much prayer Daniel had gone to bed early that night knowing he would be called upon soon. And truly, just hours later, as thunder continued to rage, he blinked awake to the additional sounds of screams and panic. Soon he greeted two regent's men at his door.

"A floating hand has written on the palace plaster," one said, "and the regent needs an interpretation, now."

"In what language?" Daniel asked.

The soldier tilted his helmet, scratched his head and said, "One of ours."

"So why, then, is there confusion?"

He shrugged. "We see the words, O prophet, but we do not know what they mean." His mate tapped his shoulder and suggested he say no more but the first went on. "Mene, Mene, Tekel, Upharsin," he said. "I saw the hand myself..." He stopped with his mouth open, unable to say more. Daniel, of course, agreed to accompany them and they rushed him to the palace. When the prophet entered the dinner chamber with his shining white hair, white beard, walking without a cane and looking remarkably strong, the guests all blinked at him in awe.

"Most of you are too young to have seen this man in his day," Nitocris said, "but my father, mighty Nebuchadnezzar, rest his soul, loved him dearly." She looked down at her hands. "Daniel is an important man from that not so distant time when Babylon commanded respect. I witnessed his god's power as a child through my father's eyes. Your campfire stories are true. This is he who contended with Nebuchadnezzar in obedience to his god and whom, even so, my father respected with all his being. He can help us tonight, I know, should he agree." She turned to her son and said, "Do it."

Belshazzar waved a hand to summon Daniel. "So," the regent began when they were face to face, "you are Belteshazzar…"

"Daniel," the prophet interrupted.

"So, you are Daniel," the regent began again, "of the exiles whom my grandfather, Nebuchadnezzar, brought from Judah. I've heard of you; that the divine spirit is in you."

"O, regent," Daniel answered, "your tone is challenging but I take no offense. I'm here not for you or Babylon but because the God of Israel demands it. You, Belshazzar, of the line of a great king, have not adopted a humble attitude. You exalted yourself against the very Lord of heaven and had the vessels of his house brought before you."

"The dinnerware," Nitocris groaned. Then, to Daniel, "I warned him."

Belshazzar pointed to the wall. "My wise men have been brought before me to read this writing and tell its meaning but they are unable to explain it. If you can read it and tell its meaning you shall wear the purple and the golden collar around your neck and rule as third in the kingdom."

"I have no use for collars or gold," Daniel answered, "but I'll read this writing as you have asked with the help of God."

"Do it, then, if you can," Belshazzar said, "and be careful of your tone."

Daniel ignored the regent's threat and studied the wall for a moment, whispered a prayer then said, "This is indeed a message from God, angered by the abomination of his holy vessels." He paused to point at the plates and goblets turned on tables, scattered on the floor and strewn in the hallways beside passed-out drunks and half-dressed women. He shook his head, remembering. "I stood as a prisoner at

Jerusalem's gate nearly seventy years ago and saw these same holy articles after they had been thrown into carts."

Nitocris lowered her eyes.

"Counted," Daniel continued in a clear voice, "a mina, a shekel and two halves."

Belshazzar and the others stood blinking and confused.

"A mina," Daniel said, "God has numbered the days of your kingship and brought it to an end. A shekel: you have been weighed on the scales and found wanting. A half: your kingdom has been broken in half and given to the Medes and Persians."

A groan went up, followed by eerie silence.

"We understand that you have spoken truly," Nitocris told Daniel. "We've failed as a nation, our days have been numbered and Akkad will be no more."

"No!" Belshazzar shouted. "This cannot be."

"For defiling God's holy items and other high crimes," Daniel said, loud enough to cause some to cover their ears, "Babylon, once the Lord's servant, is now his condemned."

"No!" Belshazzar shouted again, but his subjects knew better.

"Persia is on your doorstep," Daniel said. "This idolatrous nation has raped, enslaved and murdered God's chosen. She has leveled God's holy city and reduced her to ash." The prophet rarely scowled but he did so then, on fire with the Word, and added, "Hear, O, Babylon, for all these things, on this very night, you have been called to account."

*

The sky thundered over Azariah's home in Nippur that same night, shuddering explosions absent rain, conditions he had not seen since he was a child in Jerusalem on the day King Josiah died.

As the elements raged Azariah recalled his rage when torn from his home.

As his neighbors panicked in the streets he pictured a young Nebuchadnezzar running nimbly up the steps of the ziggurat on a sunny day.

Hearing cries for help from the throats of Babylon's damned he recalled his desperate prayers in the captive school barracks as he and his friends survived then rose to power.

As the ground shook he trembled, recalling the glory of the furnace and its flames.

Azariah cried out in empathy for those who would surely lose their world as he had lost his. A window blew open. He struggled to sit erect and look out. By torchlight he saw—he was certain—Koresh! The Persian prince himself passed on the street on horseback. Mighty Koresh of whom the Lord had said…

> *He is my shepherd and will accomplish all that I please; he will say of Jerusalem, "Let it be rebuilt," and of the temple, "Let its foundations be laid."*

"Hallelujah!" Azariah shouted from his bed. The uproar ceased. The heavens quieted. Only the rush of wind and the rumble of Persia's army marching westward remained, heralding the end of an age. Azariah thanked the Lord aloud, smiled a smile he imagined might please even the prophet, Daniel, and then closed his eyes to die.

VI. Lions

28. Koresh the Great

AS THE STORM raged outside, Belshazzar ordered a purple mantle to be fetched and laid upon the prophet's shoulders. "I am a man of my word," he said. "For reading the writing on the wall I appoint you third highest in the land."

Daniel allowed the robe to fall at his feet. Nitocris stepped forward and stooped to grab it. "My mother hated Judah," she told Daniel, "but my father truly loved you, Daniel, as well as your friends." She offered the mantle to him again. "Please?"

Out of kindness, Daniel put it on.

Belshazzar sat at the main table mumbling into his hands. The few guests who had remained in the palace after the divine manifestation either worked for the regent, lay passed out drunk on the floor or stood silently in the hushed chamber paralyzed by fear.

Daniel raised his hand and several servants hurried to his side. "Wash yourselves thoroughly," he told them, "then gather all the vessels you see lying here, in the dining room and the adjoining halls. Clean them carefully then stack them just as carefully in this room."

Nitocris rolled up her sleeves and went to work alongside the help. "Will my son survive?" she asked Daniel as they worked.

Daniel turned to look. The Regent of Babylon remained slumped upon an ornately carved bench seat, shaking with fear. "You must accept," Daniel said (as thunder rumbled and lightning flashed in the distance), "that all that has happened and is yet to take place is ordained."

Nitocris' eyes filled with tears but she carried on like a queen. After all the holy articles were cleaned and stacked she dismissed the servants and ordered the remaining guests to go home. Only the regent's armed protectors and those who had passed out during the party remained. Daniel said to the regent, "Please dismiss your personal guard."

"Why?" Belshazzar asked.

"Because," Daniel said, "there is no need for them to die tonight too."

Belshazzar whined a little then did as asked. The great hall, which not long before had echoed with the shouts of drunken revelers, stringed instruments and blaring horns, fell completely still but only for a few minutes. There came the rhythmic pounding of boots.

"Persia, here in the citadel already?" Belshazzar sighed. "That's it? They simply march in?"

Nitocris kissed her son's cheek. "Be calm," she said. "This shall end quickly."

The doors to the grand salon boomed open and scores of well-equipped spearmen and bowmen flooded inside on the quick. Finding only Daniel, Nitocris and Belshazzar awake, they encircled them, weapons held high, and seemed to be waiting for something.

"Feathers?" the regent asked, eying the intruders.

Clearly it was Koresh himself, the man Isaiah had called God's anointed in his century-old prophecy, who strode into the great hall immediately behind his troops, a surprisingly short man but impressive just the same, with a firm-set jaw and dark, darting eyes much like old Nebuchadnezzar. Leaders were leaders, it seemed.

"Nabonidus!" Koresh boomed, "on your knees for crimes against your people."

Belshazzar fell to his knees although he had been charged by his father's name.

"Shall we kill all three?" an officer asked. Daniel, by then, had long studied and perfectly understood the evolving variant of Persian spoken by the anxious officer. Koresh noticed Daniel's apparent comprehension and approached him. "I know who these two are," he said in perfect Aramaic, pointing at mother and son, "but who might you be standing so calmly and wearing a royal robe?"

Daniel grinned.

The emperor of Persia smiled back at him, intrigued by his odd response, then pointed at Belshazzar and told his man, "No, kill only him for now."

Nitocris screamed when they grabbed her son then fainted a second time.

*

Koresh's men beheaded Belshazzar on the spot. These were serious times. Poor Nitocris had revived in time to see it. Daniel, usually abhorrent of violence of any kind, watched the brutal act unmoved. Something disappointing in his spirit had kept him far from compassion for the regent, only a shade of the great men who had ruled Babylon before him. Even while Belshazzar's headless body thrashed on the floor Daniel remained detached and calm. But his heart broke for Nitocris, the regent's mother.

"Are you next?" Koresh asked Daniel as his men led the queen—the former queen—away.

"I am Daniel, a native of Jerusalem in exile," Daniel said, "Babylon's captive for nearly seventy years. I am certainly no threat to you."

"Wearing purple?" Koresh asked.

"Only as a kindness," Daniel said.

Some of Koresh's men laughed.

"Rip one of these garish tapestries off the wall," the king yelled to those standing closest, "bundle the regent's head and body inside and get them out of here." He turned back to Daniel. "A kindness, you say? This is an amazing place, Jew, tell me what you know of it."

"There's a ponderous tower in the square," Daniel said after thinking for a bit, "it's built in seven levels with a temple up top dedicated to the false god, Marduk."

"I know that," Koresh said. "I have spies."

"A glorious hanging garden adjoins the royal quarters along the south wall in that direction," Daniel continued, pointing down the hall along which Koresh's men had carted the queen. "There's nothing like it anywhere. Foliage seems to float in air above terraces which cascade down to the river in a dreamlike fashion. An amazing feat of engineering though it's now in disrepair."

"I know that too," Koresh muttered. He stepped out onto a balcony and listened. "Not a sound to be heard except for the diminishing storm," he told his men. "Swift and bloodless we attain this victory, my fine fellows." Koresh's men broke into shouts and applause. "This fat, pampered people long ago lost their spines but I must confess to being thoroughly fascinated by this grinning old man."

He turned back to Daniel. "Now I've heard your reports on the tower and the gardens," he said. "More importantly, I notice that you continue to smirk in my face, showing no apparent regard for, I have to say this, mortal danger, for I am now very much inclined to kill you too."

When Daniel failed to respond, Koresh asked, "Did you hear me? Death to you, old man, for a lack of useful information and an annoying display of pleasantness."

"I have indeed heard you, O king," Daniel said, "but to my knowledge I've assumed a neutral disposition. My hands are folded. I have averted my eyes, not out of fear, but respect…"

"All Babylon lies drunk," Koresh interrupted, "or beheaded, or shivering in corners like scared girls to save their skins yet you stand here stupidly explaining yourself as if tardy to an appointment rather than facing your execution?" Koresh began to squint. "And you continue to grin at me. Do not deny it. You do not look the moron, old one, I'll allow you less than a minute to explain why."

"I lost a friend tonight," Daniel said, "the last with whom I came here captive as a boy. It was my sacred duty to be here to greet you instead of stay with him. And so I grieve."

"With bright eyes?"

Daniel sighed. Sometimes he envied his departed friends. "Truly, O king," he said, "murder me now if you wish, I've no concern for either your curiosity or your threats. In the end you will restore Jerusalem as foretold. That is and was my only care. It is the reason I am here tonight and missed solemn time with my friend and, I suppose, it explains why I may appear to be pleased this evening. Hallelujah!"

"Is anybody listening to this insanity?" Koresh shouted.

His men looked away. No one dared answer.

"I command millions, Jew," Koresh said, "nations tremble when they hear my name and you assert that you've got no concern for my inclinations?"

"None. Whatsoever. I don't care."

Koresh seemed stunned.

"Except, as I've mentioned," Daniel added, "but the restoration of Israel is secure whether I live or die this evening. Your role has been known for ages. You are ordained to an important task and it shall be."

"Ordained! Finally I hear something of substance from your lips," Koresh said. "You see, I know more than you may think about the odd manners and exotic traditions of your people."

"Yes, you have spies," Daniel said.

"Yes!" Koresh laughed. "You Jews think you're at the middle of the world."

"We live centered in God's heart."

"You are slaves with no country," Koresh said, "yet you imagine that you are favored."

"We are God's chosen, truly," Daniel said. "You are here to now punish Babylon and restore our fortunes. An age ends this night, sir, and a new one begins thanks to you."

"Persia takes what she wants, from whom she wants as she wishes," Koresh said. "Ask Lydia. Ask the Medes. My boot replaces Babylon's on your throat and you have the brass to believe I and my army arrive at this moment to serve you?"

"It is written," Daniel said.

Koresh stood and blinked at him.

"I can show you your name if you like," Daniel said, "recorded well over a hundred years earlier in a sacred scroll at my home. It points to this exact moment. I'll bet your spies did not know that."

Koresh drew his sword. "You are insane. I will kill you myself."

Daniel smiled even more. "I've waited, I've prayed for you and now that I see you standing here in victory, I rejoice."

The king kicked a small table and sent it flying across the floor.

"Kill me if you like," Daniel said, "the end will be the same."

Again, the emperor's soldiers dared to laugh.

"Why does this chamber remain so filthy?" Koresh yelled. He pointed to the unconscious celebrants on the floor. "Revive these naked buffoons, tell them Babylon is finished and get them out of my sight," he ordered. "And post the proclamations I've prepared."

He sat upon Belshazzar's bench and turned again to Daniel. "I don't believe your fable for a second," he said, "but I confess your lie has piqued my curiosity. We've marched nearly forty miles today yet I have more than enough energy to call your bluff. Show me this scroll of yours, Daniel, I want to see my name, but I promise when your account is proven false you are a dead man."

Daniel agreed at once and led Koresh out to the gates. The sky had stopped rumbling. Black clouds flashed glimpses of a magnificent moon as they glided quickly overhead. The regent's fires had shrunk to mounds of embers, spent like Nebuchadnezzar's Babylon. The emperor ordered a chariot and dismissed his personal guard.

"I can handle this old fellow myself," Koresh told his men when they set off.

*

Persian troops waved from behind small fires at each corner as Koresh's chariot passed in the streets to Daniel's house. To a man the exhausted soldiers cheered for their king. The emperor sat on cushions as Daniel opened his Isaiah scroll and began to read aloud...

> *Thus saith the Lord to his anointed, to Koresh, whose right hand I have held, to subdue nations before him.*

Koresh leaned forward and read it on his own, scowling over the text as he followed with his fingers, mouthing each word. When finished he read it again.

"How long do you say you've held this?" Koresh asked.

"Nearly seventy years, but it is a copy of a much older text."

"I am an educated man," Koresh whispered when he had finished, "yet I have no training or experience with which to measure..." His voice trailed completely away.

Clearly Nebuchadnezzar would have accused Daniel of forgery or fraud by then. If not, the deceased king of Babylon would have called Daniel a hundred vile names. But Koresh weighed his every word before speaking, quick to think and slow to speak, showing himself to be quite a different man.

"There's more," Daniel said. "It is written herein that you, by name, will not only free my people but rebuild God's holy city, Jerusalem."

The emperor looked left and right. They were alone, of course, but he whispered just the same. "I have training not only in languages," he said, "but in magic, incantations, numerology, measurement, omens, entrails and spells…" He lowered his voice still more. "Yet I know of no god or spell capable of such as this; there is no man or god able to name someone yet unborn and put him in a place and time more than a century into the future."

"There is but one God," Daniel said, "he has done this, and his name is not Ahura-Mazda."

"You say," Koresh mumbled, but he seemed entirely undone.

"Nor is he named Marduk, Bêl, Nabu…"

"Stop," Koresh said. "I've heard of your people's stubbornness. Nothing can explain it."

"Miracles explain it," Daniel said, "it is not stubborn to heed the truth. In just ten generations, the mere blink of an eye as nations go, your people have grown from an obscure tribe in Anšan to an empire with dominion over all others. Not even Babylon's fables contemplate the scale and precision of what you and your armies, O king, have accomplished in such short time. Mighty Persia was but a notion in King Solomon's time and but a budding hope when the Lord put your name on the lips of our great prophet."

"So, you say, I…" Koresh laughed a little at the notion. "You truly believe that Persia and her millions have risen to this moment only to…"

"Yes!" Daniel said. "To restore Jerusalem."

The king stepped to the window and looked outside. "Not the first sign of conflict anywhere in the city," he sighed. "We lost not one man during the march in. Never have I seen a softer, more eviscerated nation then this Babylon."

"Yet it was a powerhouse less than twenty years ago," Daniel said.

"Even Lydia, as spoiled, pampered and self-absorbed a nation as I had imagined could exist until this moment, fought with a little dignity to preserve itself."

"Behold, then, Sire, a nation judged by the God of Israel," Daniel said, "rotted from within as she focused on pleasure and wallowed in sin. Your energy and vision should change all that in short order, I expect, O king."

Koresh stepped back to the scroll and read a bit more. With his eyes still fixed upon its text he said, "You don't fear me one whit, do you, Daniel?"

Daniel smiled apologetically and answered, "No."

*

They talked all night. Koresh told Daniel amazing things about Persia. Daniel spoke of Egypt, Moses, the unbreakable bond between God and his chosen people and his promises to them, following recent stern judgment, regarding his holy city, Jerusalem.

"Fascinating," Koresh said, "just one loving god, you people see, even after all that he has done to you?"

"We brought it all upon ourselves."

"A covenant? Cleanliness? Resting every seventh day? A proscription on graven images?"

Daniel nodded.

"I do not necessarily believe a word," Koresh said, "but..." The emperor stopped and yawned. Morning had come. The king had finally run out if steam.

The sky brightened in the east. Birds chirped here and there unaware that the world had changed. "I'm afraid you've missed sunrise at the palace," Daniel said.

"I'm at least twenty years your younger, Daniel," Koresh sighed, "and yet you look refreshed. Your candor, your energy and intelligence... So much about you amazes me, sir. Think, then, about lending your wisdom and experience to Persia for a season. Consider helping me govern this new empire."

"Before I answer," Daniel said immediately, "I will pray. It would be unwise of me to refuse you without doing so. God may have an unseen purpose in your request."

*

After the invasion, Hasdrubal, along with a score of others of privileged station among the Marduk sect, laid low. The competing minority priests who had not fled Babylon, having sensed an opportunity to gain favor, had quickly boned up on Eastern myths and rushed to offer their modified mystic services to the new regime.

These same men had been largely responsible for the bloodless fall of Babylon and now hoped to cash in. In the public sector, once it became clear that they would not be beheaded, former officials made career moves based on whichever way they thought, or hoped the wind blew. But the ordinary men and women of Babylon were simply thrilled to be alive.

"Assyria would have slaughtered us," many said. And of course they were right. Koresh's unexpected mercy made him an instant hero. Schools, markets and amusements reopened just days after the invasion. Persian troops quickly vacated the streets in favor of the familiar Babylonian guard.

Knowing prophecy, the exiled Jews in Babylon welcomed Koresh like an old friend.

"But this goodwill will only last," Koresh told Daniel when they met again the next day, "if we govern well. You're a wise and welcomed face in town. Play a role; agree to serve."

"I've prayed about it as I promised," Daniel said, "and I shall willingly serve you in order to assist the return of my people to Jerusalem."

"What, now?" Koresh asked. They sat talking in the same chamber where, decades earlier, Daniel and friends had frequently advised Nebuchadnezzar.

"Your anointing is intended for restoration above all," Daniel said. "We discussed it."

"Well and good," Koresh said. "I'll set up one hundred twenty khshathrapāvā, satraps, protectors of the province, to rule my empire."

"Why so many, O king?" Daniel asked.

Koresh smiled at what must have sounded like a naive question. "Nineveh mustered tens of thousands at arms on her best days," he said. "At her peak, Babylon was able to quickly mobilize and coordinate, say, a few hundred thousand men." He crossed the room to another window and pointed. "There are a million and a half well-armed and superbly trained warriors out there, Daniel, spreading far past Media, Lydia across the Great Plain. Yet I can step into the hall now and merely murmur an order..." For drama, he whispered, "... that will be perfectly executed in distant Anšan before the sun sets the following day!"

"There has never been anything like it," Daniel agreed, "in the history of man."

"I know what you're thinking," Koresh said, "only in fulfillment of your prophets."

Daniel nodded.

"Believe what you like, Daniel, we do not have to agree, but become one of only three men to govern the greatest empire ever known; you here, another to oversee the homeland and a third to run the frontier between. Once this nation's slave, you, Daniel, shall now rule her."

"I will do it, O king," Daniel said, "with your understanding that…"

"I know," Koresh said. "Your purpose is to help the Jews. Sit, then, Daniel. I'll summon a meal and we'll discuss your job."

29. Ugbaru

THE NEW, PERSIAN Empire's three major partitions included the original homeland, to be run by a man named Ugbaru. Ugbaru had been Koresh's top general and a principal instigator of the feints, coercion and double-dealing with local Babylonian priests which had led to Koresh's bloodless victory.

Koresh assigned the administration of Babylon to Daniel.

The third subdivision included Lydia, Media, Elam and several smaller states, assigned to another Persian, a non-military man named Behrouz. Ugbaru, Behrouz, Daniel and the king met in the palace for the first time less than a month after Babylon fell. Koresh did the introductions. Ugbaru responded politely, though detached. Behrouz refused even to look at Daniel. Each, Daniel sensed, had hoped or expected that Babylon would have been placed under his control.

They chatted around a ponderous table in an upstairs chamber at the citadel with an excellent view of what remained of Amytis's gardens. The watering transports in the gardens still functioned, much foliage remained in bloom and slaves continued to weed and trim the terraces daily, but its once dazzling array of vegetation had grown thin and sad in comparison to their former glory days. Ugly black fingers of mold had spread from the terraces' shaded corners into the light.

"I've heard such stories about these planters," Ugbaru sniffed, "but they're nothing more than a collection of cracking troughs and rowdy shrubs."

"They're nothing like they once were," Daniel sighed.

"Come, let's look farther," Koresh said, leading them onto a balcony. "See the towering ziggurat there, the broad walls about this citadel—give thanks we did not have to storm it—and notice that mighty flow, the tree-lined Euphrates as it winds down toward the gulf?"

Ugbaru and Behrouz smiled politely.

"Then here, in this garden," Koresh said, pointing at a pumping station several tiers below. "And there, up to the highest terrace, level upon level, foliage all watered, ordered and green. How on earth do you think they managed that?"

"Once impressive, I suppose," Ugbaru said, "yet we stand here as conquerors, unopposed."

"Your opponent wasn't Nebuchadnezzar," Daniel said. "It was he, not the regent Belshazzar, who designed this marvel."

"Yet it seems his excellence at hydraulics," Behrouz said, "was not enough to prevent all his people from becoming Persia's slaves."

Daniel smiled peacefully. "The men who built this nation were many things," he said, "but never slaves."

"But you were…you are, I suppose, a slave," Ugbaru said. "Isn't that right?"

Daniel had dealt with perverse men before. From the looks of these Persians, they had much to learn if they hoped to match the keenness of a Philosir or the guile of the priest, Enshunu, in his prime.

"A wise man learns from others," Koresh said, "most especially his enemies," and they moved rapidly from point to point from there, discussing the new look of the empire.

Koresh seemed unaware that Ugbaru and Behrouz were not pleased with Daniel at all.

*

Men rarely impressed Daniel but Koresh's decisiveness and attention to detail soon amazed him. "I've seen nothing like this," he told the emperor as he, Ugbaru and Behrouz reviewed the personalities, responsibilities and reporting paths of the 120 satraps beneath them. Koresh hoped to govern the diverse nations he had conquered uniformly, "but there are immense differences between them," he said, "and I'm not quite sure how to go about it."

"I say impose Persian law absolute," Ugbaru said, "and demand that your subjects comply."

"The Medes are an arrogant race, worse than Lydians," Behrouz added, "but they, like everyone, will respond to the lash." Then he turned to look at Daniel. "Almost everyone," he said, "even I have heard of the fabled eccentricity of Jews."

"What say you, Daniel?" Koresh asked.

Daniel looked across the table. Only the king observed his eyes. Daniel prayed silently for the insight to speak wisely yet boldly then said, "In customs, culture, beliefs, tax practice, language and law, all these people are different, O king, but they share human hope to remain connected to their past customs and traditions."

"Human hope?" Behrouz asked. "What concern is that of ours?"

"Whether Persia collects grain, Darics, shekels or gold," Daniel said, "it all amounts to the same in the treasury. Why change local provisions for marriage, education, property transfer, and payment of debt when they have no tangible impact on the administration of Persia?"

"And what about the gods?" Behrouz asked.

"There is but one God, the God of Israel…"

"Oh, please…" Ugbaru interrupted, but Koresh snapped his fingers.

"…and one day," Daniel continued, "all nations will bow to him." He paused, daring any of them to speak. "Is it Persia's ambition among those she has conquered to replace one set of idols with another…"

"While no one really wants change," Koresh said, "and may be deeply offended by it."

"And what is the Jews' business in all this?" Ugbaru asked.

"We will return to God's city, Jerusalem, our home," Daniel said.

"That foolishness aside," Behrouz said, "do you really propose that we allow every one of these conquered countries to do exactly as it pleases?"

"These nations were never rebellious in nature except for those in the Hatti," Daniel said. "Why not preserve their laws and customs and allow them to live under a new, nurturing, Persian peace."

"Persian peace," Koresh sighed. "Collect taxes and move on."

"Just taxes," Daniel corrected, "meaning fair and unoppressive."

"Yes, justice above all," Koresh said, grinning, "there's plenty wealth to go around." He stood up then sat down. "Brilliant, Daniel! I love it. I declare this meeting ended. I have to say we're off to a terrific start."

"Then, if we are finished, O king," Daniel said, "I'll walk the short distance home to pray now as is my daily custom."

Ugbaru parted his lips in a false smile as the meeting ended. Behrouz left the room without a word. Daniel walked home afterward wondering if ever, during his remaining time on earth, God might just once allow him to glimpse a brighter, more uplifting side to his fellow man than he had witnessed thus far among the nations.

30. Restoration

ONCE KORESH BEGAN to institute changes in Babylon and throughout his new, expanded empire he seemed to forget about the Jews. "I hear you," he would say to Daniel whenever asked about the restoration of Jerusalem, "but I face staggering challenges right now."

"You've read the Isaiah scroll," Daniel said. "Do you intend to fight the inevitable?"

"Or things may go badly for me?" Koresh asked. "Is that what you're threatening?"

"I threaten nothing," Daniel said, "but that doesn't eliminate Persia's exposure. It only makes sense that some paths leading to a certainty are more pleasant to navigate than others."

Nebuchadnezzar would have hurled curses had Daniel confronted him so. Koresh only drew a deep breath and sighed. "Give me a moment," he said. "This thing—the written revelation you showed me—the entire concept is foreign to me. I need time to think."

Daniel prayed while the king muttered to himself, perhaps thinking, as he had promised.

"I have heard a word and I shall heed it," Koresh said finally, grinning like a boy, "Persia will restore Babylon's Jews to Jerusalem."

Daniel's heart leapt. With Koresh's blessing he published a decree. In the city, in Nippur, in Birs Nimrud and throughout the districts Hebrew men, women and children cried for joy upon reading it. How amazing was God's mercy, firm his Word and glorious his power! His thoroughly chastened children, after seven decades of exile, were headed home.

Yet, it was clear to Daniel that in all but sacred memory these exiles were home. They had become Bavli, Babylonians, having planted trees, built houses and raised families as God had instructed through Jeremiah. After seventy years they spoke, ate and argued no differently than their captors. Some even dressed like them. Few had ever seen Jerusalem.

Soon it became obvious that their celebrations had been premature. Weeks passed and nothing happened. The demands of governance continued to distract the king and the enmity and opposition of Ugbaru and Behrouz did the rest. With those two opposed to everything Daniel tried to do, nothing was done at all. A year after the king's proclamation was published not one soul had returned to Jerusalem from Babylon. Daniel began to wonder if God intended for him to live to see the day.

*

The king sometimes sat in on meetings and listened quietly, hands folded for hours while his administrators bickered. His silence confused Daniel; Koresh seemed much too clever to be fooled by his Persians' posturing. One day, Daniel guessed, the king would lose his patience and pounce. So Daniel persevered at his mission hopefully, prayerfully and patiently, never missing a chance to make his case.

"In order for the transition to Jerusalem to go smoothly," Daniel said in one meeting, "we will need to clarify law regarding the disposition of exile's property, providing for their safe conduct to Jerusalem and establish a clear state commitment for financial support."

"Of course," Behrouz answered as always, "but it is now more urgent to discuss the frontier."

Table this, defer that. As time passed Daniel became concerned that he might become frustrated or lose hope. So, when his spirit troubled him he often visited Ezekiel for renewal. Nippur had been overrun by Persian military since their invasion and the city's resulting growth had made it a frantic, sometimes dangerous place. But there was always fresh news to be heard there and Ezekiel never failed to lift his spirits. They would meet out of town, far from the confusion, to sit in the shade of the same spreading tree beside the River Kebar where Azariah, Mishael and Hananiah had also spent time with them dreaming of the restoration, now almost a reality. Old Ezekiel had grown so peaceful by then he could barely stay awake. Yet, like Daniel, he always seemed to smile.

"You are usually so positive," Ezekiel said one morning after Daniel vented a bit. "It seems that you believe your calling is to simply run a resolution through your council, start our people rolling home then be done with it. But our God did not handpick you for such a simple task."

Daniel blinked at him.

"History itself is tipping in the balance as we speak!" Ezekiel said. "Satan and his minions will fight what God has kindled here even beyond the day it shall be accomplished." He nodded solemnly. "You, Daniel, sit at the emperor's right hand by design, striving not only against men but principalities. Though you face evil opposition you are bound to succeed, not because we, as a people, have earned God's mercy, but for the sake of his great name. As for your precise part in this mystery, Daniel, it has only begun. I've the feeling that you will soon face your most severe test."

"A feeling," Daniel asked, "or do you know?"

Ezekiel nodded, listening, then pretended to fall asleep.

＊

Shortly after Daniel's visit with Ezekiel at Nippur, during an executive meeting which Koresh was unable to attend, Daniel told his peers that a Babylonian born leader called Zerubbabel had offered to lead fellow exiles back to their homeland. "He's ready to go," Daniel said, "and the emperor's supporting decree is on the books."

The Persians tabled the idea as always. The agenda moved to road repair in the city and once again Ugbaru and Behrouz combined to oppose Daniel's suggestion. "This too can wait," Ugbaru said while Behrouz nodded.

Feeling a stirring in his spirit, Daniel said, "No, it will happen exactly as I say."

"But we oppose it," Behrouz said.

"And yet," Daniel said, his heart pounding (for he never enjoyed contention), "I shall issue the orders and the work will be done."

After Daniel followed through with his promise Behrouz and Ugbaru complained to Koresh at the following meeting. "We opposed this, O king, yet Belteshazzar defied your rules of conduct and without our consensus issued orders. The project has begun."

Three sets of eyes studied the emperor of Persia. "Daniel," Koresh said, "your wisdom is surpassing but I have always known that was true. Now I am delighted to confirm what I have also suspected, you are gifted with a courageous spirit too."

The emperor turned to face his two Persians. "Did you two really suppose that I have enjoyed sitting here, these months, listening to your pettiness and constant bickering?"

Behrouz seemed to consider it.

"I've been watching, waiting and hoping for the conviction to make a permanent, beneficial change," Koresh said. "Clearly this complaint of yours is my sign." He pounded the table with his fist like a gavel. "It's not the Persian way to twiddle thumbs. I expected more from you two, frankly. As of this moment I am empowering Daniel to serve as my regent over all. You two shall assist, not obstruct him, as he acts with my full authority."

"Help me understand this, Sire," Ugbaru said.

"Don't play games here, okay, men?" Koresh came back. "Think of your futures and families. Grasp this last opportunity to recommit to my service and forswear your ambition, which I am afraid has betrayed you. Work hard and faithfully now under Daniel's leadership. Try to reestablish yourselves as competent, not petty, in my eyes."

Ugbaru and Behrouz sat stunned.

"Ever it has been with men like our remarkable king," Daniel said. "Like Josiah! Like Nebuchadnezzar! Each so different yet much the same. Great men act under inspiration and accomplish God's will. Now we shall begin."

"Listen to my brand new regent," Koresh said, clapping his hands.

"Please, O king, allow us some time to consider this," Ugbaru said.

"Consider all you like," Koresh said, "but your sole option is to resign."

31. Rimush

A YOUNG MAN NAMED Rimush, a former minor official in the regent, Belshazzar's government, had been identified by some of Babylon's conquerors as having been popular among the people. In accordance with Koresh's liberal policies of occupation, Rimush was given a hasty overview of Persian law and made an official in the new regime. Like other natives drafted into Koresh's service, Rimush knew quite a bit about Daniel but almost nothing of Persian politics. So Rimush attended a special meeting called by Ugbaru and Behrouz never suspecting that he would hear a wicked proposal.

"We must completely ruin Belteshazzar," Ugbaru told the group.

They had convened at the citadel in a spacious ground level chamber flanked by arches and opening onto a sunlit court. Ugbaru had positioned armed watchmen at the entries to allow inside only those whose names appeared on a list. As the meeting began, platters with figs, dates and honeyed locusts were passed as treats.

Behrouz selected an insect and ate it. "It's true," he said, licking his lips. "The Jew, Belteshazzar, seeks to become second in the empire only to Koresh. If he succeeds we shall surely lose our power and possibly our lives."

Rimush rose to speak. "I am a descendant of that famed servant to Nebuchadnezzar, the instructor, Suusaandar," he said, "the same whose life Daniel once saved by resolving a royal dream no other man could. All Babylon knows Daniel to be a humble, holy man."

"He is called Belteshazzar," Ugbaru countered, "not Daniel, and is no friend of Persia or Babylon."

"A man of demonstrated power," Rimush shot back.

"For whose benefit?" Ugbaru asked. "What do you know?"

"I know that the God of Israel works miracles through him," Rimush said. "My grandfather witnessed one firsthand and heard of many others. I'll have nothing to do with a conspiracy." He stood to leave and several others rose to join him but Behrouz, pleading for unity, persuaded them to remain and hear a little more.

"Gentlemen, listen," Ugbaru said. "We have moved our families and fortunes great distances at the king's pleasure to serve him. Not only are our contributions ignored but we know undeserved praise is heaped upon our common enemy. Belteshazzar has deceived the king by cleverness. His invisible god threatens Persian tradition. He must be impugned."

The meeting got unruly when Rimush stood to speak again. Others heckled him down. "It is surely better to side with Persia," they said, "than trust our futures to a Jew."

Thus convinced, the majority spent the next hour trying to find a story, evidence or even a plausible lie with which to attack Daniel. But nothing came up. Finally Ugbaru said, "It seems clear we'll never find charges against him unless it concerns the laws of his god."

"It is wrong to plot against an innocent man," Rimush tried once more. "If we oppose God's own man we shall face grave consequences." But Rimush was shouted down again.

"Agreed, then," Ugbaru said, "we shall confound the schemes of Belteshazzar through exposing his beliefs."

The group chose several clever Persians to devise a trap based on Daniel's habits and customs. Rimush walked out before they began. "Tell the emperor," he said as he left, "that I stand with Daniel," again refusing to refer to Daniel by his given pagan name.

*

Ugbaru, Behrouz and volunteers quickly devised a trap based on Belteshazzar's well-known habit of praying in plain sight at his window each day. The only remaining question was when best to make their move against him. The emperor, they knew, was due to return to Babylon from Lydia later that day after overseeing an ongoing investigating into fraud.

"Missing gold," Behrouz said. "He'll be in an awful mood when he returns. Maybe we should wait?"

But they agreed, after discussion, that Koresh would likely be fatigued, thus less likely to think things through. So they petitioned to see the emperor at once, hoping to meet with him that evening.

*

Just as he arrived at the palace upon returning from Lydia, Koresh was met by an assistant saying that two of his administrators urgently wished to see him.

"Two," the king asked, "and not three?"

"Yes, and a handful of satraps, Sire," the man said.

"Tell them to assemble in the hall," the weary emperor sighed. "Arrange benches, light a fire and insist that they wait patiently. I need a meal and time to collect my thoughts."

"O king Darius, live forever!" Ugbaru said when they had assembled later (for Koresh was sometimes honored by that name to please the Medes). "Your royal administrators, prefects, satraps, advisors and governors have all agreed that the king should issue an edict and enforce the decree that anyone who prays to any god or man during the next thirty days, except to you, O king, shall be thrown into the lions' den."

Koresh blinked at them. "Urgent, you said. I'm missing a bath for this?"

"It is a great matter, O king," Ugbaru said. "As you know Persian tradition demands that you, Sire, are also a god. Prudence obliges us to extend your deity to this newly conquered land. It seems worthy of urgency, does it not?"

"I suppose," Koresh yawned. "Have you all agreed?"

"Yes, all," Ugbaru said, "a thirty day period during which we shall establish your power."

"Daniel too?"

"O king, he did not attend the meeting in which this proposal was fashioned."

"It seems odd to me," Koresh said, "that, with so many other pressing needs upon the empire, you fellows have gotten so worked up about this notion."

"We wish only to honor you, O king, and instruct and inspire your new subjects."

Koresh yawned again. He was tired and, though he did not wish to seem so, a bit confused. "I'm not convinced your proposal is consistent with my new persona; benign and enlightened conqueror? Admit it. Things are going well."

"All the more reason to act now, O king," Ugbaru said. "Issue the decree and put it into writing so that it cannot be altered in accordance with the laws of the Medes and the Persians which cannot be repealed."

"Ugbaru," Koresh said, "you and I have worked together for years now, is this not so?"

Ugbaru nodded.

"And you have thus far served me well. But I must warn you that your tone, just now, issue the decree and so forth, sounded quite a bit like an order. Surely, as a former military man, you can appreciate that my own precious mother would eventually find herself at risk if such unfortunate phrasing became her habit."

"Ugbaru does not speak for me, O king," Behrouz piped in quickly. "May all things transpire at your pleasure, in your time."

"That's wise of you," Koresh said. He snapped his fingers and an attendant appeared. "I will bathe in my quarters," he told him. Turning back to his petitioners, the king added, "Go home." They had begun to back out, bowing, when Koresh stopped them and added, "I've no time for these distractions. Do this thing if it seems good to you but never bother me concerning it again."

*

A quiet celebration followed outside the citadel, not far from the main gate on a pleasant, sun-swept green. Several satraps congratulated Ugbaru for his cleverness and nerve. "It is Belteshazzar's practice to pray to the god of the Jews each day in plain sight," they said. "Koresh has approved a perfect trap. Thanks to your courage, Ugbaru, Belteshazzar is doomed."

"But what will happen afterward," Behrouz asked, "when the king realizes that we... That you, Ugbaru, have tricked him?" All fell silent. "Surely you fellows considered it?"

"We shall do the thing in accordance with our laws," Ugbaru said. "Law, and tradition, bind our king. We will be perfectly safe from retribution."

"I have found that kings, when angry, may make laws as they wish," Behrouz said. "You campaigned beside him. Does Koresh seem to you the type who enjoys being bested?"

The celebration ended quickly after with Behrouz's pointed question still hanging in the air.

32. The story has only begun

ONE NIGHT, WHILE Daniel kneeled at prayer beside his upstairs window, someone knocked at his door. After first blowing a kiss in the direction of Jerusalem the prophet rose, stretched and answered. The interruption was no bother; his neighbors often came to chat with him, share personal stories or seek advice.

"Can I help you?" Daniel asked.

"My name is Rimush," the man said. "I live in town not far from here. Years ago I became an administrator in the city. When Koresh conquered Akkad he chose to not lop off my head."

"How wonderful," Daniel said. "Tell me, please, what brings you to my home?"

"Prophet," Rimush began, "this is our first full day under the decree..."

"Forbidding the offering up of prayer to any god save the king," Daniel said. "Yes, I well know of that one."

"Yet on my way home," Rimush said, "by the light in your room I could clearly see you on your knees at prayer. Others passing could easily see as well. The decree has been posted with trumpets and criers. For thirty days no man is to pray except to the emperor under penalty of death by lions."

"I do not thoughtlessly defy the king," Daniel said, "but you must understand that praying is more natural to me than breathing. How could I think to stop?"

The moon had come out. The evening air was damp and cool. Rimush had tied his horse at Daniel's garden rail. He hesitated to speak, looking back at it.

"You are uncomfortable," Daniel said. "I understand. Please, go. There's no need to risk your career and family's well-being out of concern for me."

"Wouldn't it be wise, prophet," Rimush whispered, "to stop your practice for just a spell? Thirty days is not long at all. Or, perhaps, simply step back a bit from your window so not to be seen?" He turned his palms up. "Surely your god won't mind if you pray from inside a closet for a while."

"I am sure he would forgive me."

"Good, then!" Rimush said. He leaned closer and spoke softly. "Prophet, this is the work of Ugbaru and Behrouz who have plotted to see you dead."

"Before you go," Daniel said, "would you like some fresh water from my well?"

"Please, sir, tell me what you'll do?"

"I will pray as always," Daniel said, "leaving ambition to men and justice to God."

Rimush clutched his fists. "But they will see you at it. They will demand your death according to Persian law. The king will not be able to reverse it, prophet, it would be a glaring inconsistency. He is officially a god, you see. He approved the decree as a god of the state and gods make no mistakes."

"My God makes no mistakes," Daniel said. "I have knelt before him every day for decades, praying for the return of my people to Jerusalem. And that season seems nigh!"

"So you've won," Rimush said. "Live to see it. You've done enough."

Tears formed in Daniel's eyes though they remained as bright as ever. He pulled a delicate chain from under his tunic and showed Rimush a beautifully polished stone.

"It's stunning," Rimush said, a bit confused.

"While King Nebuchadnezzar still lived," Daniel told him, "I persuaded his royal jeweler to bore a perfect hole through this little gem and he did so, then he strung it on this delicate chain. The Egyptians call the mineral sekal. The desert people say anbar."

"It glows with exquisite light," Rimush said. "But why show me?"

"It's just a stone," Daniel sighed, "a reminder of the holy city and nothing more. Except, I suppose, it has also served as a symbol of my faith. And as one should with faith I have polished it every day. My rule is to never compromise concerning my duty to the God of Israel. I pray that I have not. I pray I never shall. So if kneeling here as always means I may not see the day that Jerusalem is restored..."

"You certainly will not see it," Rimush said, "if you continue to follow your god."

"Who shall I follow then, friend?" Daniel chuckled. "Koresh? Mazda? The fiery bull?"

"I know better than to argue, sir," Rimush answered, starting toward his horse. "I thank you for your service to Babylon. One day I hope to tell my children and grandchildren the story of this meeting and how you stood so strong."

"The story has only begun," Daniel said, waving goodbye. The need to pray even longer and more fervently suddenly struck Daniel. Something about his parting words to his neighbor had set him trembling head to toe.

*

Koresh was still dealing with problems caused by embezzlement in Lydia when Ugbaru, Behrouz, and several satraps came to the palace one morning and demanded to see him. "What now?" he asked. "I warn you fellows, I grow weary of your pettiness, day to day."

"O king," Ugbaru said, "did you not decree that for thirty days anyone who made petition to any god except you, O king, would be thrown into the lions' pit?"

The emperor's eyes narrowed. "Yes," he said softly, "I did."

"The matter is fixed as a law of the Medes and Persians which cannot be revoked."

"I am well aware. Go on."

Ugbaru motioned for the satraps behind him to step forward. "It saddens us to say, O king, that Belteshazzar…"

"Daniel," Koresh gasped.

"…has defied your decree; praying on his knees to a foreign god before a multitude of witnesses…" Ugbaru pointed to his allies and they bowed. "…entreating the Hebrew god and thus insulting you, O king, defying inviolate Persian law. His insolence and lack of…"

"Enough!" Koresh shouted. He rose from his chair and stood eye to eye with Ugbaru, daring the coward to look at him. "You must think yourself quite clever, now, general," he hissed, "now that I see the trap you've set."

"We only wish to…"

"Stop," Koresh said. He preferred not to show emotion but he had once trusted these men. "You, of all people," he said, shaking with rage.

"O king," Ugbaru said, "we are a nation of law sacrosanct, am I correct?"

Koresh refused to answer.

"Can a god-king err? Is this Jew above our law?"

"So far, general," Koresh said, forcing a smile, "you and yours have played a clever game."

"Majesty," Behrouz said, bowing deeply, "I play no games and would never hope to outwit you. Full credit for ingenuity in this circumstance accrues only to my brilliant friend." He gestured toward Ugbaru, who glared back at him hatefully.

"You are craven, Behrouz," Koresh laughed, "but your lack of nerve may yet serve you better than your pal's daring when this ends." He called for the royal secretary. "Think fast now all of you." The king's gaze passed from eye to eye. "Each of you must now go on record with this so carefully consider your next move. I can be clever too. And while it is true I am bound by our law I also have immense resources. Hear me, kings are not accustomed to being manipulated. I intend from the core of my liver, from the marrow in my bones, to teach an utterly bitter lesson to every man here, and his entire family, who dares to contend with me now."

Every eye turned to Ugbaru who, to his credit, never blinked.

The royal secretary appeared. "So," the king shouted, "say you all as one and separately that the Hebrew gentleman Daniel, whom you call Belteshazzar, must, according to our law and your solemn witness, be cast to lions?"

No one spoke.

"Come now, you lovers of law," Koresh shouted. "Be men. Speak up."

Hasdrubal, the High Priest of Marduk, stepped forward. "O king," he said, "forgive me, for I now clearly see that I have no tale to tell today. This matter is no concern of mine."

The others frowned as he stepped back.

"You have learned your trade well, priest," Koresh said. "Out then, quickly. I expect it will be a solid career move."

"For while I revere Marduk as is my honor and duty," Hasdrubal said at the door, "I have also witnessed the power of the god of the Jews." He looked at those he had accompanied to the citadel. "Belteshazzar is his servant and I shall contend with neither. By your grace, O king, I pray that you spare Belteshazzar. I hasten to be gone."

"Any other changes of heart?" the king asked after Hasdrubal left.

"We stand together under the law," Ugbaru said, "unlike the cowardly priest."

Koresh directed his secretary to record the names of every man remaining in the room. "Each must place his seal alongside the entry," he said.

"O king, they must be ravenous lions," Ugbaru added when the business was done, "as required by your word and our law."

"They'll be hungry, my passionate servant," Koresh answered, "I promise you that, and thus we have condemned a brilliant old man to be ripped to shreds." He stopped to consider something then smiled. "But what do you fellows think, knowing his people's reliance on miracles, of the old Jew's chances to survive?"

Behrouz was the first to laugh. Soon his peers joined in. "He will be torn, O king," said Ugbaru, "completely limb from limb."

Koresh snapped his fingers and the secretary handed him the roster of accusers. "I'll remember each of you," he said scanning their names. "I confess amazement at your willingness to anger me. But keep in mind that you have also dared to challenge the Hebrew prophet Daniel and his god."

All but Ugbaru and Behrouz lowered their heads.

"If I can find no way under our law to save my brightest servant from my unwitting decree," the king said, "this drama will begin exactly as you have hoped, in a den of lions."

"Thank you, O king," Ugbaru said. "May justice be served."

"Justice above all!" Koresh shouted as his visitors hurried out. "And we shall see what we shall see."

33. No god, no faith, no magic

O N THE SAME day the prayer-ban was issued, Ugbaru had ordered the royal game warden to trap several huge cats from the southern district and hold them for the upcoming execution. The project had energized the former general; Belteshazzar had humiliated him at the council table. How sweet to arrange revenge!

"The bigger, hungrier and more powerful these lions you find, the better," Ugbaru said.

"Cats in this region feed on antelope, gazelle, warthog, wildebeest and zebra," the warden told him. "A big cat needs about fifteen pounds of meat each day, give or take, but they generally have no taste for man."

"But they will eat one if hungry enough, right?"

The warden supposed that was true.

"Then gather several, make sure that they are starving and of course we'll need a den."

"There's a good cave north, not far from the city," the warden said. "It's man made, set into a hillside, dug out for livestock long ago by a local militia."

Soon after the warden had collected the cats, Ugbaru, Behrouz and the warden rode out to the site on horseback, a short ride on mostly well-traveled lanes. The cave lay cupped against a gentle hill at the base of more severely rising slopes. The entryway was framed by rough-cut wooden planks. Beyond it a slope tumbled quickly into darkness laced with coils of spinning dust. A boulder partially blocked the entry, having replaced hinged wooden gates that had rotted away.

While Ugbaru watched, the warden's men brought up eight magnificent animals in carts, seven hunting females and a prodigious male. They parked the carts in a shaded grove not far from the cave. "They are already famished," the warden said. "They have plenty of water but will soon need meat."

"Perfect," Ugbaru said. "The king trembles like a woman hoping Belteshazzar will survive. It is impossible. He cannot."

"But he is set on revenge because of what we've done," Behrouz said. "Even if we succeed in destroying Belteshazzar how can you be sure that we…?"

"Can a king pout?" Ugbaru interrupted. "No, the emperor of Persia is above all a practical man. That has been his genius all along. When our Koresh hears the so-called prophet's screams the god of the Jews will be discredited forever."

"You are completely sure?" Behrouz asked.

Ugbaru refused to answer, sick of his peer's whining. He planned to turn on Behrouz next.

*

Koresh deliberated until sundown, weighing Daniel's fate. Persia, as Persia, was a relatively new entity but Media and its rigid traditions spanned many more centuries. Regardless, there was no precedent in either culture to allow a god-king to reverse a decree. God-kings, by definition, were never wrong. Koresh had been tricked into issuing an edict that meant his friend's death. "But it would be an unforgivable sign of weakness to do other than kill you as stipulated," he explained to Daniel, who had been summoned to the palace to hear the bad news. "If I wasn't simply shamed and run off for doing otherwise," the king said, "I'd certainly be assassinated. And on good grounds. Then what would Persia do?"

"I understand, O king," Daniel said, "and I am eager to move on."

"Eager?" Koresh sighed. "Daniel, I'm humbled by your generosity and your faith. Your god, whom you serve constantly, he must save you; but do you really think he can?"

"He is able if he wishes," Daniel answered, "but in either case I have no concern. Though my role is uncertain, the outcome, my people's return to their land, is not."

"I have never seen Judah," the king said, "but how beautiful Jerusalem must be."

*

Koresh allowed Daniel to return home before his execution. Daniel slept well that evening after spending another long spell at his window engaged in illegal prayer. In the morning, palace deputies arrested

Daniel at his door and led him out of town to join a mounted procession that included Ugbaru, Behrouz and Koresh himself.

Daniel's neighbors ran out and objected as the guards led him away. Many followed after them. When they learned that Daniel was to be ravaged by lions they shouted and threw rocks. Ugbaru ordered their arrest but Koresh forbade it.

"If only you two had a fraction of their loyalty," he said.

*

Daniel heard the lions snarling long before arriving at the cave. He could also hear Ugbaru and Behrouz as they spoke, for they rode quite near. "Do you think," Behrouz asked, "that there's any chance that this fellow, once master of Nebuchadnezzar's magicians... This man who many say is personally protected by the Hebrew god..."

"Could survive?" Ugbaru finished for him. He tilted his head to the wind and grinned. "Listen! Do you hear them? The cats smell us. They smell the Jew! There is no god, no faith, no magic... Nothing can save a man from such rage."

"But when I was a boy in Anšan," Behrouz said, "I heard of three men, this fellow's friends it's said, who laughed at Nebuchadnezzar himself while dancing in a fire."

"Fairy tales," Ugbaru sniffed. "I've heard those stories too."

*

They halted on a grassy flat before the cave. Koresh waited for the rearguard of the short caravan to advance and stop. He stood in his stirrups and saluted the man he was about to put to death and asked, "Have you last words, my friend, before we finish this?"

"I have but one word, O king," Daniel said, "Jerusalem!"

Koresh nodded. "Trust, then, Daniel," he said, "that I'll honor my decree restoring your people to their homeland." He looked toward where the blue foothills of Babylon rose to meet the gray mists shrouding the mountains of the Medes. "I understand your feelings," he told those of Daniel's angry neighbors who had followed, "and I promise you that somehow justice will be done." Then he faced Daniel's accusers. "Will anyone among you," he asked, "speak against this deed this morning, while he may?"

But the king heard only lions roaring and the sighs of the listless wind.

Koresh signaled. His game warden stepped forward and shouted an order. Oxen strained as they hauled up several pitching carts filled with frenzied lions. King's men rolled away the boulder at the cave mouth and guards bearing pikes opened the carts one by one and goaded the ravenous beasts inside.

When they finished, Ugbaru read Daniel's condemnation aloud. "It's time," he said when he had finished. "Throw him in."

Not waiting to be coerced, Daniel dismounted, stepped lively to the den then slipped inside. Guards rolled the big stone behind him and sealed the cave. Everyone held his breath, listening as leaves rattled in the trees in a nearby grove. An eagle shrieked in the distant sky but they heard not one sound from the cave.

"No noise, men?" Koresh asked. "What do you law-loving councilors make of that?"

"The rock at the mouth is so massive, Majesty," Ugbaru suggested, "the fit so tight…?" He shrugged. "The animals are starved for meat. We'll see justice by morning."

Justice, again. Koresh smiled. "Maybe, we shall," he said. "Let's finish up."

An attendant brought forward a wax pot for the king's royal seal. Koresh ordered his councilors to join him beside the pit where guards drove stakes on both sides of the boulder then wound leather lashing back and forth across its face. Koresh marked the softened wax on the central knot with his seal then required his administrators to do the same.

"What will the king do to us," Behrouz asked on the ride back, "if Belteshazzar somehow survives?"

"He cannot survive."

"But you did notice the look on that madman's face?"

"Yes," Ugbaru answered, "when Belteshazzar stepped into the cave, he was smiling."

34. Marduk pays better

DANIEL STOOD IN the pit able to smell lions but he could not see them. When one brushed against his leg Daniel fell to his knees and shouted, "I thank you, living and eternal King!" expecting those words to be his last.

The beast moved away but the next instant a blast of hot breath from behind lifted Daniel's hair. The prophet shut his eyes to die but he did not. So he whispered, instead, another quick, all-inclusive thank you to the Lord. When still nothing bad had happened he dared to open one eye. Eight pairs of glowing yellow orbs blinked back at him close enough to touch.

"I thank you, Lord," Daniel said in a whisper, "for preserving me thus far."

Nothing.

So Daniel thanked God again, this time for his mother and father, "though I can no longer imagine their faces and barely knew them."

He remained unharmed.

"I thank you, O God of Israel," he said a bit louder, "for sweet Ya'el, daughter of poor Ahiel, though I sometimes struggle to remember her face too." Again, the lions simply stared at him. After listening to the beasts breathe a bit longer, Daniel thanked God for King Josiah and Jerusalem, "though the king was murdered by Pharaoh and your holy city sacked."

His knees began to ache. How wonderful, he thought, to have survived long enough to become uncomfortable! At a bit of a loss then, having made no firm plans beyond stepping into the cave, Daniel whispered, "Thank you for Isaiah." An ear-splitting roar sent him sailing backward before a second, stronger blast threw him forward on his face. He lay where he landed, spitting dirt, ears ringing, and after a time felt fit enough to resume hallelujahs on his knees.

Habakkuk, Jeremiah, Ezekiel, Hananiah, Mishael, Azariah and even Nebuchadnezzar were brought before the Lord. "Please forgive the king's blindness," Daniel prayed, "if he really was blind, and rather reward his genius, noble spirit and unwitting service."

At that point it seemed like the animals were listening. So Daniel went on praising and breathing and wondering. How did this experience with Koresh's lions compare with his friends' dancing, long ago, in Nebuchadnezzar's raging fire?

"Thank you, thank you, thank you," Daniel whispered, surprised to be alive. Maybe the secret to survival and personal peace had been gratitude all along?

*

Koresh had an awful night; no food, no peace, no rest. On the evening Daniel entered the pit, the king of Persia... Was he not the most powerful man in the world? ...felt neither powerful, hopeful nor in control. Daniel had fallen victim to a wicked plot while on Koresh's watch because the emperor had failed to see it coming. He felt helpless at the moment, but fully able to exact revenge at a later date. He rose from bed, splashed his face and sent a runner to fetch Hasdrubal.

"What do you know, priest," Koresh asked when Hasdrubal arrived, "of the conspiracy to kill my friend?"

It was the dark of morning. The emperor's chamber flickered with soft light from candles set at both ends of the table at which the two men sat. "O king, live forever," Hasdrubal said. "I was inexperienced when I rose to this station but had already seen more than enough in Babylon to know well that the Jews, Belteshazzar, Shadrach, Meshach and Abednego, were favored by the gods."

"By one god, Elohim," Koresh said, a correction, not a question.

Hasdrubal lowered his eyes. "Yes, him."

"The one God, Creator of the Universe, say you?" Koresh asked.

"I am the High Priest of Marduk. I can say no more."

"You are a clever young man," Koresh said, "and you spar well. But I can see that you, like me, have, shall we say, doubts, about our once certain attitudes. How do we make sense of recent events? These Jews and their law, their prophets, their writings, their miracles; there are none like them in all creation for willfulness, for stubbornness..."

"And for faith."

"Yes!" Koresh answered. "Even wholesale slaughter cannot keep them down for long." The king's eyes darkened. "But tell me, priest," he said, "under the local laws of Babylon, where exactly would Marduk stand… Can advisors be summarily put to death at the king's will?"

"You want to…"

"Kill all my help, every stinking, scheming one of them, yes."

"In Babylon," Hasdrubal said, "despite our lawful traditions, monarchs have regularly done as they've pleased."

Koresh smiled.

"But it has always gone best when… The people, O king, stand most solidly behind those who follow and rule by law."

"It's the same in Persia," Koresh sighed. "With the Medes as well. They are pampered."

"One must be lawfully charged, tried and found guilty by you, by a court, or at least in the court of public opinion."

"What say Marduk and Babylon of treason?" Koresh asked.

"Always punishable by death here in town."

"Wonderful," Koresh said, "I say the lot of those who tricked me are traitors."

Hasdrubal trembled as he spoke. "O king, Belteshazzar was condemned to die because witnesses saw him defy your decree. To establish that his accusers are traitors, they themselves must be shown to have clearly lied or done a disservice in bad faith."

"Like…?"

Hasdrubal shrugged. "If, maybe, Belteshazzar survived the night…"

"No man could have lasted two minutes in that cave," Koresh said.

Hasdrubal whispered by candlelight. "The day before old Enshunu died, O king, that famous priest summoned me personally to his bedside, though I was only his assistant at the time. Enshunu confessed to me then, wracked by disease and quaking with fear, that as a much younger man he witnessed three Jews dance unharmed in a white hot fire."

"The legend of the furnace," Koresh sighed in a hushed breath. "We know it even in Persia."

"Fearless Nebuchadnezzar himself, Enshunu told me, nearly fainted away."

"Do you suppose that story is true?"

"I would never contend with their god."

"But Daniel is dead."

"You heard his screams, then?" Hasdrubal asked.

"Strangely, no."

Hasdrubal began to nod, a look so odd it first irritated, then excited the king. "Tell me every detail you heard from the old high priest," Koresh ordered, "about those Hebrew children whom Nebuchadnezzar tried to burn alive."

*

Daniel awoke flat on his face, no idea how long he had been out. By then the cave smelled powerfully of lions; lion skin, lion hair, lion excrement. He listened to the beasts as their breath blew past his ears like wind. They lay hunkered inches away, chins on their paws, so close he might have touched one by simply raising a finger. He watched as their eyes blinked randomly in pairs before him, on and off. Then he noticed a glow beside him.

"Who...?" he began, but the gleam somehow prompted Daniel to remain still. Full of wonder, Daniel blinked for quite some at the presence beside him. Occasionally one of the big cats groaned while Daniel fought to remain awake, hoping to see more.

*

When Hasdrubal finished telling the emperor of Persia all he knew, Koresh threatened to behead him for getting his hopes up. "But you've heard the same story yourself," Hasdrubal said, "Hundreds witnessed the gods' sparing of those three that day."

"One god," Koresh corrected again. "That's the whole point of this, right?"

"Again, O king, I am who I am. The high priesthood of Marduk is a wonderful job if one can avoid assassination, though it has admittedly diminished in prestige from the days of Nebuchadnezzar. But in private thoughts, Sire, much like Enshunu, I have wondered if..."

"You are afraid to say it," Koresh charged.

Hasdrubal nodded in shame.

"Having seen real miracles in his name," Koresh said, "why wouldn't Enshunu have abandoned Marduk at once and followed the God of Israel?"

"There seems to be no future in it," Hasdrubal said. "Marduk certainly pays better. But who knows? Enshunu may have embraced the God of Israel in his heart. I suspect many Akkadian eyes were forced open this past half century by these Jews in our midst. Though I have never heard a wayward Akkadian prayer I confess I have wondered, who conquered who?"

"If only there was a chance that God might have saved Daniel last night," Koresh said, "as he is alleged to have saved his friends in the fire."

"I understand that the four of them prayed," Hasdrubal said. "That they prayed and prayed."

Koresh dropped to his knees. "Let us pray then," he said. "Say one now."

"O king," Hasdrubal said, "daybreak approaches. The deed is surely done."

"You think, priest, that the creator of the universe could not reverse a matter if he wished after an especially compelling prayer?" Hasdrubal joined the emperor on his knees. "Start at once," Koresh said, "to Elohim."

"Me, O king? I specialize in chants, smoke, tricks with fire and women and, of course, entreating idols."

"God's mercy extends to the nations," Koresh said. "I read that myself in Daniel's scroll." Hasdrubal hesitated. The king became impatient. "Lower your doubting head, priest," he said, "and I'll show you how it's done." So Koresh the Great, emperor of Persia, offered up a long request to God split equally between revenge and Daniel's preservation. When finished he ordered the priest to wait while he summoned his captain. "Collect all of Daniel's accusers and their families," the king ordered. "I have a list. We will ride together to the cave, afterward, to see if the prophet has survived."

35. A fruitless exercise

WITH ONE WORD, Koresh, emperor of Persia, could dispatch hundreds of thousands of soldiers into battle overnight. After his most recent conquests, with only a nod, the king could launch a thousand ships from the coast at the Western Sea. He could divert rivers, raze cities, and erect monuments by making suggestions and displace kings by mentioning their names. But Koresh's early morning order to gather all Daniel's accusers did not go well at all.

"Dispatch king's men to the homes of those on my list," he had said. "Bring them with their sons, daughters, aunts, uncles and mothers-in-law. Leave behind only concubines and slaves." But the post-invasion chaos that had followed decades of rampant immigration had severely bogged things down. Records were scarce or sometimes non-existent.

"Many remain unfound, O king," his captain reported shortly before sunrise.

Koresh looked down into the lower courtyard from his chamber. Scores of men, women and children related to and including those on his calculated vengeance list had already been herded there by torch-light to make the trip to Daniel's cave.

"To recover them all," the captain said, "might require the remainder of the day."

Before Koresh could answer, Ugbaru appeared in the hall outside the emperor's door half-dressed, unwashed and uncombed. "O king, live forever," he spat, "I must see you now. I and my wife, my mother, my children and my Babylonian bride have all been mistreated in my home. I demand…"

"You demand?" Koresh said, pausing to consider his servant's half-shut eyes and frilly gown. "Do you really sleep in that getup?"

Ugbaru stammered.

"Never mind," Koresh said. "I've decided, Captain," he addressed his man. "We'll leave for the den in the hills with whom we have."

"This is about Belteshazzar?" Ugbaru asked. "He's dead, O king. He's plainly dead. It's physics. Why must I and my family…?"

Koresh raised his hand and Ugbaru stopped speaking. "Do you hear that chaos in the courtyard, Ugbaru?" the king asked. "Go there now, then you and Behrouz…" He stopped to ask his captain, "You did manage to take Behrouz into custody am I right?" The soldier nodded. "Good show! Hurry down to that little mob, Ugbaru, and see if you and your accomplice are leaders enough to calm them down. We will march very soon."

"And the others?" the captain asked, holding up the emperor's list.

Koresh looked down again into the courtyard at those who had been gathered. "These will do," he said. "The ones we missed can count their lives charmed if all goes well. Summon wagons and carts, Captain. The sun will soon rise. If Daniel has survived, Ugbaru, his innocence is proven, correct? And won't justice demand a like test for his accusers?"

"The question is moot, Majesty, Daniel is dead," Ugbaru said, "but for the record I will add very strongly that I could not disagree more."

"How fortunate I find myself," Koresh said. "According to the laws of Persia and the Medes, which you so highly regard, your opinion matters in this instance not one whit."

"Respectfully, O king, this is a costly and fruitless exercise," Ugbaru said. "We'll find nothing in that cave up north but satisfied beasts and the splintered bones of a Jew."

Koresh trembled with anger but answered simply, "We shall, of course, soon see."

36. The law is the law

F OG LAY IN the low spots before Daniel's cave when the king and his party arrived. Ugbaru, Behrouz, their families and the collected kin of all the others who had been collected that morning stood waiting in common carts, king's orders, shivering and in foul moods. Koresh had enjoyed observing their discomfort en route but had arrived at the cave site a bit down. He was after all a soldier, not a man of faith; had he been a fool to hope for a miracle?

He ordered the seals across the cave mouth examined and, when verified intact, he directed his men to sever the lashes and roll aside the boulder that blocked the way. A warden's man got into position up front holding a whip in each hand. To prevent an attack, men bearing pikes formed a long, secure aisle either side of the cave mouth leading back to the animal wagons but the first cat out of the cave bolted so quickly he was able to maul one of them before his peers could pull him free.

The severely mangled fellow was dragged aside and, with increased caution, the remaining animals were led out one by one with no further problems. The animals, after their transfer, nearly tipped their carts as they snarled, fought and bounded side to side.

"They don't look satisfied to me," Behrouz said.

"A single smallish man was nowhere meal enough," Ugbaru explained. "Do you see Belteshazzar or hear him? No, you do not, because he's been consumed." Ugbaru pushed against the bolted gate of his cart. "O king, justice is done," he said. "The lawbreaker is dead. Free us now and summon horses, I beg you, so our families may return home."

"Go down there, Captain," Koresh sighed, "and confirm this."

The captain started toward the cave mouth then stopped to count.

"Eight in, eight out" the warden told him. "You can proceed."

As the captain strode to the cave, Koresh noticed Ugbaru's second bride standing in a cart and holding a small child in her arms begin to weep in great sobs.

"Why cry, little girl?" Koresh asked. "It has not been that difficult a ride?"

"The man you've murdered," she answered, "is a hero of Babylon."

Ugbaru's proper family backed away from the little mother in their already crowded cart.

"A hero you say?" Koresh answered. "So I've heard. But you seem much too young…"

"I am of the royal line of Nabopolassar," she said. "My grandfather's father was brother to Nebuchadnezzar, who dearly loved the man you have so dishonorably destroyed." She sobbed again. "And though Belteshazzar ignored our gods, Babylon had no better friend. There has never been a holy man his equal; none knew what Belteshazzar knew."

"But, young lady," Koresh said, genuinely curious, "haven't you guessed by now that if Daniel had survived this morning, every one of you would soon be…?"

"This heartless murder will be a black mark against your name forever," the woman interrupted her king, "and Persia as well." She spit over the cart rail in the direction of the world's most powerful man.

"She doesn't speak for us, Sire," Ugbaru shouted as his family wailed with embarrassment. "Remove them, at once, from my presence," he said, wiggling his fingers at mother and child. "I divorce her! She is forever banished from my home."

Not to be seen smiling, Koresh faced the cave. "What's keeping you?" he shouted to his captain. Instead of inspecting the pit as ordered the soldier had stopped again, this time to speak with the game warden.

"O king," the captain called back, "your man wishes to leave at once for Babylon with the beasts. He says they are weak and starving. If not fed soon they may well die."

Koresh and the priest, Hasdrubal, who had ridden along at the king's command, traded quick looks. "Starving, you say?" Koresh asked. "Please, then, impose upon my warden to humor me a bit and hold his cats a while longer. With God's grace I may yet need them."

A child cried out, pointing toward the cave. There appeared first a waving hand then the wizened head of an old man emerging from the mist.

"Is that you, Daniel," Koresh shouted, "servant of the living God? Has your god been able to rescue you from the lions?"

"O king, live forever!" came an answer from the prophet. "God sent his angel," he said, shading his eyes from the low angling light, "and he has shut the mouths of the lions."

Ugbaru wailed as though stabbed in the heart but the soldiers, the warden, Daniel's other accusers and all their families fell to their knees to pray.

Daniel continued at a roar. "They have not hurt me because I was found innocent in his sight. Nor have I ever done any wrong before you, O king."

Koresh felt faint. Beside him, the High Priest of Marduk, the world's most thorough and accomplished pagan, put trembling fingers to his mouth and began to cry. "I have crossed the great plain and conquered millions," the king shouted, "yet I have never…" He stopped to point in Daniel's direction. The gesture sent soldiers rushing to assist him and, when Daniel stood before the king, no wound was found upon him because he had trusted in his God.

"You have killed us," Behrouz snapped at his Persian peer while still upon his knees but Ugbaru was too stricken by what he had witnessed to answer the charge.

Daniel stood before the king, his long white hair neat and glowing, his skin clear and clean. Even the prophet's robes had remained spotless and bright. After stretching a bit and, of course smiling according to his habit, he nodded thanks to those who had helped him then fell to his knees. "I thank you, living and eternal King, God of all creation," he called out, and no one challenged that notion.

In all his days Koresh the Great had never imagined such a scene, sitting his horse while grown men and women babbled, prayed and hugged one another desperately. Hasdrubal said in a voice so thin the king could hardly hear, "This is surely how it was when the Prophet Daniel's three friends danced in Nebuchadnezzar's furnace so very long ago."

"Well, then!" Koresh shouted, rising in his stirrups to meet his servants' eyes. "Throughout my kingdom all are to fear and tremble before the mighty God of Daniel. He is a living God and he endures forever. His kingdom is indestructible and his dominion endless. He delivers and rescues and does signs and wonders in heaven and on earth. He has delivered Daniel from the lions' power."

*

The emperor of Persia dismounted and embraced Daniel like a brother. "I present to you Daniel," he announced, "not Belteshazzar, who stands beside me this morning safe and strong after enduring a night with ravenous lions, delivered by the God of Israel's powerful right arm. This man is as precious to the empire, as valuable to me, his king, as he ever was to Babylon."

While almost everyone cheered, Daniel felt a sudden weight upon his spirit.

"I say, then…" The emperor seemed to pause to add drama, peering from face to face at those who had falsely charged his man, "…that the miracle we have witnessed this morning establishes beyond doubt that Daniel was wrongly accused." He shouted, eyes exceedingly wild, "Tell me, then, people, is this not so?"

No one answered. The king's horse huffed and hoofed the ground.

"Majesty," Hasdrubal spoke meekly at the king's side, "given this wonder of mercy, this answer to prayer, might justice best be served if we also…"

"Quiet," Koresh said. The priest bent at the waist while still upon his horse and skillfully reigned the animal back. "Upon the point of false witness," Koresh continued, "the laws of Persia, Media and Babylon are in accord and perfectly clear." He stopped, interrupted again by a whisper at his ear.

"What are you doing?" Daniel asked, failing to address the king properly.

"Turn the creatures back in," Koresh ordered the warden, ignoring Daniel, pointing first to the carted lions then to the den. "Captain, form your men again in lines either side to assist."

Daniel touched Koresh's shoulder, a second offense against the state, and said, "O king, I beg you, do not harm these people."

"You are a man of God, Daniel," Koresh answered. "I am an emperor with distinctly different burdens." With his eyes as cold and dark as they had been bright and joyful when Daniel appeared safe from the cave, the king of Persia pointed to Ugbaru, Behrouz and the assembled satraps and their families, saying, "Rest easy, warden, your beasts shall soon be fed."

A cry went up then, not from the condemned but from Daniel, the prophet, who had fallen again to his knees. "O king," he cried, "one of your servants already lies mortally wounded by these animals. Spare these men, their mothers, fathers, wives and children. Let us leave this site together knowing in our hearts that God's justice is perfect, knowing that nothing more needs to be done by us except to be watchful for God's mercy as he freely extends it to us."

"The law," Koresh said softly, "is the law. And these astute men have been steadily preaching to me, their king, the importance of law. Preaching to me..." he shouted. Then, more quietly, "...their king, for days, about its importance. Would you not think, then, that this judgment of mine would please them, so high has been their regard for blind compliance?"

"But vengeance is mine, says the Lord!"

"No," Koresh said soberly, "in Persia and now also in Babylon, vengeance is mine."

Upon the emperor's orders, the captain's men formed an aisle leading back from the carts to the mouth of the cave. The fractious cats were then directed back inside one by one. The witnesses against Daniel, now the king's condemned, were then led beside the cave and made to stand in rank and file to await the king's command.

During all this Daniel tore his clothes, scooped handfuls of dirt and wiped his face with them, then more upon on his shoulders, chest and hair.

"Get up," Koresh said, before issuing the order, "you are a spectacle."

"Kill me too if you must, O king," Daniel said, "but I shall not rise."

Even Daniel sensed the irony, then. He, the consistently joyful man who once calmly weighed God's justice against the murder of his parents, who as a boy had somehow found reason to smile while Jerusalem burned, who had reflected upon God's goodness when King Zedekiah lost both his family and his eyes, now kneeled wailing in the dirt on behalf of those who had wished to kill him.

"Please, great king!" he shouted. "Please, O holy God of Israel! When shall it stop? How much blood is required, O God? What purpose shall more murder serve?"

Even Behrouz seemed touched.

"If you can't decipher these mysteries, O prophet," Koresh asked mildly, "how might ordinary men such as ourselves begin to understand? Now, please sir, rise."

But Daniel remained on his knees. As a boy in Jerusalem before Josiah died, he, Mishael, Hananiah and Azariah would sometimes smile at the laments of the old prophet, Habakkuk, in the streets. Soiled, miserable and forlorn on even the most beautiful days the man of God would wail…

> *How long, O Lord, must I call for help, but you do not listen?*
>
> *Or cry out to you, "Violence!" but you do not save?*

It was possible that Daniel's grief, that morning, surpassed even Habakkuk's.

Koresh glared at him. "Once more I say to you, arise."

"Do as you please to me," Daniel sighed, for a third time that morning insulting the king with improper address, neither did he bow nor face Koresh as he spoke. "Man has dishonored God with violence since Adam. I am done with it. I am spent." He scooped more soil and let it sift through his hands. "Dust to dust," he said. "I've lost everything and even now do not doubt my Creator. Even now I revere him with all my heart, soul and strength…but surely, surely I do not understand his ways."

"These men willingly played this lethal game," Koresh said. "Do you think for a moment, Daniel, Nebuchadnezzar would have hesitated an instant to destroy them if in my place?"

"No," Daniel said, "but will you, Koresh the Great, show mercy and spare them now?"

"He challenges the king for us," Behrouz said as he waited in line to die. "Why?"

"Because he's a fool," Ugbaru said.

"Ah!" Behrouz raised his chin. "I see now, thanks to your wisdom, Ugbaru, that yonder Daniel is the fool in this comedy. But I remain a bit confused. Daniel's god preserved him against lions without spot. Shall we, then, expect Ahura-Mazda or the great bull to do as much for us?"

Ugbaru had no answer.

Koresh faced his captain. "To the cave with them now," he said, "as justice demands."

"All of them, Sire?"

"All but Daniel, your men, the warden, his men and this man, of course," Koresh said, his hand on Hasdrubal's shoulder, "a clever fellow who knew whom to back. Spare her as well," Koresh said, pointing to Ugbaru's haughty teenage Babylonian bride, "and of course her child, royal blood of Nabopolassar. She possesses the bearing and mettle of a queen."

The guards set to work. The condemned cried for mercy but the king held firm. No miracle followed. Every man, woman and child was forced down the slope and into the pit where lions fed on their flesh.

VII. Jerusalem

37. Never diddle with an emperor

SEVEN DECADES AFTER King Josiah died, Daniel finally succumbed to agony, grieving not for himself nor his people nor for his friends but for his enemies. He continued to pray at his window in town each day but found little comfort in it. The king's unexpected cruelty haunted him.

"As I've explained," Koresh sighed, as they spoke one day at the citadel soon after, "as king I was bound to destroy them by the same principle that would have killed you had God not intervened. You must remember, Daniel, the word of a monarch is the word of a god."

"There is but one God and your word is nothing like his."

"Well," Koresh smiled, "recent events prove again, Daniel, it remains a very good rule of thumb to never diddle with an emperor." He chuckled a little. "I don't expect you to approve of what I've done but I do want you to be aware that I enjoyed doing my enemies in. I found it cleansing, invigorating and renewing."

Daniel blinked at him.

"Think, now," Koresh said, "the miracle that preserved you preserved me as well. If you, a well-known favorite of mine, had died as a result of that cheap little plot all Babylon would have seen me bested by my servants. Word of my embarrassment would certainly have spread throughout the empire. Then where would we all be?"

Daniel shrugged, uninterested, unimpressed.

"I spared Ugbaru's little Babylonian bride and her child, remember that?"

"Yes. I thank you," Daniel said.

"Enough, then," Koresh said. "Remember too, my friend, that if I had lost my magnificent aura as a result of this interlude I may well have also lost the ability to grant your wish regarding the restoration of Jerusalem. As it is I can now do as I please without repercussion. There remains not one soul in the empire willing to mess with me." He snapped his fingers. A servant handed him a tablet. "I have here a roster of candidates to replace the satraps we lost to the lions. I've also jotted down a short list of prospects to govern with you. What do you say?"

"O king, I'm truly tired…"

"If you wish, then, Daniel, I shall not replace them. You can rule alone as my right hand. Egypt is next to fall you know. We'll march their way before too long."

"And that will be the end of them," Daniel sighed.

"Yes, after thousands of years!"

"O king," Daniel said, "live forever. My homeland and family are mere memories, my dear friends are gone, my joints are stiff and my body aches. I remind you again of your promise. I ask, just as the Prophet Moses called upon Pharaoh almost a thousand years ago, please, O king, let my people go."

Beyond an open window Babylon sparkled in the sun, its tall palms dipping in the breeze along Processional Way. In the square atop the ziggurat pennants flapped and a great fire burned. "Beyond these walls in all directions," Daniel said, "live tens of thousands of exiles, the sons, daughters and grandchildren of exiles from Judah, eager to return to a place they've never seen. Will you do as God has directed and allow them to go home?"

"You've served your kings, your people and your god nobly," Koresh said. "I've prayed as you've taught me and risen from my knees this very morning ready to prove your prophets and your god true. I will assist in every way."

Daniel smiled through his tears as he heard the king say, "Therefore, the restoration of the Jewish people to Jerusalem, her blood, her adopted and the workers and strangers in her camp, is now begun."

38. Ya'el was her name

DANIEL WOKE TO the sound of drums. Soon after, he heard trumpets. Mounted soldiers led a crier in the streets, reading aloud, "Hear the word of the emperor, Koresh the Great...

The Lord, the God of heaven, has given me all the kingdoms of the earth and he has appointed me to build a temple for him at Jerusalem in Judah. Anyone of his people among you, let him go up to Jerusalem in Judah and build the temple of the Lord..."

"Upon this very day!" Daniel shouted from his window.

"...the God of Israel, the God who is in Jerusalem. And the people of any place where survivors may now be living are to provide him with silver and gold, with goods and livestock, and with freewill offerings for the temple of God in Jerusalem."

Daniel dropped to his knees. "I thank you, living and eternal King for restoring my soul within me in compassion. Great is your faithfulness." After thanking God for his mercy and for prophecy fulfilled, Daniel called for the widow, Pnina, to help him close the house (then wept, briefly, when he remembered that she had died long before).

The king warned Daniel at the palace during the prophet's last visit, "Jerusalem is but rubble now. Think a moment. Stay here safe, powerful and at ease. Help me guide the greatest empire in the world."

"Safety and ease would be something indeed, O king," Daniel said. "Sadly, it is not the way of this world nor is it my way. From Assyria, to Babylon, and now Persia, all is bloodshed and brutality. The God of Israel has ordained an end to it but first..." Daniel closed his eyes.

"What?" Koresh asked.

"Earthquakes!" Daniel answered. "Discharges between planets. Famine, flood, locusts, the gathering of many armies..." He raised his gaze to meet the emperor's wondering eyes. "My friend, King Nebuchadnezzar, was so gifted... Even so, he killed my parents, leveled Jerusalem and gouged out Zedekiah's eyes."

"Yes, I would have loved to have known him," Koresh sighed. "But I suppose it would not have gone well for one of us." He ordered water for Daniel and encouraged him to sit and sip. "But the savagery will end someday, right?" the king asked. "You once said so yourself."

He pointed outside. "Look, Daniel, there's a warm, wonderful wind from the west today. See how it swirls the dust and tosses branches in the trees?"

"Dust," Daniel muttered. "Satan lives but make no mistake, his days are numbered!"

"So," Koresh said, "we'll keep a good thought."

The king gave Daniel the jeweled cylinder seal he wore about his neck. "More valuable than wagon-loads of gold," Koresh said, "but I doubt you'll make use of it except for a keepsake."

Daniel lowered his eyes. "O king, I fear I've nothing to offer in return."

Koresh eyed the little stone on the chain draped about Daniel's neck, polished and gleaming, filled with light, but before he could speak Daniel stopped him. "Rather my life, O king, or my house in town, anything but this notion from my boyhood in Jerusalem."

"Your house, then!" Koresh said. "It is in an excellent neighborhood."

"Done," Daniel laughed, "you are indeed, as everyone says, a practical man."

They hugged and thanked one another. Daniel left the citadel, never looking back after over six decades of regular attendance, for the last time.

*

At home, with the help of his neighbors, Daniel began to board windows and doors but they soon insisted that he leave at once, promising to complete the work themselves. So Daniel started back to Jerusalem with only the clothes on his back, a modest grin, his Isaiah scroll and two chains about his neck.

"How will you travel there?" his neighbors asked.

"I suppose as I came," he said. Then, remembering Mishael, Hananiah and Azariah as boys, he whispered, "Almost as I came."

"And your personal things?"

"Take from these premises whatever you wish," Daniel answered, "but remember the structures, the wells and gardens are now the property of the king. His men will come soon and take an inventory if I know Koresh at all."

He waved goodbye and soon walked past the tower at Esagila, through the gate named for the pagan goddess, Ishtar, and across the bridge upon which he had entered Babylon as a child. Crowded roads intersected where once empty fields had lain; there spread farms, markets, estates, gardens... Everything had changed.

Chaldeans called out as Daniel passed using his pagan name. "Be safe, Belteshazzar," they cheered, "and may your god protect you." Thousands of exiles had already flooded onto the broad plane beyond the Euphrates with their belongings heaped on carts. Tens of thousands more would soon follow. Daniel waved toward Babylon over his shoulder, not looking back.

"Thank you, neighbors," he said in Hebrew. "Thank You, O Lord, our God. Your people, Israel, are at long last headed home."

*

Later that day, as the sun had nearly set, no longer within sight of Babylon's mystic ziggurat, Daniel stopped beside a stream to kneel and drink from it with cupped hands. As Koresh had promised, mounted Persian guards patrolled the length of the road to protect travelers. Daniel was soon recognized by his fellows.

"We'll care for you during our journey, prophet," many offered, "if you will but honor us by riding along."

"Not an idol worshiper among them," came a voice at Daniel's side.

Daniel turned to find Ezekiel.

"So," Daniel said, "it is he from the banks of the Kebar, who has seen wheels intersecting wheels!"

"So," Ezekiel answered, "it is he from fortress Babylon, who tames big cats!"

They embraced. Once they were recognized together a greater crowd gathered and a spontaneous celebration began. Exiles danced on the roadway, some sang or played instruments. "Bright young couples and their children," Daniel said, nodding toward the revelry. "They are Babylonians really, Jews who have only seen Jerusalem in their dreams, so happy to be headed home though having no hint of what they'll face."

"Happy, sad," Ezekiel said, "what does it matter? The door has opened. God has done it. These long-chastened children, cleansed in the furnace of affliction, bearing no idols, lacking their parents' fatal vanity, all mystically long to return to a place they've never been, assured that they are going home."

"Home," Daniel sighed. "Will you accompany me?"

"My old eyes can barely see your face," Ezekiel said. "I shall go no farther." He looked at the oxcarts, livestock, and wagon-loads of exiles treading toward the setting sun. "But I am renewed, having lived to see this day." He squinted at the chain about Daniel's neck graced with a single glowing stone. Daniel removed it and allowed the little gem to twist in the pale light.

"Breathtaking," Ezekiel said, "as has been your faith throughout this epoch."

Loaded wagons rumbled down the road. "To Rezeph then Aleppo," Daniel said, "then south through Hamath, skirting Damascus, down through Samaria then home. The same route along which we boys once came."

Ezekiel took the chain from Daniel's hand and examined it more closely. "There was a young girl in Jerusalem," he said, "was there not?"

Daniel sighed. "Ya'el, was her name."

"Of the house of Ahiel?"

"Yes," Daniel said, allowing a tear to run unchecked down his cheek.

"I've some inspiration for you, Daniel," Ezekiel said, placing the piece back into his friend's hand. "I know in my spirit that the child for whom this polished stone was and is intended, now an amazing woman, lives."

Daniel smiled.

They looked west again toward the sunset. Even where they stood, miles from the city, the road was paved with fired bricks stamped with Nebuchadnezzar's name.

"My Hebrews," Daniel whispered in the dead king's honor.

"You would be wise to join a family with a cart," Ezekiel said. "It's a good five weeks' journey home."

"It seemed much longer on the way up."

"Five," Ezekiel nodded, "maybe six."

"Then I had best begin."

The two prophets embraced a final time.

"Have we learned our lesson?" Daniel asked.

"I fear that even after all the anguish of this prolonged captivity," Ezekiel sighed, "the suffering that shall yet encumber our people will be unspeakable. I do not question our God, Daniel, but so much of what we shall yet endure seems unjust to my earthly eyes. I know in the end that we are guaranteed peace if we will but heed the Light."

"And shall we?"

"Some sweet day…"

Together they recited, "We shall be his people and he shall be our God."

A young man stood upon the tailgate of a cart not far from where they stood and prophesied for all to hear. "I will return again and dwell in Jerusalem," he called out.

> *"Then Jerusalem will be called the City of Truth and the mountain of the Lord Almighty will be called the Holy Mountain. Once again men and women of ripe age will sit on the streets of Jerusalem, each with cane in hand because of his age. The city streets will be filled with boys and girls playing there."*

"Zechariah is his name," Ezekiel said with a touch of righteous pride, "born in Babylon, now a grown man. God speaks through him. Remember, Daniel? We spoke of this lad years ago when he was but a gifted boy."

"Rejoice greatly, O Daughter of Zion!" Zechariah continued.

> *"Shout, Daughter of Jerusalem, see, your King comes to you, righteous and having salvation, gentle and riding on a donkey, on a colt, the foal of a donkey."*

Standing in Babylon's blowing dust, Daniel and Ezekiel grinned at one another like children and spoke as one, "Amen."

About the Author

Cliff Keller was born in Milwaukee, Wisconsin, the son of a Jewish father and Roman Catholic mother, which didn't work out. After multiple migrations between Florida and Wisconsin, Cliff graduated from Florida State University with a degree in Engineering Science while working for NASA at Cape Canaveral. Somehow aware of Cliff's progress, Richard Nixon designed to send him to Vietnam but Cliff avoided the draft and bested the president, who soon afterward became distracted by the Watergate scandal, by receiving an occupational deferment to work for then defense contractor, Texas Instruments, in Dallas. After eight years in Dallas (and earning a Master's Degree in Electrical Engineering), Cliff spent the next 18 years in the construction business before selling the business to dedicate more time to writing.

Cliff and his wife, Marcia, now live in Jerusalem, Israel, having made Aliyah in 2011, where they are slowly improving at speaking Hebrew.

Other Books by Cliff Keller

Three Prophets Series:

Book One: *The Ivory House, The Days of Elijah*

Book two: *Faithless Heart, a love story*

*

Good Morning, Residents!

The Lion or the Lamb

Sunny Side Up!